KNOTTSPEED

KNOTTSPEED

A Love Story

JEFF JOHNSON

TURNER

Turner Publishing Company
Nashville, Tennessee
New York, New York

www.turnerpublishing.com

Knottspeed: A Love Story

Cover design: Maddie Cothren
Book design: Glen Edelstein
Cover art: Jason Walz

Library of Congress Cataloging-in-Publication Data

Names: Johnson, Jeff, 1969- author.
Title: Knottspeed / by Jeff Johnson.
Description: Nashville, Tennessee : Turner Publishing Company, 2017.
Identifiers: LCCN 2016017926 | ISBN 9781681626666 (pbk.)
Subjects: LCSH: Man-woman relationships. | GSAFD: Love stories.
Classification: LCC PS3610.O3554 K66 2017 | DDC 813/.6--dc23
LC record available at https://lccn.loc.gov/2016017926

9781681626666

Printed in the United States of America
17 18 19 20 10 9 8 7 6 5 4 3 2 1

for a mermaid, and the lamplighters

KNOTTSPEED

Part 1

1

Strangers on a Stage

I WAS IN THE BASEMENT on my mattress the morning the great Knottspeed came to live in the house on Lincoln Street. It was cold for the middle of fall, gray and wet for days, and months of it to come. I listened to the sound of feet on the warped old floorboards that were my ceiling and kept my eyes closed, as I always did when I heard people moving around up there. The house was old, and sometimes a fine gray dust came floating down. I listened to what sounded like three people and something else, something with wheels that complained in an oddly pleasant, humiliated way that's surprising to hear in a white man. I should have put my pants on and gone up to help, but I didn't. I just lay there wondering if it was the beginning of something, which is almost never a good thing. I also wondered why entertaining the notion of beginning anything was making me tired. Knottspeed had that effect on people, even through the floor, even when he was sick and crippled, as I'd heard he was.

When everything went quiet again, and I'll never know why, but I was quiet too. I dusted myself off and took a pull off the bottle of vodka I'd set on the concrete floor next to me and then gently set the bottle back down without so much as a click.

3

The small window of clarity pulled me into a state of spatial contemplation. If what I'd heard was right—the grinding and the echoes and the thumps—then Knottspeed was up there on the couch, and that would put him about twelve feet away. Our heads were that close. He had no idea I was lying in the dark, listening to him and calculating where we were in relation to each other. It was in keeping with my dealings with him thus far. Knottspeed had a way of not noticing people unless he found them interesting, and about half the time that meant he didn't like you. I have no idea why that made him such a popular figure, but it did—though not with me. Whatever kind of charm that was, as I understood it, was just about dead. I almost cursed him right then as paranoia welled up from my stomach and burned my sore tonsils. He was quiet enough to hear me in that old house if I moved, and then he'd know that I'd been there all along, listening and being a weirdo in the basement. That was how it all started with me and Knottspeed. We were listening to each other with no real idea of exactly why, and for my part, that never changed a bit.

"Goddamn!" My first words. I yawned like I'd just woken up, like that's what I yelled every morning when my eyes opened. Immediately, there was a hard pounding on the floor.

"Hey!" It was Knottspeed. I knew that voice from the thousands of stories I'd heard him tell, always when I was just another drunk nursing a beer at the edge of a crowd of more glamorous drunks. "Hello!" More pounding.

I ignored him and took another nip of vodka, careful to keep some kind of handle on the bottle. With great leisure, I put it down and started to pull my pants on.

"Little help here," he called. The request was loud and clear, like we were in the same room. There was a small edge of irritation in his voice, and for some reason I considered that a kind of victory. It was an important moment, I later realized. The quality of all small victories, the nature of them, would never be the same as that one. In many ways, it was the last small victory of the person I still thought I was. Complicated revelations with a hallucinogenic quality to them—well, I get it from my father's side.

"Hold." Short. That felt right. I didn't bother with my boots or my shirt. I did sniff at myself, but my heart wasn't in it. I hadn't showered in days, but I didn't really stink. Old cigarettes and milk. Corn. Hint of bacon. As I walked up the dirty old wooden stairs, my scent mingled with rust and tool grease, and I was glad when I pushed the door open. The afternoon light was bright and sharp with a rare break in the clouds, and the air was much colder. The house was drafty above the basement, and there was a strict law against turning on the heat. The air coming through the back door smelled like red leaves and rain dirt, and motes of dust made lazy patterns in the air.

The kitchen was every bit as charming as it had been the day before. It was a place where you cooked poison or dyed things. It made the draft a good, solid positive. The pockmarked linoleum floor stuck to my bare feet as I walked through, but there were wet spots. The alternately sticky to crusty counters were cluttered with broken lamps and mason jars of stale seeds and wine bottles with one thick sip of fruit fly at the bottom. Most of it was the leftovers of some tragic hippy woman who was around before my life sentence at the place began.

Someone had been high enough in the last day to clean the sink in a half-assed way, which was new. It was a huge double-basin porcelain relic from the same era as the Dust Bowl and other mostly forgotten tragedies, stained with any number of things that stain, and decades of it, the kind of thing my grandmother would keep out back to wire scrub horse feet and clean fish. I almost opened the refrigerator, but nothing in it was mine. I didn't want to risk getting caught looking at someone else's expired food. A moment like that could easily shatter my fragile morning buzz.

The living room was about the nicest place in the house. There was a pot-bellied stove I'd never seen a fire in, but it must work because something plastic had melted on it at one point; a big TV I was pretty sure was only good for the one video game that came with it; an old piano that had never been thrown away because people don't throw away old pianos; two mismatched lounge chairs matted with dog hair; and the sofa. The sofa smelled powerfully of unwell dog. Someone had put a Mexican blanket over it to try to keep it from contaminating the air around it, but there was no way that could ever work.

Knottspeed was lying on that sofa, the dog blanket folded over him, wretched. We stared at each other. I was dumbfounded, and he watched my reaction and waited for it to pass. The stare of strangers on a stage. Knottspeed looked very different from the last time I'd seen him. Some months ago— before he'd left town to do whatever he'd been doing—I'd seen him briefly, paying the bill at some random bar where he'd been having lunch. Then, he'd been what I thought of as a kind of shiny thing. Blond hair, nice clean clothes, an easy smile. He always had money. I thought he had style that day, just as I always did. He was doing something, and whatever it was had him reasonably excited. I'd wanted to talk to him, maybe bum a beer or two, but he flirted with the bartender woman while he waited for his change and then he left. He was wearing a tan V-neck sweater that day, and I remember how I thought that sweater might look good on me too.

This most modern version of Knottspeed was shocking enough that I almost laughed out of unfocused panic at the sight of him. He really was ruined. There was a badly put together gash across his right eyebrow, a strange looking thing that trailed into flaking scabs on both ends, like a scrape that had gone deep in the center where the hair was, like the hair had given something hard a brief traction. His other eye was black. He was wearing a dark cloth coat, and the high collar was pulled up. I was surprised to see that he was wearing slippers of some kind—well one, at least. It was tan and wet on the bottom, poking out from under the dog blanket, ringed and muddy.

He looked cold, and the fingers curled over the top of the dog blanket under his neck were skinny and foam white.

I smiled on and off. When he didn't say anything, just continued to stare, as attentive and unreadable as a focused parrot, I broke eye contact and sat down on the piano stool and then pushed on the keys to fill the awkward silence. My hands hurt a little in that kind of cold, and hammering on an out-of-tune piano in that instant would have put the wrong kind of spin on the day anyway. I settled for a lifeless sample of Joplin. It sounded like horror show circus music, so I stopped.

"FB." Knottspeed wasn't loud anymore. "I know you. Piano dude."

I lit up a cigarette, and I made no effort to suck in my stomach, none at all. The smoke was thick and blue when it rounded through the random bars of sunlight between us. I hadn't seen any sun in days. We weren't supposed to smoke inside, but as long as the landlord wasn't around it didn't matter because of the draft.

"I used to play piano." I spit a fleck of tobacco on the floor. "I guess I still do. But mostly I paint houses. Sheds. Sometimes fences."

"Huh." Knottspeed didn't blink after he said anything. It was a small thing to notice, and my noticing surprised me. It was another change that stuck that I blame on him or credit him for, depending on how you look at it.

"So I uh, I heard you hurt your back," I said. He didn't reply, and in the quiet a flange deep inside the piano popped and settled. "Didn't know about the whole eye thing, though. Some kind of car wreck?"

I'd heard that he'd broken his skull and something in his spine in one of three ways: he'd either been hit by a car, been in a car when the car hit something else, or he'd fallen out of a hot tub and had a seizure. All three scenarios had him drunk and violently disturbed about something already. People talked about it in the same way they talked about hives. Many sensible, ordinary people were frightened that he was still alive, which I found puzzling considering what I was looking at. Knottspeed sighed and shifted a little. It looked painful.

"Not really. There was a car involved, but that was only part of it."

I nodded. There were four cardboard boxes on the floor by the door. They were the cleanest things I'd seen so far that day. The living room was crammed with dust-furred flea market knickknacks, just like all the rest of the house. Knottspeed followed my eyes.

"Books," he said. "Some cooking stuff. What's left of my clothes."

"Left?" I tried to look interested. Maybe I even was. He could make people interested in almost anything, even themselves. He was doing it right then.

"Yep." Knottspeed fumbled around under the dog blanket and came up with a bent cigarette and a near empty book of matches. He pinched the filter off the smoke and torched it. "It's mostly underwear. When people steal your clothes they don't take those. I would expect the same logic to extend to socks, but it doesn't. The same variety of looter evidently has no use for certain kitchen items. Tea strainers. Oven mitts. The garlic press. But no one ever steals books, except for the people you loan them to."

I didn't really know what to say to that. Knottspeed had lived in the same house for more than a decade. I'd walked past it a thousand times over the years. He'd hosted tastefully small parties I always heard about much later. In the summertime, there were always a few interesting people on the porch in the evening, talking about the kinds of things those people talk about. It was an old place, but I thought he owned it. I had never been inside.

"We should open the door," I said. I got up.

"It's cold out there."

It was the first and last time I heard him complain about the cold. The new and destroyed version of Knottspeed didn't make much sense when it came to the obvious. It was all in the way he said it. I stuck and unstuck my way to the door and opened it. The sagging front porch was full of boxes, evidently the rest of his belongings. Someone would almost certainly see them and pick through them tonight, so the looting had only moved to a different neighborhood. I didn't want to point that out just yet, so I stayed with the weather.

"It's the same temperature inside as out," I said. "Sometimes I think it's actually colder in here."

"That's good, FB. That's what I was hoping for. Are there any more blankets?"

I flicked my spent cigarette out into the front yard. "Big stack in that wooden box."

Knottspeed glanced at his wheelchair, a stripped-down, no-frills garage sale giveaway. I did too.

"I'll get 'em."

I padded over and opened the old box. Distilled dog boiled out, a raw, angry stink that made my throat hurt again. I pulled the top blanket out and closed the lid, fast. The blanket itself was a dead thing. I shook some air through it, and I was glad the door was open. The smell that whooshed out of it was almost chokingly bad. When I put it over him, he didn't thank me and I didn't blame him.

"This place sucks," he casually observed. He didn't seem especially surprised by it. He said it in a satisfied way, as if it were part of something he had been planning for some time, and he was relieved that it was coming together. I nodded my agreement and sat back down.

"You get what you pay for," I said. Right then I realized why he blinked so little. Knottspeed was paying four times the rent as the rest of us and all of the bills. And he was in the living room. His mobile face flashed an instant of rage and something else, something that reminded me of snake. He knew. Planned or not, it was a low-down bummer. He was being ripped off so constantly that he was in record mode, with no off switch. It was another one of his many contagious qualities, so it may be that he'd always been that way.

"That's been my motto lately," he said, again in that quiet voice, watching me with his broken, unblinking eyes. "I've made a sweeping change in my purchasing philosophy in the last few months. I buy the shit no one else wants. Any sensible human stores their most valuable assets inside of them, but my head is cracked at the moment, so . . ."

"Huh." It was all I felt like saying after the intrusion of being lied to about something bad I was a part of.

"Yeah." He took a contemplative drag. The ash was half a cigarette long. "Where the fuck is this dog? It's dead, isn't it?"

"No." It came out glum. I don't like dogs, especially the one in question. "It's at work with Craig." Our slumlord.

No reply.

I looked at the clock on the TV. It was almost noon, still early for me. Knottspeed looked too. His cigarette ash fell on the blanket, and he flicked it hard with one bony finger. The inch of ash exploded and slowly settled as we watched.

"I'm hungry," he continued. "Sorry. What about you, FB?"

I scratched at the stubble on my chin. I look like an Indian, but my mother was white. Her side of the family is where the patch of multicolored stubble came from, plus both of my chest hairs. Knottspeed seemed to read my mind again.

"I'm a drinking man, FB. Especially right now. I'm suffering from a pretty bad concussion, so in addition to being partially crippled, I can't see very well, which is a righteous thing to have going for me at the moment. I'm also miserably whacked out on Valium."

"Got any more?"

He shook his head. "All gone. It's supposed to keep my brain from swelling, but I'm not so sure. It might have been to keep me from getting any enterprising ideas. But whatever. It's like this—you can either do whatever it is you're getting ready to do,

10

or you can let me pay you to be my friend. If I don't eat soon, bad things will happen. But . . ." He reached down into the black leather backpack beside him and came up with a mostly full bottle of quality bourbon. "I propose we get wasted first."

He swept the dog blankets back and struggled into a sitting position. Knottspeed was bitterly thin, a full fifty pounds lighter than the last time I'd seen him. His fur-covered coat hung on his skeleton like a bag on a clothes hanger. He took a generous pull off the bottle and held it out, smacked his lips.

And I took it. I didn't have anything to do for the next three days, but I also didn't feel like it would add very much for my sense of well-being to do anything with the owner of the bottle I was holding. Knottspeed frowned, watching me. He rocked painfully to one side, dug a wrinkled wad of cash out of his pocket, and dropped it in his lap. He picked through the bills until he found a fifty and then held it out. I took that too. It was that easy.

"Fifty bucks is somewhere in the neighborhood of what you might make for an afternoon, right? So consider the buzz your first tip of the day."

I shrugged and drank. The fifty disappeared into my jeans along with my reservations. There was no way the skeleton man was going to have enough energy to get through another couple drinks, so it was free money. I passed the bottle back. He drank again and then capped it and put it away. My next bottle, as soon as he blacked out, I thought. He smiled at me then—in hindsight, at my incredible naïveté.

"All right," he said enthusiastically. He rubbed his hands together, and I saw the afterimage of the energy I remembered. "Call us a cab. I need to get some shoes and a belt, some kind of shirt and another pair of pants. And it's Breeder's Cup race day. Even though I don't go for horse racing, I do like watching people watch it on TV. Everyone around here always dolls up like it's the Kentucky Derby—I never could figure out why. Yet another hipster defect. But big hats and skinny ties, man, and who can talk shit about a mint julep? Help me stand up, and pass me my cane."

I helped him rise and held him up while I pulled the cane off the back of his chair. He felt light, which was good, because his legs seemed entirely wrong. He set out at a bandy-legged wobble toward the bathroom. I watched him. I couldn't help it, but I was actually feeling a tiny bit upbeat. I'd never tasted a mint julep or seen a horse race, even on TV, and it struck me that sitting in a bar watching one and drinking something green would be a pleasantly unlikely way to spend an afternoon. Even the big hat thing sounded interesting.

"FB!" Knottspeed called from the bathroom. "Can you bring me my backpack?"

I picked up his backpack, and of course I looked inside. It was open. There was a sandwich on white bread in a plastic bag, his toothbrush, a couple napkins, and a notebook. And the bottle of booze. I carried it into the bathroom, where Knottspeed was gripping the sink and staring at himself in the cracked, spattered mirror. The bathroom was experimental bad. There was no toilet paper, of course. The tub was as old as the kitchen sink and boldly crossed the wide line between filthy and scary. The toilet looked like something from an isolated gas station outside of Juarez, sprayed with diarrhea of varying ages and hues. There was most of a wet curl of turd on the lip of the wooden seat where someone had been squatting over it with their eyes closed. I held the backpack out. Knottspeed took it.

"Thanks," he said. He almost touched his eyebrow and made a face instead. "This place is way better than the hotel I woke up in this morning. It has the aura of a healing Swiss spa I'm so desperately in need of. I found the rest of the dog." He pointed at the bath mat. I would have thrown up if I'd had to touch it. Craig the slumlord would need a shovel if he ever wanted to get it out of there.

Knottspeed cranked the hot water knob. Nothing happened.

The sink was full of dry hair. A lone kernel of corn sat in the soap dish.

"The water runs," I said. "Craig turned it off."

Knottspeed laughed and I smiled. It wasn't a sarcastic, mean laugh. It was the laugh of a man who had just found a bird's nest in an old shoe. Surprised, delighted, and filled with a deep appreciation of senselessness.

"Well, just get me out to the porch," he said. "I'll wait out there for our cab and guard my boxes."

"I'll get my shoes and my shirt," I said.

I hitched up my jeans and guided him back through the house, out onto the porch. There was a bright wedge of sunlight by the stairs leading down to the sidewalk, so I dragged a rickety old wooden chair into the center of it. Knottspeed sat down. He took a deep breath and closed his eyes. His coat didn't look very warm, and the breeze had real winter in it. His blond hair was a spectacular mess.

"We won't know anyone where we're going," he said mildly. "Which is good. But it will create such gossip, FB. And gossip is a tool with a numinous tip."

2

Teen Junky

WHEN I GOT BACK OUTSIDE, Knottspeed hadn't moved. Even his hair was exactly the same. His eyes opened slowly, and he looked up at me. He was still smiling at the light, which faded at that moment as the heavy clouds swallowed the patch of open blue.

"Your clothes match your psychic posture," he observed. He held out one skeletal hand and waggled his fingers at me. It sounded like he meant it as a compliment, like that was rare in his opinion.

I'd changed into my blue flannel shirt and had put on my paint-splattered work boots. I was chubby enough to make it without a coat. I nodded at him and looked at his backpack. He took the bottle out, took a quick nip, and then handed it to me. I took a good mouthful to fortify myself, swishing it around through my teeth before I swallowed. Whiskey fumes were better than their secretive vodka cousin's. They made me feel powerful. I blew them out and relished the dangerous bold. The cab was sitting out front, waiting. The driver was an old guy zoning out at his steering wheel.

"You ready?" I asked in a deeper voice.

"I am. Help me down."

Knottspeed held his arm out by the elbow, and I pulled him up. He gave me an earnest look.

"Hold on really tight," he cautioned. "Me and stairs have a one-way ticket down."

We made it down the steps without incident. The first flight was cracked, mossy wood; the second, crumbling concrete. There were no handrails the entire way, which for the first time struck me as unsafe. I'd never noticed there weren't any, and I wondered what had happened to them. Knottspeed made it to the bottom without a word, but I could tell that getting him back up meant carrying him.

I opened the back door to the cab. The driver tried to look back, but he was too fat. Sometimes people would do things like that all day, every day. He settled back down as Knottspeed folded himself in. Knottspeed had to grab his pants by the thighs to move his legs around, and silently winced when he did. When he was in, I closed the door and walked into the street to get in the other side. The driver didn't like me getting close to the non-existent traffic, I could tell, but he didn't say anything.

"Where to?" the driver asked.

"The Rialto," Knottspeed said in a friendly, breezy way.

"Which one?" The driver looked in the rearview and waited. Knottspeed and I looked at each other.

"Whichever one is showing the Breeder's Cup," Knottspeed said. "So the one that has gambling."

"A place called the Rialto—and there are three—well, they all got video poker." The driver paused to let this sink in. "So you want the Asians, the white trash dive up the street from here, or the fancy place downtown with the pool tables?"

"I'd normally say the trashy dive, but I have to change clothes in the bathroom wherever we're going, so downtown it is."

The driver didn't say anything, just started driving. Knottspeed turned to me.

"I told you I can't see very well, but I also can't remember anything, which is also all well and good, but I might forget about

16

the clothes. Keep an eye out for, like, a medium-sized place that has clothes. Nothing big, because we have to get in and out fast. Also shoes. So the display window should have shoes and clothes in it, like a secondhand store. In fact, that would be perfect. Keep in mind my size."

I was actually very likely to forget that myself, so I leaned forward and tapped the driver.

"I heard," the driver said. "Got two on the way. The Greek Orthodox place and the Challenged Child Junky place run by the Salvation Army. Teen Commie, Dope Spirit—something like that."

Knottspeed found these options unappealing and scowled.

"Team Spirit," I said. Knottspeed grunted. I looked out the window. The sun was all the way gone, and the motionless clouds looked swollen with cold rivers of raw news. I wished I'd brought my coat after all. Knottspeed looked out his window, his forehead against it. He smelled like wet dog mange. I glanced at him and knew that if I'd been able to see his reflection, his eyes would be closed. It made me want to go home.

The cab driver took a turn at a light, then another one, and I got lost in thought. I don't know why, but I wasn't thinking that afternoon about the usual things. I had almost a hundred bucks to my name, and Knottspeed had money and he needed my help, so the ever-present fear of danger-ously serious poverty was off the menu for the next few days. I couldn't remember my ex-girlfriend's name, and after three years I hadn't been able to for at least three days, maybe more, which was a record. The kid's name either. I really didn't have a care in the world, so I drifted. I'd moved from the pleasant realm of porn into worrying about one of my molars when the driver stopped.

"Teen Spirit," he announced. "Pay the meter up, and I'll put it on waiting."

Knottspeed activated like a bug unfolding. He passed a bill up and leaned down to peer out my window. I followed his eyes. Teen Spirit looked big. Possibly too big. Definitely crappy. Knottspeed cleared his throat and considered. Then he clapped me on the shoulder.

"Let's go."

I got out and dragged him up behind me. Once he was on his feet, he set out at his top speed. I walked easily beside him and held the door open.

"All right," he said as he crossed the threshold, "just follow my lead. Don't panic, no matter how bad it gets. And do not let that cab driver leave." Whatever he'd been thinking about in the cab was gone, and he was focused. He stopped me and nodded at the cash register guy.

"Dude," Knottspeed said, addressing him. "I can't see and my friend-for-hire is already wasted. Where do you keep the suits? I need a suit, a shirt, the shoes, all that shit. And a sweater. I'm in a serious fuckin' hurry too."

The cash register guy didn't smile.

"Sir, there is no profanity in the store." He talked slow and loud, like we were children or old people. "Now, if we all under-stand that and we can agree on that, then—"

Knottspeed flipped him off, long and hard. The guy stopped talking.

"Let's do this!" Knottspeed barked. He set off through the junk aisles in the direction of the clothes. The cash register guy came around the counter and followed us about twenty feet back. The rest of the store was blessedly empty.

The suits were all in a row beside the used uniforms. Knottspeed ran his hand along the row of them, then pulled one out after about thirty seconds. It was extremely dark green, the kind of relic I would never wear. It looked the size he had been all those months ago.

"Shoes," he said. We turned and looked at the clerk. He pointed without enthusiasm to our left.

The shoe section took Knottspeed about the same amount of time. He went right to the ten and a half sign, yanked out a pair of black plastic dress shoes, and shoved them into my arms and kept walking.

"Shirt." He seemed out of breath. I looked around. The clerk ambled toward the long-sleeve shirt section, dejected. We followed him. Knottspeed stopped us about halfway there.

"We should have brought my chair," he announced. He wobbled alarmingly and his legs gave out. I caught him and tried to help him up, but he started slipping out of his jacket. The clerk appeared on the other side of him and helped. There wasn't a chair handy, so we eased him down to the carpet. Knottspeed flopped back and just lay there, staring at the ceiling.

"Should I call 911? I'll call 911." The clerk began to move off, so I grabbed his wrist and stopped him.

"No," I said firmly. My whiskey brave was almost used up already, but I still had a little left. "We have a cab out front. We'll leave. Just help me get him to the register so we can pay."

"I'm not going anywhere," Knottspeed said petulantly. "Not without my fucking shirt, and I want a sweater too. Something festive. Christmassy. It's December, right?"

"October t . . . till the end of the mu . . . month," the clerk stammered, genuinely panicked. I let go of him, and he started backing away.

"I'm planning ahead here," Knottspeed continued. He crossed his hands over his hollow stomach. "You guys have wheelchairs?" He glanced at the clerk, who desperately nodded.

"Yes, we have three for sale in the front with the bikes, but—"

Knottspeed frowned at this. It was enough to stop him.

"I'd ask for a complaint form, but I realize I'm pushing it. I know that. You should not keep wheelchairs in the bike section though. You have any idea what kind of message that sends? To people like me, who occasionally have to lie on the fucking floor? They should be at the edge of the sofa area, or maybe in the back of hardware or by the vacuum cleaners. Think about it. FB! Go get me a chair, please. Cash register guy, you stay here."

"I can't let him go up front by the register unattended," the clerk whined. "He might rob us."

"Oh my God." Knottspeed was robustly disgusted. "Leave me here then. Just leave the man down. I promise I won't go anywhere."

The clerk and I walked quickly to the front. The bikes were in a row by the windows. All three wheelchairs had flat tires. I looked at them in disbelief and then stared hard at the clerk. He shrugged.

"They got them here somehow," he said, pleading. "They do roll. I know they do. They have to." Pleading to uncertain to scared in three sentences.

I pulled the first one out and pushed it open. There was something sticky on the handles. I was about to complain, but he glanced nervously at the phone. In that moment, some of Knottspeed's obnoxiousness entered into me.

"It's time for you to be a man," I said loudly. It made no sense at all, and it freaked him out. His hand went to his reddening throat and he looked at the phone again.

"You heard me." I headed out fast in Knottspeed's direction. Really bland stuff always seemed to happen to me, nothing at all like this. Even half drunk, pushing a flat wheelchair through a Christian thrift store to get some guy off the floor seemed way past my limit for a Monday—and I wasn't even sure it was Monday. I cursed under my breath and looked back to make sure the clerk wasn't calling the cops. He was trailing me, but I could tell he was at the end of his rope. We were way out on the skinny branches.

Knottspeed was right where we'd left him. He had an unlit cigarette propped up in his mouth. He looked at the wheelchair and pulled the cigarette out.

"From this angle I can tell that thing has two flat tires," he observed. "Was that the only one?"

"Let's get you up," I said. I didn't know what would happen if he found out all the wheelchairs were disabled. He'd already struck me as a guy who would go on about that kind of thing. I grabbed him under the arms and heaved him upright and then set him in the chair as gently as I could. It did something to his back and he gasped. He coughed then, long and wracking, and I thought he was going to throw up. I took a step back, and he raised one hand.

"Christmas. Sweater," he gasped. "Max this fucker out before douchebag calls the pigs."

"The shirt," I reminded him. I set off at a fast trot. The wheelchair handled fine.

"White," he wheezed. "I fucking hate a blue shirt with a collar. Can't do it."

The shirts were mercifully close, two rows away, just past the tracksuits. We were almost there when he held up a hand for me to stop. I did, and he pulled a black sweat suit out at random. It looked like a medium. He tilted his head at me.

"Nike," he said weakly. He wiped his mouth and motioned for me to continue. I pushed hard. His head whiplashed back, but he didn't say anything. In shirts, he held up two, tossed one back rather than hang it—which I thought was rude but permissible under the circumstances—and then motioned for me to continue. The sweaters were next. I stopped us in the middle, where the mediums were most likely to be if the tracksuits were any example. He pulled out a white sweater with a yarn reindeer at random and held it up, smiled grimly at it.

"I am the exact same size as most of the dead people these clothes came from. Did you notice?" He twisted painfully so he could peer up at me through one eye. "Can you believe this? Good fortune or a slap-in-the-face omen—you tell me."

"Wish I could say," I replied. "I need a new coat, but the meter is running on every front." I moved in on the clerk's position at speed. The insanity of the moment had passed for him, and his arms were crossed. He was pissed. I pulled to a stop, and Knottspeed pushed the whole mess up onto the counter. He smiled at the clerk then, really, really sweetly.

"Sorry man. This . . . this has been a bad day for me. I just got out of prison a few weeks ago, and my wife's new lesbian beat the shit out of me. I'm . . . I'm mentally unstable, I guess. And my parole officer wants me to give him head. Again. This is also the first time I've ever done what I call 'public pills,' as in shit you find somewhere and you have no idea what it is. I don't pay for anything this shitty usually, but—"

I'll never know what he said after that because I left. I walked outside and lit a cigarette. My hands were shaking. The cab was still there, and the driver leaned down to look out at me. I motioned that it would be one more minute, and he frowned but nodded. If the cops showed up, my plan was to walk. If Knottspeed made it out in time, I'd get in the cab and then we'd go home. It had started raining and I didn't really want to walk, plus I didn't know where we were. I looked back inside. Knottspeed was still talking, gesturing mildly, going on generously about something he knew a great deal about. The clerk was frantically ringing everything up.

"Meter's runnin'." The cab driver had rolled his window down to better size up the delay. Maybe he was bored. He scooched over and lowered his head a little to get a look through the windows of Teen Spirit, and a fat rain drop splattered across the bridge of his big nose. His head snapped back in like a turtle's. I didn't feel up for chitchat.

"He's haggling," I said. "Be just a minute."

The cab driver didn't reply, but I could see his fingers drumming on the steering wheel.

The bell on the door rang, and the door opened a little and closed. Knottspeed was trying to get out. I flicked my smoke out into the rain and yanked the door open, trying to hurry things along. Knottspeed was standing just inside, one hand on the door. The wheelchair was behind him, and the clerk was just behind that. Knottspeed evidently had no intention of buying a busted wheelchair, so he was relying on his cane, and the clerk had no intention of letting him out with the wheelchair on loan either, so he was holding onto the sticky handles. He may have even pushed a little at that exact moment; I don't know. Knottspeed was pushed/pulled straight out of Teen Spirit and did a face-plant on the sidewalk. His plastic bag of clothes was clutched to him about waist high, so it didn't do anything to break his fall when it came to his head, which bounced off the concrete with a sickening sound that resounded in his mouth. He hit right on his bad cheekbone, bounced once, and then he didn't move.

The clerk screamed and disappeared into the store, the counter abandoned. I looked over Knottspeed's body at the register and thought about taking the entire thing, just because I knew he thought that had been our plan all along. The cab driver started his engine behind me, and I spun around, stepping on Knottspeed's hand in the process. The driver didn't exactly peel out, but it was as close as a worn-out cab could get. I watched it race down the street and turn at the first corner without stopping at the sign. The rain picked that moment to get serious.

Knottspeed groaned. He pushed himself violently and flopped over onto his back. I almost gasped.

His already beat-up face had a fresh layer of serious trauma, very much hospital worthy. His nose was bleeding, his torn eyebrow looked brand-new torn, and there was a raw scrape down the left side of his face from cheekbone to chin, with a big chunk of black gravel stuck in the center. Knottspeed's eyes opened, and his lips peeled back over his red teeth. He spit weakly and glared at me.

"Did that fucking prick step on my hand?" he growled. There was murder in that glare.

"No," I confessed. "I did."

Knottspeed held his hand up and stared at it in wonder. His pinky was broken. He brushed the chunk of gravel off his face. Just then the door to Teen Spirit clanged open.

"The police are on their way!" the clerk screamed in a high

voice. He tried to slam the door, but it just hissed closed on the air arm without the effect he was looking for, which was only going to make him madder.

"The fucking cab is gone," Knottspeed observed. He looked at me in wonder, like it was the most unusual thing that had ever happened to anyone.

It was time for me to think fast and move faster, and I'm no good at either one. When a genuine crisis occurs, I'm usually the last one to notice, and if the situation devolves to the point where I'm in charge, well then. I sized it up and waited for some kind of plan to form. Nothing.

Knottspeed tried to sit up. If I just ran, right then and there, there might be unforeseen consequences—but then again, maybe not. That was all I had in the way of a split-second reaction. I sighed. His new old clothes had spilled out of the bag and were getting rained on. That was where I started.

Knottspeed ignored me while I gathered up the clothes around him and stuffed them back in the bag. When I was done, I hitched up my jeans and looked around. The clerk had vanished, which couldn't be good. No cops yet, but we had mobility issues. Knottspeed came to the rescue and broke me out of my meditation.

"Let's get the fuck out of here," he said. "Help me up. You hold the bag. I need a cigarette, but that can wait. Let's go! This is potentially a crisis situation! Unfreeze! Unfreeze!"

"Unfreeze" galvanized me. I grabbed him and power lifted him to his feet with the strength of the desperate. He tossed his bloody head at the residential area that started behind the building.

"Let's look for some bushes or a dumpster and call the other cab company. Get the bag and put my backpack on."

I shouldered the backpack, picked up the bag, and we set out. I had a firm grip on his arm, but he wobbled along about as well as he had that morning. Maybe all the lying around in Teen Junky had recharged him, or maybe it was the adrenaline of the chase, but he moved. We rounded the corner just as I heard the door behind us open one last time. I didn't look back.

In the lee of the side of the building, we were sheltered from the wind and the rain. Knottspeed kept going, even though I was leaning toward a cigarette break.

"Come on," he urged. "This is where they always get you. We have to do something confusing immediately. Something inhumanly stupid. Think like a monkey, FB. This is not a higher primate type of thing."

He stopped and started to turn around, possibly to go back into the store, which would confuse anyone. I tightened my grip and steered him out into the rain toward the curb. I pointed with the bag arm at a giant rhododendron on the side of the Verizon store across the street. There were two trash cans under it.

"Let's use the tree for cover," I said. "You can lie down behind the trash cans, or maybe we can hide you in one if they're empty."

"Fuck that," he hissed, pulling at me. "We need to go back so I can get a cowboy hat."

The rain was cold, and I suddenly felt sick. Knottspeed cursed under his breath with a brief moment of clarity—". . . shit piece of curb nast . . ."—as we stepped off the curb into the street, but he went where I was pulling him. We made it across the street and up the curb—". . . ucking only damn . . ."—and under the rhododendron without him falling. He looked at the sidewalk behind the trash cans. The ground was wet, and someone had eaten most of a bag of Taco Bell behind them earlier and left all their wadded bean wrappers. One of the cans was leaking what looked like coffee with creamer. Knottspeed shook his head.

"Nah," he said. "Not getting in, not sitting down." He peered out into the rain. Only one eye would open, the black one. I looked around too. There was something that looked like a park about a block down, but that was obviously out. We couldn't go into the Verizon store any more than we could stroll into the White House.

"Well," Knottspeed said, sizing up the situation, "I guess we're fucked. I didn't think it'd end this way." He patted his chest with his free hand, pulled out his smokes and shook one loose, lipped it out, and looked at me sideways, using his head as an umbrella. I dug out my lighter and lit it. He took a drag and smiled a little and then took the cigarette out of his mouth and looked at it appreciatively, glad it was finally over. His pinkie looked awful, sticking out to the side. I put his backpack down and pulled the bottle out, praying for a moment of clarity rather than amplified confusion, which can easily happen. I took a long pull off the bottle while he watched, and then I handed it to him. He took it and drained a mouthful while I blew fumes and rolled my shoulders like a cage fighter getting ready to take a dive. Something popped in my neck, and the vibration shook something loose in my mind. I focused and looked up.

"Can you climb a tree?" I asked. Knottspeed looked at me like I was crazy, which was something.

"FB, when I talk of monkeys, I want you to understand that whimsy, as a tension modifier and conversational—"

"Here we go," I went on. I pushed him the two steps to the rhododendron trunk. The first and biggest branch was just above my head, the only one wide enough to sit on if you happened to be the size of a forest elf or a down-on-his-luck whatever he was. It wasn't a tree exactly, more like a great big bush. I reached up and shook it, and rainwater fell heavy all around us.

"I'm going to lift you up and try to get you on this branch here. I'll just lift and lift and try to get your butt up on this little flat part. You grab onto something and try to stabilize yourself." Without waiting for an answer, I leaned down and grabbed him around the waist, my face pressed into his crotch. I rose and heaved and then felt him lighten as he grabbed onto something above me. I used the instant of slack to reposition my grip lower down around his thighs, and he whimpered at this. With a mighty twist, I half tossed his butt up onto the branch and landed him. He wobbled dangerously before he got his balance.

I slowly let go and then stepped back, my arms still out in case he fell. He looked down at me.

"You really need a user's manual, FB. *Cripples for Dummies*. Maybe *Companionship for Drunks*."

I rubbed my hands together. Amazingly, he hadn't lost his cigarette. He took a drag with his broken hand. His feet went back and forth, like a little kid on a swing. The slippers were past wet and beyond filthy. I took my second-to-last smoke out and fired it up.

"What now?" he asked. I was pretty pleased with my emergency solution, so I took my time before answering.

"Well," I began. I took another drag. "I guess I'm leaving you here for now. I'll walk over to the other side of the Verizon store, try to hide on that side. Call the other cab company. When they show up, I'll come back and get you. We can't just have you fall out of the tree when he gets here or he'll take off just like the last guy. We can make that part up as we go along."

Knottspeed snorted. I shrugged.

"In the meantime, try to wipe some water out of those leaves around you and squeegee some blood off. Maybe point that pinkie back in the right direction."

"Does it look bad?" he asked, brushing his face with his broken hand.

"Not at all," I lied. "But it'd give you something to do."

He nodded. I took a final drag and then pinched the cherry off, putting the stinky butt in my shirt pocket for later. Knottspeed began surveying the leaves above him. I shouldered the backpack and picked up the bag.

"Back in five," I said. He didn't answer. I walked down the street toward the park and took my cell phone out. It had four minutes left on it, which meant basically one call once they rounded the minutes away with their mysterious consumer math. I dialed the other cab company from memory. I didn't know the number of the phone I was holding, but I did know the number for both cab companies, the bagel place I had worked at more than four years ago, and maybe two or three others if I really thought about it. They answered, and I told them I was smoking outside of the Verizon store next to Teen Spirit. They knew where I was, which was convenient. I had five minutes until pickup, which would give me just enough time to circle around the block, double back, and get Knottspeed down.

I never did mind walking in the rain as long as rescue was moments away, and that day was no different. The cold drops felt good on my face, my neck, the backs of my hands. It would have been nice to have one of those cowboy hats Knottspeed had been talking about, because then I'd be able to smoke, but it was fine either way. I walked leisurely down to the corner and turned. There was a row of brick lower-middle-class apartments that weren't all that imposing. A cop car turned the corner down the street in front of me right as I was going past the lame little courtyard area, so I ducked in and walked to the mailboxes by the door and then pretended I was standing there looking at my mail with my hands in front of me, my back to the street. They rolled past without stopping. I scooted over a few steps to the buzzer and the name and button display and feigned careful consideration in case anyone was watching. Then I lit the rest of my cigarette for additional cover and smoked like I was waiting for someone.

After a minute or two, I walked back out to the street and looked both ways. The cop car had already been past Knottspeed's position and was headed toward the park, so Knottspeed had evidently made it unless they had him in the trunk. It had been almost five minutes, so I decided to go try to get him down and risk waiting at the edge of the Verizon parking lot.

Knottspeed was scrubbing his face with his bad hand when I got back under him. He actually did look better, which was nothing short of amazing. The blood was gone. While he was very wet, his hair was also wet enough to slick back, which corrected its earlier madness. He had upgraded one facial feature while sacrificing another. I shrugged inside. Knottspeed looked down and gave me his easy smile.

"I guess this is the making-up part," he said. "I forgive you for what's about to happen, FB. Is the cab here yet?"

I shook my head. "Not yet." The final part of the plan was forming. "So here's what we're going to do. I want you to slide forward, and I'll just sort of catch you. Is that cool?" I opened my arms, like a father waiting in the pool.

"No," Knottspeed replied. "I'm back in charge. What I'm going to do is this. I'm going to sort of twist and slide along my side while I roll over onto my stomach, then I actually will fall, backward, but only half as far, so that's when I need you to catch me. I don't want to risk hitting my head on the front part again, at least for today. I didn't lose any teeth, by the way. They're all still in there."

I still had my arms open. I frowned and shook my head. The way he had said "backward" was ominous.

"No, man, no."

He wriggled and began sliding, twisted all the way over onto his stomach, and caught the branch with his armpits, which stopped him for just the amount of time needed to arrest his momentum, and then his arms gave out and he tumbled backward into me. I caught him and staggered back a step and then righted us both. My hands were over his hard, bony chest, and I could feel his heart thrumming like a bird's just under his skin. Knottspeed struggled loose and straightened his shirt.

"Okay. Let's hit the street. If we see that cop again, I don't know. That was a cop, right?"

"Yeah. He widened his search pattern, I guess. Went toward that park."

"Huh." Knottspeed was indifferent. He focused on his feet, which made him quiet. I didn't mind that.

We got to the street and stood in the rain at the edge of the parking lot—a drunk Indian and an extremely white, freshly mangled cripple with a trash bag. Either a cab or a cop car would stop first. Knottspeed was making a soft kind of noise, a bad breathing, so we weren't going any farther. I kept a hold of his arm. I wanted another shot of bourbon, but the laws of street magic forbid it. Light a smoke and the bus will finally come. Sneak a shot in public and a cop car will instantly appear, even in the middle of the night in a snowstorm on Christmas Eve. So we waited. I tried to listen to the rain. It was easier if I closed my eyes. After I don't know how long, Knottspeed cackled.

"Look," he said. "It's cousin of Batman."

I was sure it was a cop he was referring to, but when I opened my eyes, there, right in front of us, was the cab. The driver was some kind of skeeby guy with oily hair and badass rainy day sunglasses. He gave us a cool dude head toss.

"Hop in," he said.

3

Rialto Slowpoke

SKEEBY GUY TURNED OUT TO be a huge fan of angry rockabilly. The day so far had a bad movie kind of feel, and this sudden shift in the soundtrack wilted me. I was just as wet as Knottspeed, and my feet were freezing. My buzz had gone nauseous, and the cab smelled like hair gel, bug spray, and the pine tree coaster dangling from the rearview. Beside me Knottspeed rolled his head, eyes closed, in no way in time with the music.

"Lincoln Street and Eighty-First," I said. Skeeb turned the music down.

"What?" he asked.

"The Rialto," Knottspeed said loudly. "Downtown. The place with the pool tables."

Knottspeed and I glared at each other as the cab lurched into motion. He easily outfierced me.

"Dude, no," I whined. "I'm not going in for this horse thing anymore. Neither are you. We can't. I say we go back to the house. Order a pizza. I don't think you realize what . . . look in the mirror, man. You're in the getting-arrested-for-going-into-public red zone."

Knottspeed struggled erect and looked into the rearview. So did the cab driver.

31

"What the fuck happened?" the cab guy asked. He turned the music down a little more.

"Nothing, really," Knottspeed said, sitting back. "I've been having trouble with my face."

"I can see that," the cab guy said slowly. Then he shrugged. "I had a similar thing happen to me a few years ago. I did a huge hit of nitrous out of a Hefty bag and face planted into a bonfire. Thought I was in a submarine. No burns except this little one on the back of my neck, if you can believe that, but no eyebrows or eyelashes after that for a few months. Looked like a Euro mannequin. Scary easy to get laid with that look."

"What happened to the nitrous?" I asked.

"Dunno," he replied. "I think I dropped it. Last fucking time I'll ever hang out with hippies."

"The nitrous bonfire dance gets really bad when they take their pants off," I said. I was going on a camping trip in a few days with my sister and her two kids—it was supposed to be a big family thing, but everyone had an out except for me—so the topic of being injured around bonfires, right then, was an omen. And every omen is bad.

"I blacked out on airplane glue once," Knottspeed said in an offhand, chatty way. I rolled my eyes. "It was an accident, but the weirdest thing was I didn't fall down. I just stood there."

"Fear change, brother," the cab driver said, as if quoting. "Fear change."

Knottspeed shook his head and hit me on the arm with the back of his good hand. He gestured at the cab guy with his head, sharply. "This dude could easily get on my nerves."

The cab guy turned the music back up. I looked out the window, hoping if Knottspeed's audience disappeared completely then he'd be quiet, and he was.

The Rialto, as it turned out, was really big, and it was in a basement. Over the front entrance was an awning with "The Rialto" spelled out in cheesy seventies Vegas disco script. The open door was mostly black, edged with a dim reddish glow from deep below. It was about as inviting as the gateway to hell. Knottspeed leaned over and peered down into it. He giggled.

"Oh no," he tittered. "Who de who de who."

"Jesus fucking Christ," I said.

"Twelve even," the cab driver said brightly.

Knottspeed dug his rumpled cash wad out and shook loose a ten and then peeled out four ones and handed it all up to the driver, who took the bills and dropped them instantly.

"Damn," he said, disgusted. "These are all wet and bloody and they smell like dog. Where in Oklahoma are you guys from, exactly?"

"Fuck you," Knottspeed snarled.

I am actually from Oklahoma. There was no way he could have known it, but that made it sting twice as bad. "Yeah," I growled. "Fuck you."

"Whatever." The cab driver punched a few numbers into his deck to look for the next fare. "Get out."

I got out on my side and reached back in and took hold of the struggling Knottspeed, pulled him to the door, wrestled him out, and then helped him stand. I slammed the door, and he scowled at me as I helped him up the curb.

"Easy FB," he said. "There's no room for both of us to be belligerent, and I'm the one who's paying."

"Fuck that guy," I said. The cab was still sitting there. "How the hell he guessed I'm from Oklahoma is . . . I'm sick of this Oakie shit."

Knottspeed nodded. "Me too," he said darkly. He leaned around and hit the top of the cab with his cane. He was about to do it again, so I gently pulled him out of range and his swipe fell short. He gave up and concentrated on hobbling, holding on to my arm with most of his bad hand. I shook rain off his clothes bag as we walked under the Rialto awning and looked down. The wide, dark, red-carpeted stairwell was daunting. We surveyed it together for a long moment, considering.

"If we make it all the way down there, we might just be kicked back out instantly," I said.

"I know," Knottspeed replied, "but this is no time to panic." He took a deep breath.

"Either way, I'll have to carry you back up," I continued.

"Whatever," he snapped. He held out his elbow. "Let's go."

Knottspeed started down, one painful step at a time. He seemed irritated with me now, so he wouldn't let me hold on to his arm after all. I crept along next to him, close enough to grab him if he slipped or his legs gave out. I was so fixated on watching his knees that when we ran out of steps and found ourselves in the Rialto proper, it was Knottspeed who took it all in first.

"Eureka," he said by way of assessment. I looked up and cringed hugely, with all of my body.

The Rialto was big enough to have a vanishing point in the haze. Dark red carpet, low lights, and wet brass. There were easily fifteen pool tables. Booths lined all four walls, and there was a section of tables to either side of a giant bar. Framed black-and-white photos of boxers and carnies and smirking women with tall hair and corsets rounded out the décor. The sprawling interior was halfway filled with hipster guys in trendy thrift store suits and women wearing lurid dresses and huge foreign hats. No one looked in our direction, which was almost amazing. There were several TVs around the room, a few of them with Keno but most were showing actual horse racing, or what looked like the prelude to it. I was instantly sucked in along with everyone else. Knottspeed hit me on the arm.

"Snap out of it," he said in a low voice. "Let's hit the men's room and clean up for a second before anyone sees us."

He struck out at a worn pace with his head down, as invisible as he could be in the low bar light. I followed, the bag and the backpack low and out of view of the nearest bartender in case she glanced our way. We made it to the door of the men's room. Knottspeed stood to one side and waited. It took me a second to realize he was waiting for me to get the door. I pushed it open, and he wobbled into the bright interior. I followed, holding my breath.

The men's room was empty, for the moment. Whoever had decorated the place had done their best to pull off swank, flapper-era brass to go with the imitation marble sinks and cracked ceramic urinals, but I guess their budget must have been tight after the TV investment, because it weighed in at really big Wendy's. Knottspeed tossed his cane on the counter next to the nearest sink and then leaned on it. After a deep breath, he turned on the hot water and let the immediate steam rise around his head.

"Help me get my slippers off," he said. He held up one foot, about an inch. The slipper was ruined.

From there it was a race. I put the backpack down and tossed the clothes bag on the counter, knelt and, one by one, took the slippers off. He pulled his belt out while I did this, then he emptied his pockets on the counter and dropped his pants and underwear, stepping out of the soggy pile. There was a square bandage on his tailbone, and his entire butt crack was bruised black. The bandage was red in the center, fading to pink around the edges.

"Toss all that shit," he said. "Hand me the underwear in the backpack."

I scooped everything up fast and paused.

"Are you sure?" I asked. He scowled.

"I've been wearing all that crap for the last ten days. I never want to see any of it ever again. C'mon! I'm showing ass here."

I stuffed everything into the trash can and got the underwear out of the backpack, nice cotton boxers with a plaid pattern that reminded me of Scotland. I handed them to him and watched as he tried to get them on. I knelt and stretched the leg holes open, and he stepped in, King of England style. Then I pulled them up to his knees, and he finished the job while I got the pants out of the clothes bag. We repeated the process, and he ran the belt through the loops and buckled it. Then he pulled his coat off and dropped it on the floor. The wet long-sleeve white dress shirt underneath was stained and stuck to his emaciated frame. I could see his ribs and every one of his vertebrae. He pulled that off too and paused to breathe and lean on the counter. I glanced in the mirror to check if he had his eyes open. He did. There was another, less bloody bandage on his stomach. There were also bruises all over both of his arms and a big yellow-and-orange splotch on his sternum.

"Shirt," he croaked. I hurried. Knottspeed swayed dangerously.

I helped him get the shirt over his head. While he tucked it in, I untied the shoes and pulled them wide apart and set them at his feet. He stepped in barefoot, and I started tying them while he struggled into the suit coat. When I stood up, he had his hands under the hot water. He washed them with soap and then washed his face, like a torn-up hobo cat grooming. When he was done, he rinsed his mouth out and spit pink water into the sink. Lastly, he squirted two big pushes of hand soap into his palm, rubbed his hands together, and then worked the soap into his hair. While he did he smiled into the mirror.

"Little soap will keep your hair shiny all day," he said. "Smells good too."

It smelled like a janitorial product, but he seemed to like it, so I didn't say anything. When his hair was preened to his satisfaction, he rinsed his hands off and blotted himself with a paper towel from the dispenser, studied his teeth for a moment, and dabbed at his eyebrow. He looked remarkably better, like a skinny guy who had been in a bike wreck.

"Toss the rest of this shit," he said. He picked his backpack up and stuffed his Christmas sweater and the tracksuit into it. "I'm ready. We have to get some socks on the way home, FB. I'm getting blisters just standing here. Normally not a huge bad, but the flophouse has pounds of active bacteria per square foot."

I put on my best poker face and opened the door for him.

Knottspeed pulled himself together and did his best to strut, an inviting smile fixed on his pale face. He wasn't even leaning on his cane too hard, and he tapped along like it was a prop that came with the outfit.

The race either hadn't started yet or was already over. It was hard to tell, but most of the people were talking and only halfheartedly paying attention to the TVs. It seemed like more people had shown up while Knottspeed was changing, and the place was about three-quarters full. I followed in Knottspeed's wake as he moved through the loose crowd, past the bar to the booths lining the back wall. He collapsed into the first empty one we came to and winced as he resettled his scrawny butt to the greatest relief for his tailbone. I sat down across from him and looked at the nearest TV. Some really little guy was leading a huge, oiled horse around. It was vaguely dangerous looking.

"What can I getcha?"

A waitress had appeared. She was pretty in the way that always made me irritated. Hair as blond as Knottspeed's, slender hips and a short dress, pert boobs and red lips, big blue eyes. Hard. A gum chewer. She was pretty enough to know it, and that meant if you smiled at her, you were suggestively over-friendly; if you didn't, you were disdainful because she wasn't the right brand of good-looking; if you looked confused, it could be mistaken for smitten; and if you looked immediately irritated, it could be taken as juvenile come-hither. I looked at Knottspeed instead. He didn't suffer from this problem.

"Hello," Knottspeed said smoothly, smiling with his entire broken face. He was one of those men who transformed with ease in the presence of a beautiful woman. Even his fingernails looked suddenly clean, his suit amazingly tailored. He batted his pale eyelashes, and I noticed how startlingly blue his eyes were in contrast to everything else around his head. The waitress noticed too.

"What happen to your cheek, sweetheart?" She cocked her hip, ready for the whole story, the other customers forgotten. I

was almost afraid she was going to sit on me, since I was forgotten too. Knottspeed shrugged, as though what he was about
to tell her was a daily occurrence.

"I was ejected from some sort of Christian thrift store," he
said lightly. "I was never popular with religious people. It wasn't.
like I was thrown bodily from the place. My exit strategy was
off."

"I see," she said. Her painted lips cut a smile as she took him
in. "Happens to women more often. Heels."

"I bet," Knottspeed actually looked her up and down and
got away with it. "And then, to top it off, we had to wait in the
rain for a cab. My friend here wanted to throw in the towel, but
I wasn't turning back after the door debacle. Every wipeout has
a silver lining. I'm betting that actually hurting myself before the
race will minimize my hangover."

"Right," she said. "Booze karma."

This threw Knottspeed for an instant, but he didn't go
down. Instead he leaned back and put one arm over the back of
the booth, slouching professionally.

"I think," he began, "we'll have two mint juleps. And can
you bring us some pretzels or peanuts or some kind of snacky
thing?"

"Sure," she replied. She leaned at the waist to get a better
look at his eyebrow.

"Is it bad?" he purred. Both of their faces went oddly slack.
Knottspeed slowly raised his good hand and lightly brushed two
fingers under his eye. I was riveted as she raised her hand and
did the same, brushing just underneath her own eye. They'd
hypnotized each other.

"Probably too late for stitches," she murmured. Knottspeed
nodded, not breaking eye contact. Their faces were drawing
imperceptibly closer together.

"Figures," he almost whispered. She straightened up and
bounced a little. I almost risked a smile myself. Almost.

"Two mint juleps and bar snacks." She gave Knottspeed one

more smile to hold him until she got back and went to get the drinks. I blew out a breath, relieved she was gone. Knottspeed turned those eyes on me, and they dimmed a little. He smiled a different smile.

"She seems nice," he said. I snorted.

"What the fuck was that?" I was legitimately curious if his answer would make any sense, and I was astonished when it actually did. It made so much sense that it changed my bitter outlook on women and things of the heart. I never knew if he was aware that some of the things he said had that effect on people, but there is no way he would have cared.

"I fall in what I call 'tiny love' really easy," he said. "Every ten minutes on average in public places, and sometimes even when I'm alone, like thinking or reading or whatever. It makes me lovable."

"Well, I'll be." I was pondering this and absently looking at the nearest big screen when the waitress arrived with our drinks. It looked like two bourbons on the rocks. I glanced up at her, momentarily confused; she scowled and then flicked the pretty back on and turned her attention to Knottspeed.

"Let me know when you need another round," she said. Knottspeed held up his hand for her to pause. He picked his drink up, drained the glass, and then handed it back to her while smacking his lips.

"At your leisure," he said. She laughed.

"Ronnie is getting out the pretzel bowls. Be just a sec." She seemed delighted that Knottspeed was such a flagrant alcoholic. He nodded appreciatively. When she was gone, he turned back to me and gestured at my drink.

"Give that a try," he suggested. I picked it up and looked at it, gave it a sniff.

"It's not green," I said.

"I didn't have the heart to tell you earlier," he said. "It seemed too . . . dickish. But go ahead. You might like it."

I took a sip. It was sweet and tasted like cheap whiskey with a breath mint or a Rolaid in it. I scowled and set it down in front of him. He picked it up and took a sip.

"The mint julep is a powerful antifungal," he said. "French people carry these everywhere in the tropics."

I had to laugh at how stupid that sounded. It could even be true. I was beginning to have a good time, I realized. I loosened up a little and fished my last smoke out. Knottspeed did the same and lit mine, then his. He did it with an animated flourish. Bars with low light and weird shit going on suited him.

"Glad you're finally smiling, FB. You're going to get the wrong kind of wrinkles if you keep up with the sad-to-pissy spectrum, wind up like that Mutual of Omaha guy. Check this out." He made a series of facial contortions and then pointed to the side of his mouth. "See that?"

I squinted. "No."

"Then you at least see my point. I have a broken finger right now, among many other things. These shoes are really pinching too, but do I look like I'm thinking about it? No. I know I don't."

The waitress came back with Knottspeed's mint julep and set it next to my unfinished one in front of him. She put a bowl of pretzels down in between us, but just a little closer to him. I was invisible again.

"Can my friend get a vodka or a bourbon or something?" he asked. "His people fought against the French."

"Sure," she purred. After a parting exchange of haunted eyes, she disappeared into the thickening crowd. Knottspeed watched her go and kept watching for a moment, lost in thought. With a small sigh, he turned back to me.

"So, FB, I've been meaning to ask. What does FB stand for?"

I admit I was taken aback. It had been years since anyone had asked me that question. The last person had been my boss at the bagel place. I considered.

"I won't laugh," he said. He picked up the shorter mint julep and leaned forward. "Is it Francis Bacon? No, no way. Fredrick Buntworth? Forbes Bosun? Fernando Beaner?"

"Not even close," I said. The waitress returned and set my drink down, a vodka. She didn't pause to chat this time. It was my drink, for one thing, but the energy of the crowd around us was changing. Something was getting ready to happen on the TVs.

"No," I continued slowly. "My name is Fencepost. Fencepost Beckenshire."

Knottspeed let out a howling laugh that brought a few grins out of the people around us.

"Holy shit!" he cried. He slammed his good hand down on the table with surprising force. "Fencepost Beckenshire! No shit. Is that like an Indian name—I mean, the Fencepost part?"

I had to smile at his delight, which seemed genuine and even a little innocent, like I was the first half-breed with a strange but authentically Indian screwy name he'd ever sat across from.

"It is an Indian name. My father, he . . . well, the story goes that whenever he got loaded he'd talk about the old days, that kind of shit, about how the land never used to belong to anyone. Now that's horseshit, of course. You went on some other tribe's land and it was tomahawk time. But he was fixated on the fencepost as a symbol. In his mind, it had a new meaning when used as the name of an actual human being."

"Just like my name," Knottspeed said, grinning hugely. "So you're supposed to be, what, like . . . some kind of . . . I don't get it."

"A fencepost, on the line between here and there. My mother was white."

Knottspeed nodded. As he considered this, his euphoria diminished. He took a sip of his drink without tasting it and then looked at me, set it down, and slowly held out his good hand.

"Pleased to meet you, Fencepost." I shook his hand. It was thin, of course, and remarkably cold.

"FB," I said. "Please."

Knottspeed shook his head.

"I don't think so, Fencepost. You have a righteous name, a solid fucking Indian name."

I had to agree, although he was the first person to feel that way in a long time.

"Fuckin' way superior to Squatting Turtle or Headlight Deer," he continued. We both laughed. He looked up at the big TV.

"Here we go," he said, gesturing with his drink. "I think we were supposed to be paying attention to what they were saying or maybe reading the racing form, but I don't see any forms and I can't hear a fucking thing over these people, so I guess I'm voting for green. You?"

"I dunno," I said. I turned and studied the screen. The horses were all in the gate, getting whipped and cursed and revved into fury. One of them reared and tried to get out early, and the rider scrambled to force him back down. "I'm not voting for the people. I hope those horses kill one of those little fucking guys. That's who I'm voting for."

Knottspeed looked like he'd been slapped. I took a breath to apologize, but then his face changed. He squinted at me and cocked his head.

"Fencepost," he said evenly. "I can't believe it, but that might actually be the first thoughtful thing anyone has said to me since I checked out of the hospital." He looked back at the screen. "I'm voting for all those horses. I'm voting for every fucking horse that was ever born."

The crowd exploded as the gates flashed up and the horses surged out. I admit that I got swept up in the tide of shouting people. There was a poorly modified frenzy in the air, and it took me. I focused in on the horse with the green rider and felt my jaw go tight and my lips curl back over my big teeth. I could feel the bit in that horse's mouth and feel its rage at running against its own kind with its stupid haircut and the tiny madman whipping the shit out of it, and I so wanted someone to get their head smashed flat and hear the people scream in a different way. Knottspeed could feel it too, and he howled across from me; I would have been scared at that sound if I hadn't been so horribly pissed myself.

The horses rounded the bend. People around us were shrieking now, shaking their fists and grabbing each other, and I felt my guts go cold and thick like I was about to fight a wild dog. The horses churned down the stretch, all majesty gone, running flat out and graceless like some coal-fired prison stove was scorching their organs. I turned away and looked down at my drink. I didn't care who drove their delirious animal the hardest. Knottspeed looked as angry as I felt, but his anger was different than mine—bigger, on the same scale that they measure earthquakes. His pale face was twisted with something below unforgiving and to the far left of sane, but he never looked away. We locked like that, and I watched the race on Knottspeed's face and saw in him an animal surging through weeds that cut its eyes raw. It was amazing that he could even watch something he so obviously wanted to will from existence, and it was amazing that I couldn't look away from the lightning fanning through him.

The crowd roared together. The din staggered after a collective breath, ratcheting down into a loud pig's festival, at once congratulatory and lamenting, with bright spots of sloppy drunken fury and lurid sexual whine. Knottspeed blinked. He'd risen somewhat, and he dropped back down into his seat. He looked down at his drink and picked it up in a daze, drained the glass, scowled, and then looked at me fiercely, remembering I was there. His eyes flicked back to his glass, and he set it down and then smiled suddenly with great joy.

"Mint julep my ass. This is a whiskey with sugary tap water and breath spray." He looked around. "Where the fuck is that hot-ass waitress?"

I always thought it was a sure sign of madness in someone when they flicked from enraged to happy in a single heartbeat like that. Whenever I saw the dark side of anyone, all the rest of it just seemed like paint on the windows, and I more than suspected the darkness was still inside. Really, everyone was like that. I sometimes think the first time you see someone scream the bad kind of scream when you're a kid is probably the last

43

time you ever truly trust anyone. It was that way for me, anyway. But if the good side of everyone was just paint on the windows, at least Knottspeed had the uncommon decency to paint something interesting. I guess that's right about when the Rialto booze came home. I raised my vodka.

"Knottspeed, I like drinking with you. You're not as ugly as most of the people I know."

Knottspeed raised his fresh mint julep.

"Very observant, Fencepost. I'm an impossibly vain man, inside and out, and being crippled has made it even worse. I like drinking in general, and since you seem just smart enough to keep me out of prison tonight, I find you quality company as well. I'll never look at horse racing the same, but . . ." He shrugged.

We drank. Knottspeed lit another cigarette and passed me one and then casually looked around. I did too. The horseracing crowd hadn't been what I was expecting, but then I'd had only a vague idea of what we'd find. Old people, maybe. Leisure suits and faded dresses, lots of generic cigarette smoke. Maybe a few East Coast greaseballs and a black dude with gold teeth hustling pool, something like that. Not this.

"What the hell is up with these women's hats?" I asked.

Knottspeed shrugged again and pointed a woman out as she walked by. She was wearing a tight yellow dress with a floral pattern that reminded me of a church picnic tablecloth and a huge hat made out of a model wooden galley festooned with plastic roses. He frowned.

"It's a tradition," he said thoughtfully. "Like all traditions, it's pretty hit and miss. I don't know how it started, but whenever I think about shit like that, I get lost almost instantly. Why the hell do we eat canned cranberry jelly, whatever the hell that stuff is, every Thanksgiving? You're an Indian. Answer me that."

"One of the higher mysteries," I said, "never to be revealed to the unanointed. But I see your point. I always wondered about the deviled eggs. How the hell did they sneak in there?"

"Whatever. Tell me something spooky, Fencepost. Tell me something deep, way gone, fucked-up Indian crazy. You must have some version of these perverse hats." He looked on expectantly, fully assuming I was going to deliver right off the top of my head.

Unfortunately, my head was full of booze. I lit the cigarette to give me a little time to maneuver. I'd never seen a peace pipe. I'd never been in a tepee or a sweat lodge. I'd been in a hippie sauna once, but that didn't count. Nothing came to mind. I could go for a deviled egg. I thought about that boat hat. My father hadn't had a boat. He'd had a beat-up blue pickup truck—a Ford, I think. It looked like he'd driven through every desert on earth in that thing, or at least in places where it never rained. And that's when it came to me, a story from the distant past I'd heard when I was a kid. The only Indian story I remembered.

"Okay," I said, "I got one."

"A creepy Indian tradition?" Knottspeed looked relieved that I wasn't going to let him down.

"Yep. Sort of. Mostly." I wet my lips. "No. Not really."

"Tell it good," he said enthusiastically. I leaned in and looked both ways like I was about to tell a secret. Knottspeed leaned in like he was ready to hear one.

"Okay. So the reservation where my dad's people are? It's kind of shitty out there. Cattle land, way the fuck out in the middle of nowhere. But the old people—and I'm talking like Civil War old—they all live up in the hills in the same houses they were born in. The young people live in single wides down by the gas station, right off the highway. Anyway, about once a week, the highway patrol stops by, cruises around stirring up shit, and sometimes . . . sometimes they open the cattle gates and go all the way the fuck up into the hills to screw with the old people. And every once in a while, they get hit with a tradition." I paused for effect.

"Serves them fucking right," Knottspeed said, his eyes glowing. I nodded.

"It does . . . it does. So anyway, this one night the new guy on the HP decides to go up there and monkey around with the old people for his very first time. I can only assume he was pretty excited about it, but he had to be a little nervous too. The white side of the story has him nervous, anyway. Old Indians are spooky as hell most of the time, and late at night, when there's no moon at all, dark as fuck—well, you get past that first cattle gate and out of your car, you close the gate behind you and as soon as you hear that 'click' and you're inside, you get back in that car fast because it feels . . . it feels like there's something right behind you, so close that you can feel the hot off it on your scalp, feel the hands reaching out of the black to touch you, maybe wrap around you and yank you in."

"Aw goody," Knottspeed murmured, his stare open.

"Oh yeah. Oh yeah. Thing is, there are four fucking gates about a mile apart from each other out there. So you drive on the dirt road, and all you can see is your headlights. You bump along and get to the next gate, get out and unlock it and open it, and it gets worse and worse. That feeling . . .

"So our HP rookie douchebag is at gate three. Every time he has to call it in—tell whoever is back at headquarters that he's getting out to open the gate then when he's back in his car, et cetera. He gets out and starts walking to cattle gate number three, and he sees something, right there in the road on the other side of the barbwire, and it's walking right toward him." I licked my lips. "It's a fat little midget, he thinks. But it gets closer and he realizes the legs are too long, as skinny as a wrist and about ten fucking feet too long, like stilts. It stops in the headlights and it smiles at him, and its teeth are big and blunt and yellow. And then it screams, high and long, like a strong baby with a fever."

Just then a woman screamed and a glass shattered. The laughter around us sounded faint, the chatter of mostly drunk hipsters and big-headed women drowned in the boozy horror at our table. Knottspeed's eyes were unfocused, and I knew he was envisioning a midget on stilts in the desert, screaming mouth with oversized teeth shining with mucous in the tangled fans of the skewed headlights.

"It was the devil," I whispered hoarsely, "and it was coming for him. It stepped over the cattle fence. He screamed and ran, and it screamed and went after him. As he ran and ran, he could feel it reaching for him, and the lights of his car faded away and he was charging through all that blackness, stumbling and falling and tearing his clothes and blind, but he knew it was right there on top of him, leaning in."

I sat back. Knottspeed did too.

"They found him at dawn. By then everyone knew something was wrong. They sent out all the cars they had, but he was right there, just inside the second cattle gate. He had only one boot on. Lost his gun belt and his hat, shivering cold, piss all over him. Couldn't even talk. They took him to the hospital. Found his car. Some HP went up and talked to the old people, and they weren't surprised. They said the rookie was an Evangelical and told them to send only Catholics to fuck with them."

Knottspeed looked suitably horrified, but also confused.

"Catholics?"

"Everyone brings their own devil when they pay a visit."

I thought the punch line would make him laugh, but it didn't. His confused look deepened, and I could tell he was thinking about other things. Eventually, he shook himself out of it.

"I'm not a religious guy," he began. "I mean, it would be nice to believe in something, but I could never quite manage it. But that was creepy, Fencepost. You're a creepy fucking dude for even telling me that."

"You asked," I said.

"Yeah, but that barely even qualifies. I was talking about hats and garnishes. A fucking toothy midget on stilts chasing some poor shithead around in the desert is just grim, dude. Way to go to the dark side."

We looked at each other for a minute. Finally, he leaned in again.

"Is that your only Indian story?" he asked.

"Pretty much," I said. He looked away, leaned back.

"Shit."

Sometimes when I'm more than half drunk, I space out. It might be my Indian side. That night it happened. I snapped out of it when the waitress gave us new drinks and then again later, when I realized that Knottspeed was no longer sitting across from me. He must have gotten bored, because he'd dragged his withered body over to the bar and was shamelessly flirting with the waitress, who was laughing, her hard edge gone to the point where she was almost girlish. Knottspeed himself was transformed again, and I wondered how I of all people had wound up as his friend-for-hire. I watched them for a while. At first, I thought it must have been terribly difficult for him to lean against the bar and be the kind of breezy shithead who could make such a woman laugh; gradually, it came to me that it wasn't really hard for him at all. That made me resent him just a little. Finally it dawned on me, as I watched him conclude some epic story that had her holding her sides, that he actually couldn't help himself. Of course, I immediately wondered if he was using some of that charm on me. Then I became suspicious, and, because of the booze, that made me angry. When he finally wobbled back to our booth and sat down, I gazed at him through slitted eyes, ready for his line of bullshit and pissed in advance.

"I'm drunk enough to go lie on the frozen dog carcass again, Fencepost," he announced. He looked back at the waitress, who was watching us. "She sure is some kind of human. From Minnesota. I barely escaped before she launched into the sorry story of how she wound up here. Minnesota to the Rialto. Hard to believe."

"Why would that be hard to believe?" I asked in the most measured tones I had in me. He shrugged, indifferent to my attitude.

"I don't know. I guess I always think of upright cows when I think of Minnesota." He gave me an appraising look. "Does that make me a dick?"

"Yes," I said. "Maybe you should keep those kinds of observations to yourself."

He cocked his head. "Fuck you, Fencepost. If this is your way of bucking for a raise, it's not working. Maybe you should keep your opinions on my observations to yourself. Asshole."

So he didn't want the help getting uppity. I sneered.

"Or what?" I asked.

Knottspeed's vague indifference evaporated along with the residue of the charm he'd been smearing all over the waitress. His broken face hardened, and his eyes glittered dangerously.

"Or what?" he hissed. "Or I beat that nasty look off your fucking face with my cane and you walk home. I've clawed my way over bigger sacks of shit than you just to get into a fight, pussy. And I'm talking recently. I'm not in the mood to take any shit from anyone, as you may have noticed. Use both of your brain cells, dumbass."

I realized there was vodka in front of me, so I drank some. The last thing I wanted was to get attacked by a mean albino cripple in a bar called the Rialto. Way too depressing.

"I was just watching you work that waitress, and it occurred to me that you might be working me," I confessed. He looked instantly exasperated.

"Of course I am! That's why I'm paying you! I'm teetering on the brink over here, retard. This is no time for me to rely on the altruism of my fellow man, because with a single exception I actually don't know those kinds of people. It's a lifestyle choice, and a very inconvenient one at this time. So I need a deadbeat brand of mercenary, and as shitty as that sounds, you need a job. Are we clear? Can you try to enjoy yourself and not be a lame fucking bummer about our arrangement? I don't think I could stand this going bad so fast."

I was still grumpy, but everything he said made sense. I hate it when anyone is right at my expense, but especially people like Knottspeed, who was sure to gloat at any sign of victory. I nodded, reluctantly. He looked relieved.

"Thank God," he said. "It's settled. I paid us up, so it's time for you to carry me out of here. I had Cherry call us a cab in case we're blacklisted from both cab companies tonight. Let's get a move on."

I finished my drink, and he finished his. All the flirting seemed to have energized him. He scooped all the uneaten pretzels out of the bowl and put them in his pocket and then stood and looked at me expectantly. I smiled, got up, and stared down at the fierce little man, who was a full head shorter than me.

"Backpack style, or you just want me to carry you *Gone with the Wind*?" I asked. He considered.

"Embarrassingly enough, we'll try you holding my good hand first. If that fails, then we go Scarlett O'Hara. I don't think my spine can handle backpack, and you seem pretty drunk—I don't want you to fall over backward right on top of me. I'd rather just be dropped if you wipe out."

"Makes sense," I agreed. We started toward the stairs together.

"Did you get Cherry's number?" I asked.

"Nah." He waved at her. "Got this heart problem—not the physical kind—and I'm too fucked-up for pussy anyway. Plus, she's sarcastic. I really don't like that in a woman. She also has a dog, which is a major red flag in single women, in case you never noticed. On top of it all, she seems to be in need of rescue, as in she hates her roommates, thinks her job is unlawfully shitty, can't fucking stand this city for a second longer, and even the weather is wrong, like every drop of rain has her name on it. I'm in no position to mount such an operation, no pun intended."

I shook my head.

"Cynicism is beneath you, Knottspeed," I said. He nodded.

"I agree," he said. We got to the bottom of the stairs and beheld them with mutual dread.

"Once again," he said, "I forgive you for what is about to happen."

4

Clairol

THE CAB DRIVER WAS ANOTHER garden-variety fat guy with a mustache, listening to a boxing match blaring on the radio. It was raining hard, so we didn't hear it when we staggered out of the red mouth of the Rialto. Knottspeed must have sensed it, though. Amazingly, he'd made it most of the way up the stairs before I had to drag him. When we paused under the awning, his head snapped in the direction of the cab; some of the fury I'd seen when the horses ran lit in his face, and then abruptly his bright eyes went dead. The bouncer looked up from where he was huddled on his stool next to us, just clear of the downpour. He seemed sad. Knottspeed snapped out of it and looked at him and then patted him on the shoulder.

"I wish I had a hat I could loan you," Knottspeed said.

The bouncer untucked a little and shivered. He shrugged, his hands deep in his jacket pockets. "Me too." He hunkered back down.

Knottspeed cursed under his breath and wobbled out into the rain. I jogged the ten steps to the cab and opened the door and watched his approach, squinting through the rain. It was then that I heard the boxing. I leaned in to ask the driver to turn it off, but I couldn't think of a plausible reason why, so I pulled my head back out and decided to make no decisions.

"My sock crisis is real now!" Knottspeed howled as he made it to the cab. He held his elbow out, and I wrestled him in, both of us cursing, and then slammed the door and ran around to the other side. By the time I got in, Knottspeed was already laying the groundwork for a tirade.

"The fights," he said with mock enthusiasm. "Man fights! What kind of desperate minorities are donating blood and brain cells for our amusement here, cabbie?"

"Lincoln and Ninety," I said. "Thanks. So the rain, huh? Any flooding? Streets good? Seen any lightning?"

Knottspeed scowled at me. The cab driver started the meter and pulled us out. He turned the match down a little.

"Streets are good," he said. He had an East Coast accent. "No lightning, but we never get none out here."

"We were just watching the horse race," Knottspeed said. "Epic animal whip down."

"Oh yeah," the cab driver said. He glanced in the rearview, glad to hear it. "Who won?"

"The devil," Knottspeed replied. I rolled my eyes.

"I saw the big hats," the cab driver continued.

"So back to the boxing," Knottspeed said, picking right up where he'd left off. "Is there any way we could just listen to the rain?"

The cab driver looked in the rearview, slightly miffed but prepared to switch to wounded. "What, you guys don't like boxing?"

"No," we said together. He turned the radio off.

"Suit yourself."

We rode along in silence. Knottspeed looked out the window at the passing streets, shifting now and then, his bad hand wrapped around the head of his cane. At some point during the evening, he'd pushed his pinky back into alignment. The hand looked swollen all over and as white as soap with a hint of blue around the knuckles. I was glad he hadn't gotten us kicked out of the cab; evidently, he still had some instinct for self-preservation. My shirt had soaked up as much cold rainwater as it could while I was getting in, and it was running down my back in small rivulets that converged in my butt crack. It was miserable. And the house was going to be so cold we'd be able to see our breath. It was always warmer in the basement, out of the constant draft and with the added warmth of the old water heater, but it was still going to be a long night. Knottspeed was in for worse. He must have been thinking the same thing. He turned to me and smiled.

"I have my sweater," he said. "And, if I'm not mistaken, we are going to pass a Rite Aid here in a minute. So I have one more mission for you, the last one of the night."

"You want me to go into the Rite Aid?" I asked. He nodded.

"Sorry," he said, "but you have to. We have critical needs."

"Jesus," I whined. "Like what? Rite Aid is terrifying at this time of night."

"I know," he said grimly, "I know. I was kicked out of a Safeway two nights ago for the same phobia I see in you now, so you're not alone. Those fluorescent lights, the hacking old people in line, the one sickly fat guy paralyzed in the Doritos selection, and those damn people talking code over the loudspeakers. It's always you they're talking about. Everyone knows that."

After everything else that day, a Rite Aid might be too much. Knottspeed watched the phobia take root on my face and started fumbling with his backpack.

"I guess we have to stop at the Rite Aid," I announced to the cab driver. He nodded soberly, like he thought it was a bad idea too. Knottspeed handed me the bottle. I coughed a little and then leaned over and tried to take a sip but only succeeded in sloshing some on my pant leg. I put the cap back on and gave the bottle back to him. He silently put it away.

"What do we need?" I asked flatly. The smell of the spilled booze rose up into my nostrils.

"I need socks," he said. "Black ones. If all they have is white ones, forget it. I also need a jumbo Ensure for vitamins and minerals, and I need one of those short rayon-type throw blankets, the little ones obese people with diabetes put over their legs when they watch *Jeopardy*. That's right in our price range for disposable bedding. Essentially I need something in between me and the dog putrefaction. And get yourself a candy bar. And I need something for my face."

"Superglue?" This kind of list was guaranteed to get the loudspeakers going.

"Antiaging cream. Moisturizer. Only total pussies go in for the ointments. I knew a guy who got shot in the back of the head one time, execution-style with a twenty-two. The bullet bounced off his skull and went right down his back, just under the skin, and shot out next to his tailbone. When he woke up, he rubbed hand lotion on the entry and exit wounds and put toilet paper on 'em, taped it in place. He was fine—sort of."

"I read somewhere motor oil is good," the cab driver said.

"Oil of Olay," Knottspeed said forcefully, trying to erase the motor oil from my mental list. "Or Clairol. Just don't get anything for hair."

I closed my eyes, but I could feel him watching me. The hiss of the tires changed after a period of time, just long enough for me to forget the source of my anxiety. The cab driver snapped me out of it when the sound of motion stopped and all that was left was the drum of rain on the roof of the cab. He even paused dramatically.

"Late-night Disneyland," Knottspeed said brightly. "Next stop, anywhere but this."

I opened my eyes, and the garish lights of the Rite Aid pissed into my retinas. I burped. Knottspeed was still staring at me.

"We need cigarettes too," he said softly, sympathetically. His wide eyes were bright with longing for the items on his list and the hope that I could function long enough to get them. I steeled myself and set my face into Indian poker mode.

"Cash," I said. I held out my hand, and he slapped a few wet twenties into my palm.

"Check," he said.

"Fluid level," I said. He fumbled the bourbon out of his backpack and spun the lid off, took a generous sip, and then passed it to me. The cab driver was watching us in the mirror.

"Don't drink that in here," he said. I took a swig and passed it back to Knottspeed.

"Too late," I said. I opened the door and paused to meet the cab driver's eyes.

"You need anything?" I asked. He didn't even bother to shake his head. "I'll be right back."

I got out and hitched up my wet pants like a gunfighter, ignoring the rain. It was go time.

The sensory assault upon entering the Rite Aid was impressive. To my left was a Ms. Pac-Man machine, chirping with the bubbly crisp sounds of eighties arcades. The screen was smeared with layers of small greasy handprints. The two checkers looked up at me. One was a fat kid with acne scars and thin, rat-colored hair, probably the night manager. Across from him, a scrawny brunette with a scar on her mouth and fish-eye glasses, meek, years older than the zit, but still hot. The Muzak version of "The Girl from Ipanema" cut out— replaced with "code forty-one, code forty-one"—and then resumed. I realized I was transfixed, mad dogging the manager guy, who was nervously avoiding my eyes. I went through the turnstile and had the presence of mind to grab a handbasket, which was a good sign.

The very first aisle was beauty products, positioned for high exposure due to their popularity with thieves. Strategically not the wisest item to add to the basket first, but I was pressed for time and my memory was hemorrhaging, so I sidled up and started scanning. Clairol had a nice-looking squeeze bottle of moisturizing sunscreen for a bargain price, so I plucked it out and dropped it into the basket with a flourish for the cameras and the clerks. Next up, stuff deeper in the interior. Something was sure to stand out.

The Rite Aid began to seem clean right then, a sterile place to lie down and clip my toenails or get a haircut. I had no idea where Ipanema was, but I knew what the lady looked like: as brown as me but different, more golden, with hands that danced and wide hips, a grass luau skirt and bare feet with splayed toes that had never seen the inside of a shoe, and perfect tits, as round and firm as peaches right off the back of a truck heading to the paradise of grocery stores. I paused in the frozen pizza section and stared at them.

"Can I help you find something?"

It was the woman with the scar on her mouth. She looked like she was on her way somewhere else in the store and had stopped randomly to interrogate me. I shrugged and smiled.

"I think you can," I said. "I need a Hawaiian shirt, a bandanna, and some kind of vitamin drink that goes good with whiskey. I'm thinking of a snack of some kind too. An electric heater or a hair dryer. I have about forty bucks to work with."

She wasn't expecting this. The scar on her mouth looked old, and I realized she was pretty because of it. She had a shyness that came from a mark on her face, and that shyness made me feel good in my stomach. Her baggy shirt was a functional old lady blouse, dark and featureless, and her shoes came from Payless. I bet naked she had the unspoiled body of a woman half the age of her face.

"Socks too," I said. "The socks are a priority." Her face lit up, and I wanted to touch her.

"The socks I can help you with," she said. "Right this way."

She set out at a leisurely stroll, and I followed. She walked sort of hunched forward, shoulders high.

"It's really pouring out there," I said. She nodded.

"I had to go out there earlier to take the boxes out. I had one of those raincoats from the dollar aisle, but my feet got all wet."

"Bummer," I said. "I need a couple one-dollar raincoats. Good thinking."

"We had one-dollar umbrellas too," she went on, "but they sold out a couple hours ago."

We turned onto the clothing aisle. It was all no-label track-suits and sweatshirts, a small section of women's flip-flops, and three different kinds of Hawaiian shirts. At the very end was a panty hose display with a few kinds of one-dollar three-packs of women's socks. There was one pair for women with big feet, black tube socks that were on the thin side with machine-embroidered pandas. I looked down at my feet and judged that they might fit me and thus Knottspeed. I took them as she watched. She looked like she wanted to ask about them, but she didn't. I kept going, and she followed. I could hear her walking, feel her watching. I stopped at the shirts.

"I don't really like any of these," I said. They all had Mexican beer ads on them. I fingered the polyester briefly and envisioned it sticking unpleasantly to Knottspeed or the cab driver.

"They're way too big for you," she said. "All we have left are the Big Gulp sizes. Happens that way."

"Eh." There was some kind of observation I could have whipped out there, but I passed. "How 'bout those umbrella shirts?"

"Right over here," she said. She set off the way we had come, her hands folded behind her back. She didn't wear nail polish, and it looked like she was a chewer. I found this oddly soothing. She was definitely my speed. At the very least, she was unlikely to turn on me right away. We turned on the aisle with all the remaindered junk, and I slowed into drift mode. She followed suit. I plucked some toenail clippers out of a bin and dropped them in my basket.

"I can never have enough of these," I said. She nodded. We went past the empty spray bottles, paused for mutual consideration at the pink hair curlers and hair clips, and finally made it to the raincoats. They were one size fits all, yellow plastic, and about as thick as a cheap trash bag. I took two.

"Right on," I said. She nodded once and raised her eyebrows.

"Sports drinks?" she asked.

"More like old man juice," I replied.

We wandered past home appliances and then down greeting cards—which, for sentimental reasons, I never look at—and took a left at office supplies. That's where we ran into the zitty guy. He was setting up a plastic Christmas tree at the end of the aisle. It somehow made me want to like him, to include him in the surprisingly good vibe I was generating. He looked at my guide and back at the tree.

"I put all the candy canes by your register." Not friendly, not rude—just bland. My mood began to erode, so I pushed past him. She skipped spryly to catch up.

"Here we go," she said. We stopped, and I looked down an aisle of denture glue, rash cures, and hair dye. The old man juice was somewhere in the center of it all. I tried to not touch anything as we closed in. This would be the aisle with the most rarified germs. The Ensure was right next to the adult diapers. I got a jumbo strawberry one and put it into the basket.

"Not for me," I said.

"Same as the socks?" She started walking again, toward the pain relievers on the far wall perpendicular to us.

"Yeah. I need a few more things . . ." I stopped at the Advil and got a generic bottle of ibuprofen. "Good. Now beer and cigarettes and I'm out of here. That zitty dude your boss?"

"Yeah," she said, a little coldly. I knew it was just a matter of time. We got to the orange juice. The beer was right next to it. I took two forties of Bud and put them in the basket.

"I shouldn't even sell those to you." She couldn't look at me.

"I shouldn't even buy them, but I actually have to. I have to rinse the memory of a horse race out of my head. Budweiser has medicinal value to Indians."

She snorted, from cold all the way to disgusted just like that. I was glad our relationship was over. It had lasted for about a minute and a half too long. We walked to the register in silence. I sat my basket down on the counter, and she took her station and started ringing me up. I took two sticks of beef jerky from the plastic can by the register and tossed them in with the rest of my crap.

"Two packs of smokes too," I said. "Cheapest ones you got. I have money today, but generic smokes add to my street cred."

She ran two packs of generic one hundreds across the scanner and dropped them in the bag. I checked out the magazines until she was done.

"Twenty-two seventy-nine."

I pulled out Knottspeed's money. It was wet and a little bloody along one edge. I opened the fold and passed her a twenty and a ten. Disgust ramped up into the genuine preamble to shun. She made change and set it on the counter so she didn't have to touch me. I took it. "The Girl from Ipanema" faded then and gave way to a Glen Campbell song. I winked and took the bag. She stayed looking down.

Knottspeed was standing outside the door, smoking a cigarette and looking out at the rain. I took a deep breath of wet parking lot and then joined him in his survey.

"That was fun," I said. "What happened to the cab?"

"He's gone," Knottspeed replied. I nodded and took one of the packs of smokes out and began gnawing at the cellophane.

"But I didn't have to pay," he went on. I mumphed my approval. "I told him what I thought about boxing. He took umbrage to my pointing out the indisputable middle-class draconian voyeurism inherent in watching the classically disadvantaged beat the shit out of each other to the point of brain damage for money, and he told me that all of us fags should go back to Jerusalem. I challenged him to a real fight and spit on the back of his head to get things going. So now I'm standing here. Big fat pussy."

"I got beer," I said.

"Good," he replied. "Did you get my socks?"

I took them out and handed them to him. He studied the pandas.

"These are kind of thin, but there's two pairs here. I'll double up. Blanket?"

"Forgot," I said. "But I got us big-ass raincoats."

"Hmm," he said. "That's actually an improvement on my idea if the plan is to have something in between me and the dog problem. I can wear it to bed." The thought seemed to brighten him. I decided to run with my positive momentum and took out one of the raincoats and passed it to him.

"Yellow," he said.

"Yep. Let's hit that bench there and get your panda socks on, suit up, and go hide by the dumpsters and drink this beer."

"Good idea," he replied. "That cab driver hit me, but that in no way means he didn't call the cops."

"Then these yellow raincoats will be the perfect disguise. It's all coming together."

He hobbled over to the bench and dropped down on it, winced, and pried off one of his shoes. His foot was amazingly white in the fluorescent lights—not ghoulish, but definitely a stylish cadaver. He flexed his toes.

"I tell ya, Fencepost, a month ago, maybe six weeks, I never could have guessed that I would be on my third disguise of the day and changing into panda socks in a drugstore parking lot accompanied by a wily and resourceful Indian who was bravely acting as my squire."

"Really?" It somehow surprised me. "You . . . I keep getting the impression that you planned it all. That this is actually the middle of the opera, and I'm a character who just took the stage."

He struggled into sock number one and then paused for a break. I lit two cigarettes and handed him one. He took a drag and then gestured at the parking lot.

"This empty parking lot is just another backdrop, is it?" He shook his head and pulled a second panda sock on over the first, paused again. "Everything is this way, Fencepost. It's the nature of reality. You might have failed to notice that an 'opera,' as you call it, is in progress, but I don't blame you. Almost no one ever notices. It's why they hire people like me."

I laughed. Then the smile faded as I let the words tumble around in my head and mix with the booze and the rain. Gradually, I frowned.

"What the hell do people hire you for again?"

"Dreams." He got the shoe back on and got after his other foot.

"I guess I don't get it." I watched him pause and then get back to work. The second foot went faster. When he was done, he flicked his cigarette out into the rain and rose on his own. He leaned heavily on his cane and gave me a strange, almost sad look.

"Don't worry, Fencepost," he said quietly. "You will."

"I will?" I was relieved for some reason. Then it sank in too. Everything was on delayed reaction. "Why?"

"Because it's part of the plan."

5

Recycled Buildings

PEOPLE HAVE ALWAYS TOLD ME the kinds of things they never tell anyone else. When I was younger, I thought it might be my simple face or maybe my plain clothes. In some ways I was only half present, standing on the border between anonymity and the wide territory of possible embarrassment. I was also generally unsure of what other people may have been telling each other when I wasn't there. As I got older, I reasoned that the truths inside of the lies that poured out of relative strangers were brought forth due to my fondness for booze and my general proximity to it.

However it happened, a handful of odd and otherwise unnoticed characteristics combined in me to form the perfect confessional, the deaf and distracted priest who absolved through the act of shrugging indifferently. In this way, I was eventually led to a heightened understanding of the nature of evil. After a thousand and one stories told in just as many ways, I can say with certainty that evil, and the measure of it, stems entirely from lies. Not the lies we tell everyone else, but the ones we tell ourselves. A really convincing liar can justify anything, and right there the nightmares in the newspapers are born. And all people do this to some degree.

Knottspeed was different, even singular in this respect. He obviously didn't believe a word he said, even if it was true, and I don't think he believed anything anyone else said, either. To him, the concept of truth seemed to be a flavor, to be selected in favor of dirt or dog shit, but one of many. His understanding of the moment was subject to his internal moment, and he knew it. It colored everything he said, everything he did, and he seemed to know that too. But that made him so easy to trust, easier than anyone I had ever met, because he wasn't going to put any cave dirt in his mouth, and nothing like that was going to come out. But . . .

"I really like it here," Knottspeed said. He inhaled deeply through his fine nostrils and coughed. "It feels like camping. I even have an Indian."

I did feel a tiny bit bad about the mess we made behind the cardboard recycling bin, but I admit to being shallow, so it was only for a second. I had taken a few boxes out of the recycling and made a floor, a few more to make some walls, and then some plastic to make a partial roof. The poor woman I'd just gone through an entire relationship with at warp speed would probably have to clean it up at the end of her shift. Mutual admiration, flirtation, the period of mutual discovery, the awkward phase, and then rejection staggering into shun, concluding with her cleaning up a mess I'd made while I was drunk. I was getting better at relationships. Start to finish in record time. I handed Knottspeed the beer. He nodded at the bag as he took it.

"Food in there?" Knottspeed's almost-white hair was wet and plastered to his skull. In the dim parking lot light, it looked like cellophane over a bulb of pale-pink Halloween candy. There was a big blue vein pulsing in his temple. I nodded.

"Jerky," I said. I passed him one.

"Perfect," he said. He took a long pull of beer, passed it back, and then took the jerky and bit at the wrapper until it peeled back. He took a thoughtful nibble and chewed.

"Outdoorsy. Teriyaki."

"I got you the Ensure too. And some fingernail clippers."

"We can share the clippers," he said.

He chewed for a long time in silence. I drank and kept quiet. The rain was loud around us and it was cold, but I felt peaceful and I think he did too. He swallowed and then stared out at nothing. The wind picked up a little and rattled our strange little urban hobo shelter. The lights from the laundromat across the parking lot smeared all the way over the black in blurry strips of green and fans of muted gold. I thought about the rain and the boat hats at the Rialto and then drifted peacefully along into my usual random nonsense, watching the fireworks, when I suddenly blinked, drunk. Knottspeed had been talking for some time, but he'd ending whatever it was he'd been saying with a question.

"What?"

"Flat-out hallucination, Fencepost. You ever seen anything that you knew wasn't there?"

"What, like a UFO?" I shifted uncomfortably. "UFOs are real, man."

"Excellent answer. So I'm sure you'll see around the edges of my next point." He sipped and shifted a little, his eyes still fixed far beyond anything. "One step past that, one big step over the edge, and you spread your wings and glide out into everything important. The future and its trillion momentary friends. Love. The inside of the inside of the atom. The far side of everything you forgot. What's hiding inside you behind what you're actually trying to hide. So much of what's important is just like your UFO, Fencepost."

I thought about that. So did Knottspeed. He was right, of course, but it was the first time anyone had ever been right about anything so clearly that it filled my head. We listened to the slow hiss of a passing car and then the soundscape of city at night.

"So," I said slowly, "if that's true—and it is, I'm sure of it— is that . . . is that why you're so crazy, Knottspeed? Because you can see around the edge?"

He turned his broken eyes on me, and it was like he was looking right through me, at my snail's trail through time, at all my coming Monday mornings.

"No, Fencepost. I live there."

I looked down at my hands. I suddenly thought about pianos and how when I was a boy I'd believed whatever was inside of them that made the sounds was alive. And that if I could see inside of one, it would have a canyon inside of it, something large and wide and deep and full of shadows, and warm. Tiny mammals or teakettles with eyes and chests full of voice would live in it. I hadn't thought about that in two and a half decades.

"I fell in love twice last month," he said quietly, almost to himself.

"That all?"

"I was busy," he replied in the same soft voice. "A coma for part of it, then just totally somewhere else with a wraparound concussion. So yeah. Only twice. The first one was more of a 'little love,' I guess I'd call it now. Not to be confused with 'tiny love.' But in my entire life there's been only one big one. The kind that makes you dream with your eyes open, almost like peyote. The kind that makes you feel different forever, about everything. 'Big love.'"

"Hmm." I listened to the rain and toyed with the fantasy. "Big love."

"Yeah." His eyes got a faraway look as he stumbled around inside his wrecked memory. "When I woke up in that East LA discount shithole of a hospital, I dunno man, I didn't know where I was. There was a no-visitor deal, because everyone there was either a convict or a mental patient. A few people with TB, that kind of thing. Junkies galore. Anyway, I had no idea where I was. The tip of my spine had ripped a hole through my skin just above my butt crack, and I was on some kind of plastic mat, just stuck there in my own piss and blood. I was all alone and shackled because I evidently bit some guy on the hand when they tried to move me."

I'd always wondered what I'd do in a situation like that. If I woke up in agony with no idea where I was or how I'd gotten there. If I didn't know my name or what I looked like. I hoped I wouldn't be the kind of guy who cowered and wept hysterically, unmanned by the experience. I probably would be. Knottspeed wasn't, and I can't say I was surprised.

"I don't remember biting him, if that's what you're wondering, so in some ways I didn't do it on purpose. Anyway, I was fucked-up bad. One day they pried me out of my nest and hosed me down, and then somebody wheeled me outside. It was so bright out there, Fencepost. Hot too. This guy gave me a smoke, some guy named Clark, maybe Ken. I ate some food that day, first time in a few weeks. A sandwich. It tasted like pure salt."

I didn't say anything to encourage him to keep going, but he did.

"They wheeled me back in before I passed out, and this woman came around and checked the bandage on my head. She was Mexican, with long black hair and big brown eyes. She had cold hands that felt so good. That was the first time I'd ever seen her. First I remembered, anyway. She was wearing tight jeans, but not like she was showing off her ass. More like it was the only kind she had, the only kind she'd ever worn. Mexican uniform. God, she touched me and I knew, I knew all about her in that single instant. Some small apartment where she ate soup alone at night at her kitchen table. Falling asleep watching TV with her slippers on. All alone because she had no idea what kind of guy she wanted, but it wasn't the vato peacocks around her or the white-trash-chasing Margarita-flavored Saturday night poon. It was me. Someone who knows she's sad about things she can't find the right person to talk to about, who would understand. A person who isn't looking around that edge we were talking about, but lives in there and can't ever get out because there's no such thing. Someone who would touch her face like she touched mine, with cold hands when I was on fire and soft hands when I was hard as a stone. A person who knew why being good wasn't the kind of thing she did on purpose, and how close to the statues that made her, and why that's so frightening that it's hard to swallow. She was all I thought about for a week. I talked to her every day for hours, and she listened, Fencepost, and kept looking and looking at all of the many things in my mind, turning them over and . . . her breath. And that magic grew until one day I had to split. I had some queer black dude to bust me out, and I bribed one of the other patients to call me a cab so the raging gutter outside the gate didn't eat me alive. She wasn't there that day. I never even got to say good-bye."

"Mmnn." I'd never felt that way about a woman. I'd never even felt anything that complicated. I didn't know if I wanted to.

"Maria," he whispered to the night.

We were quiet for a long time, listening to the rain and drinking. I thought about the bagel place . . . the horses . . . the mint julep. And then I realized that it had been more than a half hour and Knottspeed hadn't said a thing. I glanced over at him to make sure he wasn't dead. He was still staring out into the dark, seeing something I couldn't.

"Why did you come back?" I asked. "I mean here, to the fucking rain and the shitty wreckage of, you know—your life. To the house on Lincoln Street." He didn't answer for so long I thought he might have fallen asleep with his eyes open.

"I was in LA on business," he finally answered. "Fobbing off some shitty paintings on a high-end hotel. I knew my friends and my now ex-chick would have landed on my place like vultures and taken everything, even fought over it, when the news came out that I was in a coma in an East LA trash bin and was probably going to die. They did. But they never found the cash I had stashed in the heater intake, and I still had one bank account no one could get to."

"So . . . what's with the boxes?"

Knottspeed shrugged and sipped his beer. Then he lit a cigarette under the cover of his plastic hood.

"Cover. Leaving a ghost trail. If everyone thinks I live in that shithole where you do they'll leave me the fuck alone. Plus, it will scare the fuck out of everyone if they think I've gone insane enough to give up my old place and go into what might be considered hiding in plain sight."

I considered for a few sips.

"I thought you were supposed to be smart," I said eventually. "Or at least, I dunno. Enterprising."

Knottspeed wasn't insulted; in fact, he seemed pleased. He gave me a genuine smile that turned thoughtful and then just a little sad.

"You see, my plan is working perfectly. I've even fooled you, my Indian friend-for-hire. And so it begins."

6

Graveyard with a Buddy

WHEN I WOKE UP, I felt especially terrible. I didn't move for I don't know how long as I measured the level of physical fucked-upitude. My feet hurt, so I started there. They were wet, and one of my boots was still on. The foot inside it felt hot and swollen and itchy, straining at the laces. The other foot was cold. My knees ached. Generalized pain through my guts and my chest. My face felt puffy, and it was hard to tell if my eyes were working in the pitch black. The feeling in my head was what I imagined a rattle-snake bite might feel like, and there was rodent in my gums. I was in the basement, I realized. On my mattress. In the house on Lincoln Street.

Bad. I'd gone from drunk to serious bender, crazy Indian style. It happened from time to time, but at least I hadn't been arrested so far. I reached up into the darkness and found the twine dangling from the lightbulb and pulled it.

Knottspeed. The last thing I remembered was hanging out in the Rite Aid parking lot behind a dumpster. We'd evidently made it back. I listened, but there was no sound from upstairs. He was either uncon-scious in the belly of the dog cocoon or he'd died in it. I doubted I had the physical strength to leave him anywhere else; the little demon bastard would have beaten me to death with his cane first.

First. It was a good place to start. A hangover this bad had only one cure—to keep going. It required stamina, willpower, and the nervous system of a Marvel superhero. Vodka Man. Dr. Wad. The Hangman. I blew out diesel fumes and picked up the vodka. My knuckles cracked like little eggs full of dry rice, and my hands palsied as I fumbled the plastic top off and let it fall to the concrete floor. I took a mighty double chug, and two minutes later my heart slued into a human rhythm and the raging tic under my eye stopped.

"Goddamn!" I thundered. Nothing. The old house was ominously quiet. The rise and fall of a low whistle of cold pushing through a crack somewhere above me sounded like a poltergeist warning me, and then it faded. The echo of stone-cold empty honed through the enormous, beautiful flower bloom of the first drink of the second day in a crazy train derailment, and I rose. My other boot was nowhere to be seen. Smears of blood had dried across my arms and my naked, hairless chest. I charged up the stairs two at a time.

The kitchen was extra wrecked from my passage. Bottles on the floor, an upside-down plate from where I'd staggered into the counter. I careened into the living room and stopped, aghast. The vodka bottle dropped from my hand.

Knottspeed was . . . gone. I went to the front door and opened it. It was raining steadily. Half the boxes had been stolen. The remaining ones were torn open, many of them empty. There was no sign of him. I closed the door and looked for clues, and as I did I was relieved, then amazed, then alarmed again. I sat down on the piano bench.

The wheelchair was gone. His backpack was by the couch, open and empty. The shiny new shoes were absent. Knottspeed was alive. He'd made it back with me, and somehow, when I'd been unconscious, he'd made it back out.

I took my boot off and rolled my ankle around. Sore, but not sprained. Crunchy, but not busted. The dried blood on me amounted to less than half a cup. He'd been bleeding, but it was possible that I'd had a nosebleed in the basement. I was poking around my nostrils for crust when I noticed a bottle of quality bourbon sitting in the greasy dust on the piano. Half full, and nothing half full or half clean or partially destroyed survived here long. Quality was stolen instantly. There was an envelope next to it. A good-bye letter, I realized. The maniac had abandoned me.

I snatched it up and opened it. Forty dollars and a note, written in perfect, flowing script on the back of some junk mail. I squinted.

Fencepost—

Order a pizza and drink this hooch. I'll be back just shy of midnight, and it would be best if you were loaded and full of calories. We have grim shit to do. Run and I'll find you, and I'll light this unhealthy place on fire before I start looking.

—KS
PS I have tons of money.

I read it a second time, then looked up. After a moment, I took a thoughtful sip of the bourbon.

"Grim shit," I repeated in a cracked voice. I glanced at the winking clock on top of the TV, the only clock in the house that worked. Five hours to kill. I turned to the keys and put my bare foot on the sustain pedal and started playing.

"Mysterium Luni," early seventies jazz, with that rambling, incomprehensible quality so useful to heavy drinkers; easy to play and magical in some way that made me seem incredibly competent. A sucker's tune. Rubetones. My fingers wandered over the keys and loosened, my mind clearing as much as it was going to. The dog smell was bad, but the draft was carving at the edges of it. Distorted details of the night came back with the right soundtrack.

The devil midget on stilts. That story had left a stamp in me so big and so deep and so old it was like the meteor crater in Mexico that ended the dinosaurs. I couldn't see it, or what it had done, and I'd been standing in the center of it for as long as I could remember. Bring your own devil. Maybe it was the rage in the horses, the horrible jeering and the terrible pageantry of the goddamned hats, or Knottspeed's glowing, torn-up eyes, but somehow it came up and out of me. Fencepost the dog shed painter, newly awakened and delivering a high-octane beating to a hangover in a freezing dump, temporarily employed by a demon, and playing piano for the first devil that had ever walked my way. I muscled into a hard B-flat hammer stroke and let the old box ring.

I was Knottspeed's friend-for-hire, and somehow that had made him my default therapist. It was why my ex-girlfriend had the "ex" attached, why the bagel shop had taken the keys away and weaned me off the schedule. How I'd become a sort of codependent slave to Ken the slumlord. Lost was a commodity in the same way as welfare cheese, apparently; no one wanted to eat it, but making money off of it was acceptable.

I took another swig of booze. If Knottspeed was my new head of soul management, then . . . what? Suicide? Quit drinking, shave my entire body, and stow away on a banana steamer bound for India? Make YouTube videos?

Order pizza. I needed those calories for the grim shit. I took everything out of my pockets. Four bent cigarettes. A book of matches. The change from last night's many transactions and my buddy payment added up to more than three hundred bucks. I was rich.

There was no phone, so I couldn't order a pizza. And the oven had cute little mice in it, so I couldn't get a frozen one. I found my lost boot in the kitchen and put it on and then went to the 7-Eleven and ate four microwave burritos in the parking lot. By the time I got back I was wet and cold, so I put my coat on and went back down into the basement and sat down on the mattress. After a minute, I turned out the light.

======

"Tonto!"

I was sitting up before I was awake. Knottspeed pounded on the floor.

"Get up here, you horse thief! You heathen offspring of next door and nowhere!"

I obediently headed up the stairs. Unbelievably, I felt a lightness of being in my chest. No matter what happened next, it didn't matter. Knottspeed had come. He sounded animated, and something of his giantness was already working through me.

I entered the living room firmer, like a breeding problem with a cure, a bright new madness coursing through me. I grinned and tasted blood.

Knottspeed sat just inside the open door. He'd bribed someone, probably a cab driver, to get him and his flea market wheelchair inside. The black plastic trash bag he was wearing like a poncho billowed majestically in the wind at his back. His white hair was soaked and scraped back flat over his skull, his damaged eyes wild.

"Ready," I reported.

"The booze, kemosabe." He held his hand out, and I passed him the remains of the bottle from the top of the piano. He killed it and tossed the empty on the couch. A cab was waiting down the street. "Go find a shovel, and let's get the hell out of here."

I nodded. He rose, and I helped him down the stairs, noticing as I did that his legs were worse than yesterday. He was tired, which I didn't think could happen. Something had punched through his rabies. Once I got him in the cab, I brought the wheelchair down and put it in the trunk, leaving it open an inch, and went quickly through the rain into the backyard. Ken's toolshed was a rickety piece-of-shit chicken coop. There

75

was a padlock on the outside, but it was just for show. I pulled the warped door open and stepped back. Much of what Ken had stolen from the previous tenants was stored inside, including everything he had already stolen from Knottspeed. Almost all of the missing boxes were inside. I stepped forward. One of the boxes was open, and for some reason I glanced in and then took something out.

It was a picture of a younger Knottspeed wearing a tuxedo. Part of a wedding. Smiling, healthy, two dozen pounds heavier. Clean. Ken had been after the frame, I'd guess. Antique brass.

My mood tumbled like an empty box down the stairs. Gone. It was all gone. Knottspeed had been stripped bare, reduced from the proud, arrogant, prosperous man so many people had admired to a skeleton in a trash bag waiting for a shovel. I took one of the spades out of the leaning stack in the corner and slammed the door. When I got back down to the street, I put the shovel in the trunk and got in, quiet, angry. Knottspeed was silent and motionless, but his eyes were open. He was in that place he went to again.

"Sixty-First Street and Market," he snapped, coming out of it. The cab pulled out.

"I found most of your stolen stuff," I began haltingly. He glared at me.

"What stuff? The shit my unpaid friends stole from my old place or the shit Ken stole last night while we were gone?"

"Ken." I shook my head. "Eight or nine boxes out in the toolshed."

"Ah. How fantastically reliable." Knottspeed looked back out at the rain. "I wondered if the frog would peek out of his pussy. This is good."

"It is?"

"Yeah. I've been encouraging that kind of thing. Spread the valuables far and wide."

"And there's a reason? Other than crazy?"

Knottspeed leaned over and whispered under the radio. "It

makes me harder to find. The trail leads in dozens of different directions now, all of them made secret because they're loaded down with shame. Manufacturing liars is as easy as making cake."

I laughed a little. His reasoning actually made sense, which was scary. He smiled at my reaction, reading me like he always did.

"You think that's nutty? By the time this night is over . . . well, you'll never be the same. And I'm not sorry for that in the least. There's a chance you might like wherever you wind up when you finally run out of gas." He cackled then, and the sound gave me the chills. The cab driver's eyes flicked to the rearview and then back to the road, and he turned the radio up. Knottspeed flipped him off out of reflex.

"Where the hell did you go?" I asked, leaning close enough to keep it private. Knottspeed radiated cold.

"Long day, Fencepost. I had to go break into my old place, which is still in my name by the way, and steal my own briefcase out of the heater duct. Then I had to mail it to LA. So, of course, I needed help. The waitress from the Rialto—and God, that was ugly. She had a terrible hangover."

"Aw, man."

"Yeah, I know. Her car smelled like dog, which was convenient." He shook his head. "The looting of my old place is very nearly complete. All the antiques are gone. I even found a few notes on what was left. Nobody's been there for a few days. Anyway, from there I had to hit the post office by the train station. After that . . ." he drifted off, remembering.

"You fight with the post office people?"

"Nope. Couldn't. Everything I had to mail was a felony."

"Explosives? Guns? Briefcase full of coke?"

"No, you idiot. Cash." Then he smiled in triumph. "Man, you know that bar Dun Tiki? Over off the interstate? Bartender there owed me a huge favor for years. Paid off her debt about a year ago. I had a standing order with her for three years—if a guy who looks anything like me comes in and he's foreign and using a passport for ID, get that fucker wasted on the house and lift it. Yens Browar. Guy could be my half-brother."

"Gnarly."

"Yeah. So after the post office, I carried on with the camping theme."

"Jerky? Build a little fire?"

"Beer with the hobos at the switchyards." He sighed. "This city has a magnificent train station, Fencepost." The cab slowed and came to a stop. Sixty-First and Market had an out-of-business tile store on one corner and a breakfast diner, closed for the night, across from it. The rain falling through the lone streetlight made me feel like I was in a movie about something I couldn't quite follow.

"This is us," Knottspeed said brightly. He passed up a twenty and shot me a warning look that could only mean that I should be quiet, so I was. I got out and pulled up the collar of my old army coat. The driver popped the trunk, and I took the wheelchair out and then instinctively hid the shovel low as I took that out too, rightly predicting that a shovel could not be used for anything legal at this time of night. I stuck it on the side of the chair with the head of it hidden by my legs and then wheeled over for Knottspeed, who cleverly ensured that the cab would depart swiftly by declaring sudden nausea. We watched it speed away and round the first corner with a brief flare of red.

"Where to?" I asked.

"Under the awning of the tile place," he suggested. "Let's collect my thoughts while we smoke."

I pushed and pulled him through the gutter and up over the curb until we were out of the rain. Knottspeed dried his hands under his trash bag coat and came up with two menthols and passed me one. I lit mine, then his.

"So." I smoked and watched him do the same. Unless he had a flask, we were completely out of booze, which was bad. It was cold and the temperature was dropping and we were both wet, which was also bad. We had a shovel, which was both ominous and bad.

"So," Knottspeed repeated. "We have about four blocks to go before we reach our actual destination, Fencepost." He felt around under his trash bag and came up with a second trash bag. "Wrap the head of the shovel. We can stick it out front, and it will look like my leg."

I did. Like all of his plans, it worked unusually well, especially after he propped his leg up on it. Once he was comfortable, he pointed out into the dark.

"That way. We see anyone, just don't make eye contact. Cops stop us, let me do the talking. And no matter what I say, no matter how bad it gets, don't run for it without trying to save me first."

I shot my smoke out into the street and started pushing. Knottspeed began humming, happy enough to be traveling through the rain in a trash bag. I needed a drink.

Three blocks later, I stopped. He twisted painfully and glared up at me, trying to read my mind. I stepped around in front of him in case he tried to go on alone and crossed my arms over my chest.

"No," I said firmly. "Just no. This is not happening." Behind me was our destination: several acres of graveyard. The mystery of the shovel was a mystery no more. Knottspeed seemed unimpressed with my resolve. He considered for a moment before he spoke, composing.

"Elton was an old guy I met at the university. Janitor. Thirty years of floors and toilets and getting gum out of the carpets. He was one of the smartest human beings I've ever known. Total cliché, I know. Elton helped me out from time to time, and I'll be damned if he didn't predict this very night, Fencepost, in exacting detail. Five years ago, he predicted that everyone I know would betray me if I was ever seriously damaged and that— because of the nature of my work and, worse, because of who I am and what that means to people—I certainly would be harmed eventually. He surmised that in the end, all of those close to me are, in fact, just like you—friends-for-hire who I accept because they owe me, so I think I can trust them. Elton believed that all people operate in this way, but that I'm worse in that I make so little effort to hide it and thus subject myself to the inevitability of the cruelest of mutinies. I trade in favors, the imagination, hope and salvation, the redistribution of lies and the shifting of blames, the obscuration of the maps leading to the awful things people are running from or toward. Elton predicted that a night would come when I would be in a wheelchair or bleeding in the back of a stolen car and that my last hired friend in the godforsaken town would be the first person I could actually trust, because my desperation would lend a cleanliness to that association, a truthfulness historically absent in my dealings with other people, himself included. How uncanny is that?"

Knottspeed gestured at the graveyard with his chin.

"I repaid his wise ghost, Fencepost. I volunteered to dig his grave and, of course, to fill it in again once he was at the bottom of it. One foot in and one foot down from the front of the headstone of Elton Eugene Davies is a plastic SentrySafe. One of the things I stole from myself today is this key." He brought his hand out and showed me, closed it again, and recaptured my eyes with his.

"Tonight you dig, Fencepost Beckenshire. You dig for me. But mostly you dig for yourself. Know why?"

I shook my head, mute.

"Because you aren't an Indian, dumbass, or even a delusional spiritualist who shuns the dead or mocks their ghosts. You aren't a white lady, either, with a mind bound by panty hose and the gospel according to television. You aren't even a shed painter. You're a piano player, Fencepost. It's the only thing you ever discovered about yourself, the only real part of you. And if what really is behind your beady eyes and your lost expression is music"—he tore the shovel out and thrust it into my stomach—"then you might be capable of anything."

I took the shovel and looked away from those eyes, out at the rain-swept, empty street. A thousand shades of gray. All kinds of wet. Going that way alone was wrong in a big, cosmic way. I never wanted to be the kind of man who was tormented by big thoughts. It was an intrusion. I didn't care what a classic book was, and I didn't give a shit about philosophy or why the bumblebee shouldn't be able to fly. Knottspeed had shared some of his curse with me. I sighed with all of my lung capacity.

He was quiet as I went behind him and began pushing us toward the graveyard. When we got over the curb, he indicated with a gesture that we should travel away from the locked gate and down the side. The rain slacked and the darkness deepened as we went under a row of overhanging trees. Eventually, he held his hand up for me to stop and pointed through the bars of the wrought iron fence.

"There. The tall, pointy stone. Hello again, Elton."

"How do I get over the fence?"

"Climb," he replied. "Use my wheelchair to get high enough up there to grab that lowest branch, and then pull yourself up higher. As soon as you're on the other side, I'll pass the shovel through."

"Aw, man, what the hell is it with you and trees? I mean, the—"

"I was in the last tree," he snapped. "Your turn." He rose unsteadily and leaned heavily on his cane, motioning for me to hustle.

I passed him the shovel and then pushed the wheelchair up to the fence, stood up in the seat, and steadied myself. Using a wheelchair to break into a graveyard had the kind of poetry to it that I'll forever associate with Knottspeed. I reached up and was just able to grab onto the lowest thick branch. I pulled down, and a shower of collected rainwater blinded me. I blinked and kept pulling.

"C'mon, man," Knottspeed urged. "There's a security service that rolls by every once in a while."

I caught hold of the thickest part of the branch and grabbed on with both hands. Over the next five minutes, cursing steadily, I managed to get all the way up to where I was standing between the spear points on top of the fence, holding on to the tree and looking down through the leaves. The six-foot drop hadn't looked so bad until right then. I looked down at him. He made an exasperated winding motion with his hand.

"This is the stupidest fucking thing I've ever—"

"Fencepost!" He turned. "Lights!" He slung the shovel through the bars of the fence and yanked the wheelchair free of the mud, scrabbled with it over to the sidewalk, and dropped into it. "Car on the corner! Jump!"

I couldn't see anything that far to the right from where my head was in the lowest part of the canopy, but my legs were certainly visible from any direction. Panic seized me and I jumped, flinging myself out into the darkness in a kind of dropping hop, like a fat gorilla, my arms out and ready to take part of the impact. My feet hit with a numbing shock and my hands a fraction of a second later. I splattered hard. My hands shot wide to the sides in the mud and wet sod, and I face planted with tremendous force. For a second, maybe more, there was nothing. I lay there, blank.

"Fencepost!"

I moaned and rolled over. It was like I'd just been tackled in a rugby game. My chest hurt, and the first breath was gummy and rattling. A racking cough followed, and my sinuses were full of a detergent ozone and copper fume with every painful breath. I reached up and cautiously felt my nose. Bleeding warmly, but unbroken. Miracle after miracle.

"Get up, you sissy," Knottspeed hissed. "You're halfway there, so haul some ass. I'm way too pretty to spend the night in county lockup, and they'll be mean to you. I should remind you at this point that you're trespassing. Possession of a shovel after midnight in a graveyard is beating material at the very least, so . . ."

I sucked in some air and got to my feet. Nothing broken. Without a word, without any more preamble, I picked up the shovel and went to the headstone of Elton Eugene Davies, looked both ways, and started digging. It took less than three minutes to completely unearth the safe. I hit it almost right away, and then I used the top of it as a guide, running the shovel along the hard surface and powering soil out in heavy strokes. When the top was clear, I used the shovel to lever it free and pulled it up. It was made out of an off-white plastic and was smaller than a suitcase, not nearly as heavy as I thought a safe should be. I carried it over to the fence, turned it sideways, and slid it through. It just barely fit, and I knew then that Knottspeed had measured it all out. The plan was so precise. That's when the rest of his plan dawned on me.

"How the hell do I get out?"

Knottspeed blew sludge out of the ring-shaped keyhole, fitted the key in, and popped the lid. I couldn't see what was inside, but whatever it was narrowed his eyes. For an instant, for a flash that was as fast as lightning and left an afterimage, he looked frail. Then he reached in and pulled out a towel and tossed it to me.

"And so it begins in earnest," he said to himself. Then he stared at me and blinked. When he spoke, his voice was full of wonder. "What a thing, Fencepost. What a place to find what we have." He took out a bottle and held it up to the faint light filtering through the leaves. The bottle looked expensive. "Lagavulin, seriously old now. Distilled from the fruit the angels use for ovaries." He savagely tore the cork out with his teeth.

"Knottspeed," I began firmly. He ignored me and drank, smacked his lips, and drank again, savoring this time. Then he passed it through to me.

"This night will only seem long, Fencepost. They open the gates at dawn. Wrap yourself in that trash bag we used for the shovel and find somewhere dry to sit on that towel.

Two-hundred-dollar bottle of scotch and your thoughts to keep you company."

"You knew this was going to happen," I said, wounded. "That I was going to be stranded in here."

"I had the foresight to buy whoever you were destined to be some quality booze for your trouble," he replied. "It had to be this way, man. If I ever needed this box, I was going to be too fucked-up to fight over what's inside. I had no idea who you would be, but that old janitor was right about all of it. I should have put a rope ladder in here instead of the towel and the bottle. I'm sorry, buddy."

I sipped the scotch. I had never tasted anything so fine, never even dreamed of it. It dawned on me that I'd comically missed the point about getting drunk, and that made me shake my head. Knottspeed closed the lid on the safe, and we watched each other.

"Sorry," I said. He cocked his head like a curious sparrow, fast to still.

"About?"

"I don't even know, man." And I didn't. I don't know why I even said it.

"If you weren't such a shitty climber, damn . . . you could have played piano for us while we finished that thing." He patted the lid of the box. "I got a spare, but no music. I would have scratched out some lyrics." He shrugged and smiled. I smiled back.

"What should I tell them?"

He thought about it. We listened to the rain for a long time. Then, without a word, he pushed away, down the sidewalk. When he reached the corner he paused, and then he was gone. He never looked back.

I didn't sleep that night. I put the trash bag on like a poncho, like he had, and drank on the steps of a mausoleum until I heard a guard open the gates as the gray dawn came on. No one saw me as I walked out. I took a bus downtown and had pancakes and sausage at a random shithole. While I was eating, I listened to the conversations around me. The quiet, muttering busted-heart babble. Truck talk. The waitress went on a date the night before, and something saucy had gone down. She couldn't talk about it, but the other waitress, the little fat one, was crazy curious. The dishwasher with the hairnet was glowering and jealous.

I rarely really listened to the people around me. But I'd always wondered how the hell anyone could endure a life that spun off a hundred sad songs, or even mean, clever ones. It occurred to me as I looked down the long lane into the kitchen and watched the dishwasher slam the grate on his big, steaming machine, that a great many songwriters might have done what I was doing right then—watching a man with a misplaced heart feeding the machine while the whore he was in love with looked right over his head again. There were songs everywhere. There was an opera in my last forty hours. The world was full of birds, and all of them were singing.

I finished eating and paid. My money was filthy, but so was I, and no one seemed to care. I got cigarettes at the little place next door and then smoked under the awning for a few minutes before taking a bus back to the house on Lincoln Street.

There was no sign of Knottspeed. He'd come and gone, and the living room had returned to a lifeless place full of dust and bad news. The empty safe was on the dog couch with his empty backpack. The house seemed so much more forlorn, dirtier and colder and more hopeless than it ever had before, and it was almost as if I was seeing it for the first time. I sat down on the piano bench and stared at the empty safe for I don't know how long before I turned to the keys.

The cover was down. I lifted it and slid it back and there, right in the middle, was a small fold of bills and the strangest postcard I'd ever seen. I picked it up, glanced at the back and then at the front again. It was old, maybe from around the time of the first color postcards. The edges of the paper were fuzzed out, as soft as denim. The faded picture on the front was of someplace with palm trees and a fountain. The sky was a washed-out blue. The information had all been scratched away with something rough, like the edge of a coin. Even the scratch marks seemed old.

It wasn't anything Knottspeed ever said that meant anything at all in the end. It was who he was and what he was doing, how he was doing it. The potency about him, the driven conviction that there was no right or wrong direction. There was, for him, just the direction he was going, and he was rolling hard and fast; and he knew, he *knew* he was going to get there. I put the money and the postcard in my coat and got up, went to the door, and opened it. The clean rain smell gusted in. It was gray out, like it always was, but it looked different than it had last night, when I'd looked down the zero boulevard and turned away from it. For some reason, it looked a little like a black-and-white television with a magic picture, too clear for technology, or the work of a camera that came from somewhere no one had ever heard about, a camera used to take pictures of the things none of us knew about. I walked out, leaving the door open, and then I walked down the stairs and just kept walking. I was going to where the postcards came from, and I didn't know where that was.

Part 2

7

The Daily Hollow Point

MY EYES WERE FIXED ON something else when the first wand of sunlight pierced the dim blue-and-orange smear on the far side of the canyon across from the White Palace. The surface of the small but insanely expensive swimming pool shivered with glitter; trillions of goldfish dancing in a sudden formation, filled with the eerie mathematics of dawn. The light did the same things it always does. It made the sound of the freeway at the bottom of the canyon louder. It made the brain tissue behind my eyes ache rather than sting. I closed my eyelids and rolled away, feeling around in the pocket of my bathrobe. Xanax. One left. I put it in my mouth and chewed it dry. Bitter as the crust around a car battery terminal. There was still something in the glass of melted ice on the bone-colored ceramic tile next to the vanilla lounger where I'd slept, but I wasn't brave enough to touch it. There were a thousand reasons why. I remembered them all in the same instant.

Ten seconds passed before the primitive chemical bit into my brain stem then bubbled forward into the middle and then the front of my head. I sighed and opened my eyes again.

White. The floor-to-ceiling windows were all that stood between me and Wanda's abandoned temple of glass and ivory furniture, white carpet, and abstract paintings rendered in the uncountable shades of white, the testimony of the self-proclaimed genius of an Argentine artist with one name, like Marko or Junik. I couldn't remember seconds after I bought them. Across the living room and over the divide, Tay Tay was operating the coffee machine. The bald, muscular black man was evidently singing too. He did a seriously gay pirouette, shot me a grin, then held up two white mugs like trophies. I watched as he sashayed up to the sliding glass door and hooked the edge with one big, pedicured toe and danced it open with one smooth move that was part kung fu and part eighties *Soul Train*.

"Doctor Resner," Tay Tay sang, looking me over. He wrinkled his wide nose. "All about as yummy as a hot tub full of leukemia." He tutted and held out a mug. "Black is back." Tay Tay was wearing bulging, bright-yellow Speedos. He turned his huge brown eyes on the pool and the sunrise and took a deep and satisfying breath and then looked back down at me. I sat up and took the coffee.

"Clarence," I began. I would never, ever call anyone Tay Tay. "If we could remember even one single aspect of my morning ritual, just this once." I sipped and winced at the sudden hot in my face. "I mean I—"

"Yes, yes," he interrupted. He sipped his coffee and closed his eyes, raising his face to the sky. "In two months, we chip and sand and paint and pick at your shitty little ritual of doom. We preen it. We comb the lice out. Like I tell you every glorious morning, Simon. Wake up and fill your belly with wind. But I'll try something different today. Imagine . . ." he said thoughtfully, looking up. "Imagine this morning that you're a little blue pot full of dirt. And this morning I pluck out the weed and drop in the good new seed." He looked down and grinned at me. "In your face, white man." He made a plucking sound and pantomimed the same thing with his hand.

"Clarence . . ." I was already defeated.

"Part of my rent," he reminded me. He set his coffee down and rolled his huge shoulders, preparing.

"You don't pay rent." I rolled my neck and something popped. I winced.

"I am Tay Tay, the Human Prozac," he proudly declared in a deep boom. "Now get up an' go get dressed. We have another day in paradise, baby, just ready to get its groove on. Don't want to get in trouble with the boss."

He saluted the dawn and then clapped his hands together in front of him, dove into the pool, and swam underwater in powerful sidestrokes. After coming up for breath on the far side, he sighed and then struck out in a leisurely backstroke, humming softly. Cindy Lauper. I lay back and looked at the sky too. Blue again, with a ring of LA rust around the edge. Contrails. I listened to the humming and the splash, the morning commuters. Clarence Farrow was an orderly at Sellwood Hospital, and low in the pecking order in that already low profession. I was the chief administrator, answerable to no one—except, evidently, Clarence.

After a minute, I slowly got to my feet and went inside, mostly to avoid any more of his morning joy therapy. Only one slipper this time, which would have been embarrassing if I had any shame. Through the glaring-white living room, down the alabaster hallway, past the three guest bedrooms— one of which Clarence had taken over—and into the achromatic master suite, where I still kept my clothes even though it had been more than four months since I had lain in the snowy white bed. Everything looked perfect. Immaculate. A maid of some kind came three times a week. I'd never even seen her, and I didn't even know her name. Clarence never added anything to the house, other than in the refrigerator, but I had a feeling a time would come when an orange vase would appear on the dining room table, or maybe an errant, fruit-eating tropical bird would materialize and start singing in Arabic, or even a picture of something that had been alive. At that moment, the turn in the road I had taken that might lead back to color would take the form of material objects less complicated than a giant gay black man who called himself Tay Tay. Sterility is a hard mirror to crack.

My suits, all still in their transparent dry-cleaning wrappers, were in the huge closet behind the spotless rolling mirrors. Everything was in wrappers, even my shoes. I rolled a mirror back. Clarence had thoughtfully placed the shoes I'd worn yesterday neatly back in the shoe section. They had mustard on them, so the maid would take them later, and then they'd reappear in a day or so in a wrapper. I had no idea where my suit from yesterday was. Possibly in the front yard, possibly in the trash, but probably in the hamper waiting for the nameless maid's attention.

All courtesy of Clarence. I thought about him as I fingered through the suits, finally selected a gray one, and padded into the bathroom. We had, certainly, the most unusual symbiosis I'd ever experienced. It was true that he was saving me from something, blocking my path down a fast and lightless road I'd been headed down since Divorce Day. I still wondered from time to time if I was saving him from something in return or if he just liked the pool, the cars, the life I wasn't getting around to living in. It was likely he'd eventually tell me in some oblique way. He certainly talked enough. But it was something we never discussed. I'd assumed for the first few days that he would just go home. When he didn't, we just steered clear of the topic. It had been over a month.

I turned the shower on using the key pad, hung the suit on the back of the bathroom door, and then stared at myself in the mirror while the twin water heads heated up. I knew what I was. I sucked in my small gut and scowled at myself, trying to see some cheekbone. A forty-seven-year-old potato man scowled back at me. A doctor, an oncologist no less, who had given up on all things healing to become a plutocrat. And I'd done it all for the worst reasons. And I was good at my job—at least I had been, anyway.

Not exactly ugly, but in no way handsome. I turned sideways.

Given to an overall pudge if I didn't work out, which I didn't. Mostly bald, with curly, mouse-colored hair that poked out of my scalp in sparse patches and random units of one to sixty per square inch if I didn't buzz it every few days. And to top it off, the rest of me was hairy. Bad hairy. I inspected my back and scowled in earnest. The one waxing session Wanda had forced me through resulted in a six-month rash I was forced to combat with sophisticated antibiotics. Bacteria invaded the cratered landscape of gaping follicles and dug in, started families and mining operations. For six months, I'd looked like a plucked baby bird with acne. The antibiotics had temporarily discolored my teeth.

I turned away from the big mirror and looked into the light-framed one above the sink. My eyes were on the small side, a crappy, flavorless mud color. My teeth had always struck me as a little square, and my voice was high for such a hairy man. It had given me a boyish quality I could work with up until my mid-twenties, but after that it was decidedly obnoxious, even to me. I sighed and dropped my robe and shorts on the floor, stepped out of my slipper, and got in the west end of the shower.

The maid took care of everything, now under the paternal direction of Clarence. My best friend, Gary, had found her for me a week after Wanda left with her new lover and husband-to-be, Jack, to live in Hawaii. I lathered up with expensive soap that smelled like lavender and cinnamon. Clarence's doing. He'd "interfaced" with the maid and modified things after his first week. They talked. They even had coffee. He knew her name.

The soap was only one of the changes. Steaks had appeared in the refrigerator, along with bags of organic produce and weird juices that were good for your hair and fingernails. The wet bar had an assortment of foreign liquors and flavored vodkas. The coffee was different, African rather than the awful traditional hazelnut of the White Palace. There were actual spices in the cabinet, ones used by human beings, to be applied to food that was actually cooked on the six-burner stove. I was no longer a takeout and delivery man.

Clarence cooked almost every night, a strange mixture of the Caribbean and Texas, and he sang the entire time. The food was good too. Other than Cowboy Bob, Clarence never had any visitors, and Bob had visited only once, on that first night. Clarence had been forced to beat Bob up that evening, and I suspected that might have something to do with his extended stay, even though he had referred to the cowboy as "the flavor of the week" and only once, in passing. But I owed Clarence for that night and he knew it, so he could stay forever if he wanted to. I think he knew that as well. He'd been forced to choose that night between a relative stranger on the brink of suicide who was ultimately his boss and a dictatorial one at that, and Cowboy Bob, who exuded money, blazed with style, but also had a malicious slant that came out when Clarence extended his hand in charity. He'd felt inclined to slap Clarence's hand for that, and Clarence had returned the sentiment by breaking Bob's wrist before he smashed his head through a pearly coffee table.

Gary had dragged me out that fateful evening—two months after Wanda left, six weeks after he'd gotten me the maid, and the day the divorce had closed. Divorce Day. I scrubbed behind my ears and then just stood there, letting the hot water pound on my back and my chest. Four months of sleeping on patio furniture had done nothing for my back.

Jack was far more wealthy than I would ever be, a terrifying, GDP-of-a-small-country-style rich, a hotel magnate with resorts all over the world and sailboats in every sea. Jack was, in fact, so rich that most people had never even heard of him. His Swiss lawyers rammed the divorce through at light speed. Wanda wanted nothing when she left, not even her clothes or her jewelry. Nothing at all, not even a single picture, and that had shaken me on some deep, disturbing level, miles below my skin, in a distant place where I never knew I had anything at all. The divorce papers were delivered to my office by one of

Jack's impeccable couriers, who was probably also ex-Mossad with a PhD in economics. An hour after I signed everything, an envelope arrived via an equally impeccable courier. I can clearly remember the Windsor knot in his tie, his tight smile. I was sitting at my desk, in shock.

Inside was a thank-you card from Jack that looked handmade by a Japanese artist, himself more efficacious than me, and two all-inclusive tickets to one of his resorts in Martinique. A voucher for a private jet service was attached. I'd put everything in my desk and called Gary, who laughed and said we should go and trash the place, that maybe this Jack guy wasn't so bad after all, that we were going out for drinks at his favorite bar later to celebrate and get started on some "fresh poon." I stashed the envelope in a drawer in my dresser, and I hadn't opened the drawer since. Never even touched the handle. It made me nervous to even think about it.

Gary was wealthier than me too. He lived in a sprawling mansion in Malibu, and I wasn't his best friend anymore, even though he was still mine. He hung out with Bruce Willis and Jay Z whenever they were in town, other Hollywood types when they weren't. He went to those kinds of parties, and even though he always invited me, I never went, because I knew he actually didn't want me to go.

We'd grown up together, and at first I thought Gary was going to turn out to be a bum. He drank, as in rivers. He fought in bars over women he didn't really know. He dropped out of college after three weeks. At the time, three weeks was also the longest he'd ever had a girlfriend. It still was.

Fortune smiled on Gary in the oddest way. He'd gotten a job at a skate shop in Santa Monica while I was premed. One day a Japanese man had come in and examined all the boards and all the shoes, the shirts, the shorts, and the stickers, and then he approached the register and sized Gary up.

Gary was never a big guy. Five foot seven and 150 pounds for the last twenty years. That day he'd been wearing trashed Vans, worn Dickies shorts with a few patches holding them together, and a Ramones T-shirt with holes in it. The man gave him his card: Isozaki Imports. He explained that in Japan, the worn versions of these garments and accessories, if the wear was authentic, were worth far more than any of the new items on display. Gary's longboard had been leaning against the wall behind him, a truly abused thing, and he wanted that too. The Isozaki Imports man took his wallet out and removed a stack of crisp, new one-hundred-dollar bills, his eyes gleaming, ready to do business with the young man he mistakenly assumed was an idiot.

Gary did several momentous things that day. First, he told the Isozaki emissary to go fuck himself and that if he ever saw him in Santa Monica again, he'd make sure the man was raped to death. Then he called his boss and politely quit, saying something had come up. He was so smooth about it that they're still friends to this day. Then he went across the street to Sander's Café, where all the waitresses continuously fawned over him (Gary was and will forever remain impossibly handsome, with piercing blue eyes and a smile every actor would trade two souls for), and approached Kathleen, who was just finishing her associate's degree in the then-esoteric field of web design. She was delighted to go out for drinks whenever he was free. She still works for him and lives in a mansion of her own. Then he boarded down the street to the bank and withdrew a sizeable amount of money from his savings account, more than half of what his grandparents and his mother had put in his college fund over the previous two decades and had successfully shamed him into never spending on anything else.

The rest was easy. As a hard-drinking bong hit champion and all-around good guy who was everyone's go-to at the skate shop, he was something of a fixture in the skate scene. He boarded around Santa Monica and Venice Beach all afternoon and far into the night, spreading the word. Cash for old boards, skate clothes, and Vans. Starting tomorrow at his place, 10:00 A.M. until the money ran out.

By the time I graduated, Gary had offices in LA and Osaka, and he'd mentioned a new one coming together in Bangkok, where he spent weeks on end doing sordid things and getting away with it. His clothing and skate lines had expanded from those early days, from a reeking one-bedroom rent-controlled apartment, filled with what looked like trash to me, into an empire with warehouses in three states and two countries. Last year he acquired a sailboard company and a snowboard company in the same week. Gary wasn't at my graduation ceremony; he was surfing in Costa Rica with two strippers, but he did send me a Rolex with twelve diamonds in it.

When I was done showering, I buzzed my head and shaved. I could hear Clarence singing in the shower in the guest room two doors down, also getting ready. Every morning it was show tunes. Sometimes, at night—if he was drunk enough and had smoked enough weed (outside)—he would play Wanda's white Steinway. I'd heard her play it only once in the two years we'd had it, and she'd been good, in the classical sense. She knew just one song, something she'd been forced to learn for a recital after years of childhood training. A single song, though when played with the precision of a robot, it had sounded oddly like someone typing. Clarence was slobular on the piano, but he more than made up for it with soul.

We were getting ready at the same time because we carpooled to work in my BMW. Clarence had no car that I was aware of, and besides, we worked at the same hospital. He was an MRI assistant, which was part lab tech and part janitor. He'd taken a class for it though, so at least he made more money than the desk clerks or the actual mop-and-squeegee bottom rung. I started getting my suit on.

Gary's favorite bar in the world was called the Matador. LA's rich weirdos hung out there and smoked thousand-dollar cigars and experienced molecular gastronomy cocktails and hobnobbed about futures algorithms, the latest in Southeast Asian architecture, yachts, wine, and all things halcyon in the coded language of the elite. He'd picked me up from work on Divorce Day. I'd left my car at the office thinking I would take a cab in the morning, knowing I'd be in no shape to drive after an evening with him. His ride at the time was a pink convertible 1969 Mustang. Gary rode in back, as always. His driver, a guy named Freddy, wore a black suit and cap. He also had tattoos on his neck and hands, and I suspected he did more than drive.

"Lana," Gary had gushed to our incredibly hot waitress. The Matador was cliffside in Malibu, overlooking the ocean. The sun was setting low and gold over the water, and the woman shimmered like a model in a lotion commercial. Her smile for Gary had been genuine. "Two Midori martinis with no olives or crap of any kind."

"Make that one," I'd said. "I'll have—"

Gary had flashed two fingers, and she'd vanished. He turned his bright eyes on me, eyes as blue as the Mediterranean on a summer's noon. "She's available. Trust me, I know."

"I believe you," I'd said cautiously. He leaned back.

"Too bad we're officially too old to do coke," he'd continued. "That would make this the perfect sunset." He looked at me, keenly. "We are too old, aren't we?"

"Yes, Gary," I'd said firmly. "We were too old more than a decade ago."

Three of those foul martinis later, we were in the bathroom snorting Gary's coke while Freddy stood watch. That had been a central part of how I'd gotten so wildly intoxicated that night, and how later, when Clarence "Tay Tay" Farrow arrived with the extremely wealthy Cowboy Bob and found me stranded and crying in solitude on the edge of the balcony looking down, why he'd given me a ride home. He'd never said anything about the terrible events of that night to me, to anyone at work, hopefully not even to the maid. And he'd never gone back to where he came from, either. I finished tying my tie and inspected myself.

"We're gonna be late!" Tay Tay called.

"Shoes," I called back.

"On my feet. My orthos."

"No. I'm getting my shoes on."

I got my socks on, selected a pair of new root beer wing tips, custom-made in Singapore and part of Wanda's now-abandoned effort to make me look like a suitable male counterpart. I idly wondered what I'd paid for them while I listened to Clarence humming as he locked up the Palace and turned off the coffeepot. We filed out silently to the car, parked slightly askew in the driveway. He ignored my parking job.

Clarence was usually quiet on the way to work, as he psychically adjusted from flaming gay and flamboyantly loud to a modest and professional neutral. The transition usually took the entire forty-minute commute and had surprised me at first. But I'd gradually begun doing the same thing, transitioning from a depressed and bewildered pill-popping yuppie into a scheming, soulless administrator. My transformation took the entire drive too, and sometimes it ate up the rest of the morning. I made the entire commute on autopilot while Clarence looked out the window. My privileged parking spot was right to the side of the hospital entrance, just south of the nonemergency waiting area. I parked and glanced at Clarence.

"Five?"

He shook his head. "Nah. Half day, then I'm over to Saint Francis until six."

Saint Francis was deep in East LA, a hood hospital for minimum security convicts, junkies, prostitutes, and the generally hopeless. The critically uninsured were also routinely steered their way. I knew he had another part-time job, but until then I had no idea it was in a place so far below the poverty line.

"Is . . ." I cleared my throat. "Are you doing community service, Clarence?"

He laughed, gay again for an instant. "No, but I get paid nine bucks an hour more than you pay me—they call it hazard pay—plus I have some friends on the staff. 'S how I got the gig."

"Ah." That would account for his occasional late nights out. I'd thought he'd been off doing gay things.

"Your dinner is in the fridge. Steak fajitas, and I made the barbecue papaya salsa last night. After you passed out."

"Okay."

We got out and split up. Clarence went down to the emergency entrance; the staff showers and locker rooms were located past the chaos. I went in through the main entrance next to my car. For two years, I'd carried a briefcase through those doors. I didn't have one anymore.

Doris and Lai were at the front desk, a raised, imposing affair. They both nodded and smiled politely before returning their attention to their computers. The lobby was quiet for the most part. Two elderly women in formal burkas were dozing, obviously waiting on someone who was getting dialysis or a boil lanced, something not critical or worrisome. A lone man was calmly reading the new *TIME*. I couldn't remember his name, but I knew a lot about him. He was post chemo for leukemia, waiting to get blood work done. The hospital was up on him somewhere to the tune of half a million. Insured.

The only interesting person in the lobby was a big man with shaggy brown hair and a short beard, wearing a flannel shirt, a battered Carhartt jacket, jeans, and work boots. A construction worker. He had a wadded-up bloody T-shirt on his meaty thigh, and I couldn't tell if the injury was on his leg or on his hand. On impulse, I approached him. For whatever reason, I'd been doing that a lot lately.

"Hi," I began. He looked up at me and squinted. He smelled like beer and sweat and tree sap. "Being taken care of?"

He shifted. "Signed in. Just waiting."

"Good." I sat down next to him. "Where are you hurt? Hand or leg?"

He briefly lifted the T-shirt. A little blood welled up out of his thigh, but not much.

"Keep the pressure on it," I said. "Sting some?"

"Yeah." He smiled a little. "I had a few beers rolling around in my truck so I chugged those in the parking lot. Took four Advil."

"Can't hurt. What happened?" I crossed my leg and struck up my listening pose.

"Nail gun. Not even that deep, but my boss wanted me to come down for a stitch and a tetanus shot. So, day off. Least I did it on-site instead of at home. We're redoing the bathroom."

"Hmm." I didn't tell him that their premium would go up. That stitch and a shot were going to cost the company more than a quarter of a million dollars, spread out over a decade. If it was the third or fourth time it had happened, even if it had previously happened to someone else, a sharp accountant might recommend him for firing to set an example. "Well, hang in there. I'll see if I can get someone over to you."

He shrugged.

I got up and wandered in the direction of the elevators. Sellwood was three stories, and I was generally too lazy to take the stairs. I pressed the up button and waited. When the doors opened, Dr. Schwanitz of the old guard looked up from his chart.

"Morning," he said.

"Swan." I tried to stay on a first-name basis with the doctors I'd worked with before I became the administrator. Swan was one of them, a nickname in this case. "Who you after?" I held the door while he looked back down at the chart.

"Larry Fowler. Puncture wound. Thigh. Morris and Dell Construction."

"Ah. I was just talking to him."

Swan looked surprised. "How's he doing?"

"Had a couple of beers and some Advil in the parking lot. He's okay. Tough guy."

"Good." He made to move past me, and I stopped him with a gentle touch on his forearm. "Swan, could you explain to him about his company premium? He seems like a decent guy. Tell

101

him about accident numbers and frequency of visits, see if he gets it."

"Keep it . . . low?"

"Wedding ring tan line. Probably in his pocket. Probably has kids. Just tell him."

Swan lowered the chart. He drew a breath to say something, and I clapped him on the arm.

"Have a good day," I said. I let go of the door and pressed the button for the third floor. Swan stepped out. When the doors closed, he was still looking back at me. I listened to the Muzak, blank, and restfully so. Talking to the construction worker had put me in the right frame of mind. Asking Swan to give the guy the inside scoop on his insurance had been a questionable move, but I didn't care. If he bothered to tell anyone, which he probably wouldn't, they would think he was being an asshole.

Hospitals, especially midsized ones like Sellwood, were not accurately depicted on TV. Our emergency room was mostly car wrecks with facial or cosmetic. Real trauma was shunted away. We did lots of therapy, lots of blood work, chemo, dialysis, and since I'd taken over we'd begun some treatment for alcohol and drug abuse, high-end only, and the always warm by noon cosmetic surgery action. Liposuction to tummy tucks, four residents and three surgeons steaming away, profits up by 217 percent, big bonuses for me, and a little less stress in general for everyone else. It was, I knew, a very boring hospital. My job—after getting it that way in the first place, which took a solid year—was simply to keep it that way. Chase the numbers.

And it was easy. As soon as I'd lost interest in everything, my previous momentum had been taken up by Dayleen, my primary secretary, and the department heads. Everyone thought they were doing a good job and that I was leaving them alone for the most part to let them do it. Dayleen was a completely type A, middle-aged mother of two, divorced but reconciling, attractive, energetic, and impossibly power hungry. The right hand I needed at the moment—though if the day ever came when I wanted to focus again, taking some of that power back was going to be brutal. But for the moment, she could have it.

My office had a nice view of the landscaped park behind the building and the Cyprus windbreak beyond. Clean expanse of uncluttered desk and cabinet, modern furniture, a tasteful, zero shade of gray. An artificial plant or two. A bookshelf full of obsolete medical texts. Dayleen wasn't around, so I went in, took my coat off, and sat down at my desk. I looked at my phone. Five lines, two blinking. So she was in the building somewhere. I checked my messages. Nothing. I looked at the tidy stack of folders on the blotter. Dayleen had already gone through them. All of them needed my signature. There was a time when I would have reviewed every one of them in great detail, bounced ideas off of Dayleen all day long, gone and asked people questions, researched and double-checked figures, looked for easy steals in the gossip trade winds, and harassed every single person I talked to. Right around the time Gary had gotten me the maid, I'd told Dayleen that she knew enough to go through most of it and then I'd given her a big raise. Now the folders were reviewed by her. They all had tabs. Green ones meant "sign here." Yellow ones meant "consider signing here." Red ones meant "reject and return."

I looked out the window for a while and then signed all the green ones. By the time I was done, it was just after ten. Then I signed all the yellow ones, pausing over only one—a training program for the new MRI. Calibration specimen: an intern with a negative post mammogram biopsy. I signed it. The red ones I pushed to the side without looking at. Then I stared out the window until noon, when Dayleen finally breezed through my door without knocking.

"Simon," she said. "I see you got through the stack." She sat down across from me. "Coffee?"

"Sure," I said.

"Me too." She leaned out and picked up my phone, punched an extension. "Hi, Rose. Can you bring in two black coffees? Resner's office. Thank you."

Rose was Dayleen's secretary, a harried young spaz of a woman. She had another month or two in her before she cracked. Dayleen gathered up all the files and pushed them to the side of my desk. I leaned back in my chair and studied her, my face carefully expressionless. I knew what was coming.

"So, do anything fun last night? Square dancing? A pot roast? Out with Gary?" She didn't know about Clarence.

I shrugged with my mouth, an expression I knew from watching home videos made me look owlish. "Watched some TV," I lied. "Caught up on some periodicals. Reports. The usual. You?"

"Dave came over for dinner." She didn't seem especially pleased. I'd had a feeling for weeks that Dayleen's new power at work was translating into a fresh series of hurdles in the tortuous preamble to the reunion with her ex-husband. It was the least of my problems.

"And?"

"More of the same. I made meatloaf, which he loves. My meatloaf, with the swiss cheese spears. Then . . ." She sighed. "Then I felt like I was pandering, which pissed me off."

I'd tasted Dayleen's cooking at various staff potlucks for two years. She was no Martha Stewart. Dave was either generous or just plain hungry.

"It turned sour at dessert," she went on. "Fruit with two scoops of ice cream. I don't even eat dessert, as you know. So at that point I knew I'd totally caved in. I was being servile."

"Servile," I repeated.

"Servile." Her mouth was a hard fuchsia line.

"What was in the red tags?"

"Crap."

"Huh."

We looked at each other. I knew she was afraid of my waking up again, of the fiery, caffeinated work machine I'd been before. I also knew that she was anxious that she had become presumptuous in too many ways. Women like Dayleen were fearful of something almost as much of the time as they were angry about something. Many men were too, so it wasn't a sexist observation.

She stood. "Making rounds?"

"Nah." I looked back out the window. "Tuesday. Never that much going on. All the glory hogs are sharking around down there below us in a dance they all know pretty well. I'm going to lunch, and then I'm heading over to Tecsegate to talk to Travis Holston about their catalog before I head home and go through some spreadsheets, watch the swimming pool." Meaning show my face in the cafeteria and then head over to a bar in West Hollywood, someplace loud and shitty where no one would recognize me, slowly slurp down the legal limit, and dink around on my laptop, which was still in the trunk of my car, and then go home and start working on a serious buzz that would lead to Clarence's fajitas and eventual blackout on my white patio furniture while staring at the lights across the canyon.

"Wish I could do that," she said, smiling. I knew what was behind that smile. Judgment. Satisfaction. I didn't care at all, but I kept talking anyway, mostly because she was waiting for me to say something in the way of a conclusion.

"I haven't taken an entire day off in . . . almost a year. I miss it."

"Then take one," she suggested. "Take a week!" I could hear the hunger in her voice. She wanted to sit in my chair, I realized. At my desk. "What, you have like six weeks-plus of vacation time saved up. You haven't gone anywhere since . . ."

"Since Wanda and I went to Costa Rica." I returned my attention to the window. A moment later, my office door closed. I waited for a full sixty seconds before I took out my Xanax bottle and popped one. A couple minutes later, it was time to get lunch over with. Afterward, my personality exposure period would be done for the day and I could quietly slip out.

The cafeteria was on the second floor, just past a row of outpatient exam rooms, around the corner from radiology, and down past a small, sunny waiting area that had always seemed like an architectural design flaw to me. I nodded at interns and the slow-moving and distracted attendings, frowned with authority I didn't feel at every nurse and orderly out of reflex, and generally acted like the person I used to be. Afterward, as I went through the cafeteria archway, I felt drained.

The cafeteria had been transformed very early in my iron rule. When I first became administrator, it had been little better than a prison chow line. Within a week I'd made it an example of the sweeping changes to come. The head cook at the time had been a great big woman with a hairnet and a giant pre-cancerous mole dead center between her oily nose and her thin upper lip. I never learned her name. I'd fired her with great prej-udice, much to everyone's approval, and hired a peppy young cooking school graduate, fresh out of the chute and eager for a job. I'd explained to him the great challenge of feeding the snobs who worked for me, that they were vastly more important than our patients or their families, and then had gone on at length about the unfortunate concessions to the nuances of dia-betic dining and, finally, the vagaries of dealing with the speci-ficities of the dieticians.

Troy understood immediately that it was the springboard to his dream job: resorts or cruise ships. He went at it with great gusto, and the results were spectacular. He procured an espresso machine and emulated the modern cheffing trend of buying local and organic, at farmer's markets no less, which in Los Angeles was a time-consuming and possibly fraudulent enterprise.

The cafeteria was half full. It was always about half full, even at four in the morning. The tables had flowers, and there were paintings on the walls that were original, tasteful, and inex-pensive, mostly because they were for sale as part of a rotating charity gallery program curated by Troy's wife—a pleasant, moonfaced little woman whose name I didn't remember. I got my tray and cutlery and joined the end of the line. Troy saw me and waved hello. He came down the line a moment later and handed me a single short espresso over the divide.

"Administrator," he said, beaming. He was always that way, energetic and overflowing with speedy positive verve.

"Simon, Troy, I keep telling you. What's good?"

"All of it, of course, but I like the roasted butternut squash soup. And we have a sort of special—apricot pork roast with red kale, lightly steamed in balsamic, unsalted."

"I'm hungry today," I said. I downed the espresso and considered. "I'd like to try both."

"Have a seat," he said. "I'll have one of my robotrons bring it over."

I nodded and carried my empty tray over to a table by the window. As soon as I sat down, I wished I'd had the presence of mind to bring some reading material with me, something to make it look like I was hard at work, even while I was eating. What would people say when they saw the hospital administrator staring pitifully out the window, alone, without even a laptop? I was making that kind of mistake too often. While inwardly cursing myself, I felt a presence just behind me.

"Administrator?"

I turned slightly and looked up. It was Clarence, and he was holding a file. I smiled up at him and took it, flipped it open. It was nothing, a detail file for a minor surgical inventory he was probably taking to records.

"Thank you," I said, peering closely at the data.

"Cut it," he said softly. "You taking off after lunch?"

"Yes," I said quietly, without looking up. "A bar in West Hollywood and then home to work on my tan. Why?"

"I need a ride to Saint Francis. My homegirl usually gives me a lift is bogin."

"Absolutely no way." I flipped to the next page.

"I'll make that flank steak with the red sauce you flipped out about Friday . . ."

"No."

One of Troy's people appeared and set a tray down before me, cutting Clarence off. I smiled at her, and she nodded and went back to the line. Troy was a chef, but he was not the same kind of cook as Clarence. Still, it looked good. I continued reading as I sampled the soup.

"Why?" Clarence asked quietly.

"I'll get carjacked, Clarence. A white man in a suit in a brand-new BMW?"

"With a big, bald black man who can beat the fuck out of a yeti, Simon? C'mon man."

"I'd still have to drive out of there alone. So no."

Clarence took a breath and tried to look casual, like he was waiting for me to finish the file. "You cowardly shit," he continued in the same tone. "I can't even believe this. Let me borrow your car. You're rich. Take a cab. Then you can get as wasted as you want."

That was an idea. I could spend the entire afternoon at the bar of my choice. I snapped the file closed and handed it back to him. When I looked up into his big, pleading eyes, it suddenly occurred to me for the first time that Clarence had never asked me for anything. He was certainly too poor to take a cab himself, and it was LA. The bus could take days, if it was even possible. I took a bite of the unsalted pork roast and stood.

"We can get some In-N-Out on the way," I said quietly. I gave him the file back.

Clarence smiled ever so slightly and adjusted the file under his arm. "Taco stands, Simon. Realio dealio. I know the best ones."

"Out front in ten." I gave Troy the thumbs-up as I strolled out, quickly, a man on the move. Clarence followed a moment later and peeled off toward Emergency and his locker.

Back in my office, I found a new stack of files from Dayleen, who was absent again, no doubt out on patrol. I signed the first three green ones and dropped them on her desk on the way through. I kept a red and yellow one tucked under my arm for appearances. Then it was more of the draining nods, the artificial smiles, and the harried frowns, all thrown out randomly along my purposeful march. I ignored the desk staff in the lobby and pretended to be listening to grim and important news on my cell phone.

The hospital was reasonably busy by then, inside and out. I didn't want any of the staggering, zombified swing shift residents or the orderly cluster of smokers down from the entrance to see Clarence getting into my car, so I got in and pulled out, drove down past Emergency, and put my blinker on.

East LA. I was taking a gay black man into East LA. Without knowing it, I had begun some kind of journey on the night Clarence found me. I had no idea that we were about to hit fast-forward.

8
Saintessa of Birds

LOANING CLARENCE MY CAR WOULD have been the best idea. My bank account had swollen to record levels with Wanda out of the picture. Her hair, kept so blond it was glowing, her perfect nails, the eight-hundred-dollar sushi lunches she had with her friends, the endless multistarred places where we'd dined out almost every night . . . The BMW was fully insured, and even if the insurance didn't cover whatever happened when the car was in Clarence's care, even if he drove to Mexico and never came back, I realized that I didn't give a shit. It wasn't the Xanax. I didn't really like the car. I certainly didn't like Wanda's white on white Carrera, still parked in my garage. All through college and my residency, I'd driven a yellow Volvo station wagon. My favorite car to date, and I hadn't really liked that car, either. I was thinking along those lines when the passenger door opened and Clarence hopped in. He smelled like fruity bubble bath, and he'd put his earring back in.

"Let's roll, baby," he said, clapping his hands together. He sank low, anticipating my anxiety about publicly associating with him. I glanced down at him.

"Stealth comes natural to all creatures like Tay Tay," he said, giving me his floodlight grin. His teeth were almost blinding.

"Good to know," I replied.

"Just don't you go abusing my powers."

We got on the freeway and headed east. Tay Tay gradually rose into a relaxed slouch, flipped the visor down, and started putting on glittery blue eye shadow. He was gay again.

Sometimes the right question can be framed only when in the right frame of mind, which is an odd redundancy. It was the opposite to generating a series of questions without answers, which I'd become a recent and unpaid specialist in. I'd never actually seen Clarence apply makeup, though he often appeared with it on around the house, especially on his days off. He contorted his face with great concentration and tremendous dexterity. Witnessing the demonstration while pretending not to, after feigning so many other things all morning, formed the foundation of my thought process. The panic I would have ordinarily felt on penetrating deep into hostile minority territory accompanied by a gay black man contorting his face was partially hazed out and garbled by the pills, and the hangover lent an additional sense of disembodiment. The structure was reasonably complete, at least enough so to produce one rarified inquiry.

"So, Clarence, we're heading way into the hood, and I'm just wondering, just wondering, if your . . . whatever you called her . . . your ride . . . if she flaked out or whatever happened, exactly how are you going to get . . . what are you going to do when you're done with your shift?"

His eyes flicked to mine in the mirror and he paused, mid-application. "You mean you fear for Tay Tay? I'll get back to the White Palace before last call, dummy. Two buses and one cab. Someone has to tuck yo' dumb ass in."

I was incredibly relieved. I leaned back, and a little of the tension flowed out of me. "So do you like working at Saint Francis?"

"Yeah." He finished with his eye shadow and began the puckering and smacking application of honey lip gloss. "Like I

112

say, friends. Plus, I seen all kinds of crazy gay in my day, but Francis is like a raw homo soap opera. Some of them sturdy men in from county minimum on a two-day pass . . . well, they can't get down on nothin' inside 'cause of the rep. We all find love where we can. And the ancient queer population is just too damn funny for words. The junkies too. Humor and desperation be historically bound."

"I see." Sometimes I sincerely regretted hearing the details he disclosed about his personal life, though they were rare and I often suspected he was joking.

"Plus the money," he continued. "*And*, at only seven or eight shifts a month, I get some crappy health insurance."

That was a dig at me. The insurance at Sellwood was below crappy for people at Clarence's pay grade. As in there wasn't any. It had gone out the window in my second wave of cost-cutting measures, and the sizeable bonus I'd received had paid for the pool he'd gone swimming in at sunrise. I didn't tell him that.

We were both quiet for a few minutes—me with one of my many secrets, and Clarence with his gayness, which he made no secret of at all, except at Sellwood. The amount of graffiti on the freeway edging began to steadily increase. So did the number of dented older cars and the number of splendid, sinister lowriders.

"There," Clarence said eventually. He pointed at an exit. "Welcome to taco county. Look as tough as you can." He put on a face that was part scowl but contaminated with pout. He didn't look tough at all, especially with the eye shadow and the lips, but I knew better. On the terrible night that concluded Divorce Day, he'd beaten the very athletic-looking and larger Cowboy Bob soundly, with a mechanical efficiency rather than any kind of fury. Bob claimed to be a black belt in something too, and he made a great show of it. Clarence's father, he summarized one drunken evening a week later, had been a marine drill sergeant who had tried to "beat the unholy faggot out of him," starting young. Clarence had developed an understanding of combat that couldn't be taught, only grown, though two more bottles of Wanda's hideously expensive Bordeaux had provoked no elaboration.

"Like this?" I set my face in what I thought might at least pass for upper echelon drug dealer. He studied me with a pained expression and sighed.

"Naw, baby. Naw."

I tried for the severe, judging contemplation I directed at the nursing staff. He snorted and rolled his eyes.

"Simon, that only works in mirrors, you pinkie pokin' dummy. Boy keeps his nads all tucked up like . . ." He trailed off, shaking his head.

East LA was more colorful than the rest of our plastic kingdom. Clarence pointed out a few unhygienic fruit stands and rhapsodized about them, directed my attention to a seafood place where we would meet certain death if we dared enter, and finally went into a spasm of "Oh there, oh oow eew!" and bounced up and down in his seat and almost grabbed the wheel as we came up on a dusty lot with a single taco wagon and picnic tables. I reluctantly pulled in, disappointed at how nervous I already was.

It was an old UPS truck in disguise, with an awning that looked like it was constructed from sprinkler system tubing and a deluxe shower curtain. There were two filthy plastic picnic tables. The outside of the truck was covered in a dense field of colorful graffiti, the imagery so layered and convoluted that it could take hours to unravel the overlapping chilies and sombreros and chicanas with clown makeup, the smoking guns and wild donkeys. It was singularly threatening in almost every way, and exposed, right at the edge of an empty liquor store parking lot.

"Now you won't believe me until it gets in your mouth, but you'll thank me for this." Clarence checked his makeup one last time. "Just don't ever come here alone."

"Has a health inspector ever been here?" I could hear the worry in my high voice.

"Get out."

Clarence didn't slam his door, but he closed it hard. This was where he was eating lunch, and I was free to either join him or cower in the car—my choice. I scanned the area for signs of hoodlums, but the only people on foot were two scrawny old guys exiting the liquor store and a pimply Korean kid skating down the sidewalk. I took a deep breath and got out. It was hot, and the air smelled like red meat and onions and smog. My gray suit felt like a beacon, an invitation for trouble. Trying not to scurry, I went quickly over to where Clarence stood under the awning, jabbering with whoever was inside.

"—an I said bring that shit," Clarence was saying. "Ain't never been a pepper could hurt my metal tummy." An aging Mexican man was leaning on his elbows in the window. He had three teardrops tattooed on his face, and he was wearing a black hairnet that I was pretty sure was a fashion statement. He leered at me. Gold and brown teeth. The still air under the awning was thick with circling flies.

"Puerto Ricans," the Mexican said in a smoker's loud whisper. He tossed his head at me. "Who's your new ride?"

"Big shot at the other hospital. Head of the whole janitorial." Clarence glanced back at me and smiled. I nodded in nervous greeting.

"What's good?" I asked. Both of them frowned. Clarence shrugged at the man, who pointed a craggy scowl at me. His glassy eyes were nightmarishly hard. I almost giggled. Sweat bloomed up my back, starting in my butt crack.

"White boy don't know it all good," Clarence said, apologizing for me. "We'll take four pastor tacos, two lengua, and four carnitas."

The Mexican man looked back at Clarence and swabbed the tiny metal counter with a wad of greasy napkin. He looked dubious. "To go?"

"Fuck no," Clarence said. He spread his arms encompassing. "Ambience, baby. Atmosphere. And two Oranginas. And from the back of the cooler too. I want my soda sweaty with cold."

I slumped down into a chair at one of the picnic tables and tried to look natural. Clarence settled on a bench across from me, obviously enjoying my discomfort.

"This place is great, idn't it?"

I grimaced. "I ate at a place like this outside a resort I was staying at with my ex-wife. I was picking up a rental car so I could drive her to someplace where they had horseback riding. I was so hungry after the flight I thought I was going to pass out, so I risked a single taco."

"And?" Tay Tay's plucked-to-pencil-line eyebrows went up. His smile was full of evil anticipatory delight.

"I'm a doctor, Clarence. At least I used to be. But even I was not able to figure out exactly what happened to me."

"Do tell." He was delighted.

"No."

He sighed and casually looked around, content. Even peaceful. I was nervous. I wanted another pill and a tall whiskey. I glanced over at the liquor store, but I knew that if I walked across that hot, dusty parking lot and went in, it would be robbed at that very moment. I turned back and attempted a smile.

"So I guess you're a regular here."

Clarence made a toss of a gesture. "My peeps roll through. I dig it."

I nodded. Small talk had never been my strong suit, so I waited. He left me hanging, still enjoying himself.

Fear, greed, pride, regret, love, shame—they all had the same dynamic for me. Love could often lead to deeper love at its inception, whether I wanted it to or not. It could also awkwardly begin eating itself out of existence, as it did for most people. Joy led to a dangerous excess of itself. Sorrow was the gateway to depression and points beyond. And all the rest, the vast pantheon of humors noble and vile, all of them were the same. So

I will forever blame Clarence's delight at my sweaty discomfort's transition into genuine terror for what happened next. It wasn't the gardener of his emotional landscape that led us right then; it was mine. His mirth was only the catalyst.

A seriously low Lincoln Continental, circa 1970-something, purred at a throbbing jungle rumble into the parking lot. The midnight-blue and buffed-chrome sled idled just past the entrance while Clarence and I looked on. Then it vectored our way, like a trolling shark that had caught a whiff of pink. It pulled to a halt right next to my BMW.

I looked at Clarence. He flicked a withered chunk of dried tomato off the table in a distracted way, but his body language had changed. He seemed bigger somehow, and more negro. His eye shadow didn't look funny or cute in the set of his large, deep eyes. His wide, fat lips didn't seem honey dipped, instead greased by boar fat from a rutting swamp animal he'd hunted barefoot through the lost deltas of the Congo. I couldn't help but marvel at the transformation, which I knew played over my own face like a sad film on a drive-in movie screen comedy with no sound. Clarence clacked his teeth together. His great white teeth. I winced.

"Soda!" the Mexican in the taco truck's voice rang out as the doors to the lowrider opened, huge doors almost half the size of a jet wing. A small carnival piled out, but without the rodeo theatrics. Three button-collar skinny Mexican teenagers, their motions the poetry of sinister grace. Then four more came out of the back, along with what could only be an underage Latino hooker. Their plaid shirts were fastened at the top button only, flowing like capes as they moved. Underneath them, they wore skintight titanium-white T-shirts. Loose belts, baggy black pants, and pointy dress shoes. The harlot wore a red plastic mini, a scarlet halter top, and half a can of hairspray. She was the only one who looked drunk. The seven young men were zoned out but curiously aware at the same time, perhaps on a combination of opiates, speed, and something else, like PCP or expired mescaline.

117

"Ain't they adorable," Clarence said, half to himself.

The entire group stared at my BMW for several heartbeats. Then they turned one by one until they were all facing us. The ringleader made himself known by cracking a dead smile and slapping one of the other guys on the arm with the back of his hand. He tossed his head in our direction and set out toward us with a practiced, arrogant swagger, so menacing that it looked like choreography. The others followed.

I tried to catch Clarence's eye, but he was staring hard at his fingernails.

"Shush now," he said quietly.

"Maybe," I began, trying to sound relaxed and failing, "maybe let's move on while they order."

Clarence looked up. "This is Tay Tay's taco time, Simon. Jus' you follow my lead. Like ballroom dancing." He leveled his eyes. "You're the girl."

The girl. I'd passed into the kingdom of lost Caucasian wimps and somehow I never even saw the sign. Six of them went to the taco truck window and ordered in machine gun Spanish. The leader and the girl peeled off to greet us.

"Sweet ride," the boy-man purred. The girl smacked her gum, once, and then rolled the wad around in her mouth. Her fingernails were bright red and over an inch long. Her bare feet were two days' dark with street grime.

Clarence looked up at him. He didn't speak. He burped.

"Order!" The taco man rang a bell. Clarence turned back to me.

"I'ma get some of those pickled jalapenos. You want some?"

"Sure." The high voice again.

"Hot sauce—you got hot an' super fuckin' hot."

"Super fucking hot is fine." A little deeper.

The gangster and the girl nodded, as if they approved. She drifted off to join the others at the window. Clarence rose and went to the window too, strutting more than a little himself and cutting a neat path through the group. As he passed between them, I noticed how much taller and wider he was. They did too.

"Cars." The leader sat down at my picnic table, right where Clarence had been. He gave me a tight smile and lit a cigarette he'd pulled from behind his ear with a wooden match he ripped across the tabletop. "Cruise? Real leather?"

I shrugged.

"My Lincoln," he went on, exhaling at me, "is way fucking bad on gas, man, but I love that bitch."

I glanced over at his car. "S'nice."

"Nice?" He chuckled bitterly. "Fucking nice. You like it so much, maybe we trade."

"I, uh . . ." His twilight zone eyes bored into mine. I blinked, and they left afterimages.

"Muthafuckin' lunch!" Clarence was suddenly there, a looming black meat tower carrying a red plastic tray laden with tacos wrapped in wax paper, a small paper plate piled high with pickled jalapenos and what looked like carrots, two sweating Oranginas, and a crusty squeeze bottle of something deep red and painful. He looked down at the vato.

"You in my seat," he said warmly, like he was talking to a child.

"It's a big table." The kid gestured at the empty seats.

Clarence set the tray down in front of me and then settled back on the bench, lightly, gracefully, extremely close to him. Then he smiled and slowly ran his fat pink tongue over his wide upper lip. The kid's eyes narrowed.

"I can get down on some brown," Clarence assured him, "but no kissin'. That cigarette is the wrong kinda nasty."

The Mexican's eyes shot wide, and he leapt to his feet and backed away with a startled laugh. I grabbed a taco and unwrapped it, squirted some red sauce on it. The taco was small and doubled up, about the size of my palm, and stuffed entirely with mystery meat. I bit into it, and fire filled my sinuses. I chewed solemnly, trying to give off the impression that I was

119

thinking about something else, something far removed from whatever the hell game Clarence was playing.

The Mexican shot some rapid-fire Spanish at his friends, who howled with laughter. The taco guy stuck his head out the window and lasered me with menace and warning. Clarence had his wide back to all of them and didn't notice. I ate fast, working through three nuclear tacos in less than two minutes. Clarence was deliberately slow, almost nibbling, completely oblivious to the gathering storm.

"Let's take the rest of these and eat them on the way," I suggested quietly, keeping my eyes down. I flicked my gaze up to Clarence, who shook his head.

"Nah."

"The, uh . . . those guys. Is this some kind of macho gay thing?"

"Yep. An' fuck 'em. I ain't gettin' taco grease in a BMW, and neither are you. We ain't crazy, Simon. Least I ain't." He picked up a jalapeno by the stem, pinkie cocked out, and took a dainty bite. I wiped my hands on the single tiny napkin that came with our order and drained my Orangina.

"Done," I said.

"Pussy." He said it warmly.

"If you don't hurry the fuck up, I'm leaving you here, Clarence."

He shrugged. "I can't walk the last two miles and be on time, but I don't want to jog it and get there all sweaty. Them *putas* might be able to squeeze me in their boat." He used the vaginal slur a little too loud, and I knew he'd done it on purpose. I realized something awful right then.

Clarence Tay Tay Farrow was spoiling for a fight.

"Shit." It was all I could think of to say. Clarence glanced at me with an innocent expression. He took another bite and talked around it.

"You need to treat this like an administrative matter," he said. He was obviously enjoying himself. "Let the help do their work their own way. Get the best out of them by being encouraging. That kind of thing."

120

The leader of the Mexicans slowly approached his car, almost dancing on the tips of his shiny shoes. He glanced over his shoulder to make sure the others were following. They were. The taco vendor slammed the iron gate on the window of his cart closed. Clarence picked up his last taco as the Mexicans got in the lowrider. The engine roared to life, and Latino rap boomed out over the parking lot—loud enough, I suspected, to cover the sounds of gunfire and screaming. Clarence finished his taco and rose.

"Just a sec," he said. He turned to the lowrider and hitched up his pants, rolled his neck.

"Clarence!" I hissed.

My heart was already hammering, but it began pounding at a truly alarming rate as he walked over to their car and rapped on the hood. He leaned into the driver's window. When he stood and stepped back, there was a second of a pause and then the lowrider slowly reversed. Clarence ambled to my BMW and motioned for me to join him. I did. Fast.

"That was fun," he said mildly. He casually fastened his seat belt. I started the engine and pulled away, not fast, but not slow either. The lowrider fell in behind us.

"What the fuck did you tell them?" I was furious. When we hit the street, I stepped on the gas hard. The lowrider did the same, rolling a tight ten feet behind us. Clarence flicked the sun visor down and checked his eye shadow in the little mirror and then inspected his teeth.

"I told them that you were a purely psycho detective-grade pig with a death wish and that I was the leash assigned to you by the department therapist. Now, that's almost about three-quarters of the way true. It came off as real, anyway."

"You . . . you . . . you're fucking crazy!" My scream had more shriek in it than anything else. Clarence flipped the sun visor back up. We were less than a mile from the hospital.

"No, Simon. You're crazy—I am Tay Tay. The difference is unimaginable for you, especially right now. Breathe. Think of how good dinner is going to be after such an exciting lunch. We're on a culinary roll here, man. Lighten up."

"Oh my God." I couldn't think of anything else to say.

"Prayer never hurts," he said. His heart rate must have been hovering in the low sixties. He even yawned. "It never works, of course, but the power of positive thinking does. So maybe something can be said about the practice after all."

I saw the gates of Saint Francis, and my heart fluttered. There was an actual guard at the gate booth.

"Better come in with me for a few," Clarence suggested. "Give the ghetto a chance to flatten out."

And that was how I entered Clarence's second world—which was, of course, what he had been planning all along.

9

Lamp in the Circus Maze

THE GUARD LET US THROUGH, and the gate closed behind us. The lowrider kept going but slowed to a crawl. I could clearly see them in the rearview, watching. It looked like they were smiling. The driver blew some kind of smoke out the window in a slow plume. As I pulled into a space, Clarence finally looked back himself. Then he turned to me and grinned.

"They're parking," he observed with evident pride. "Looks like you get to hang here for a few hours. See a real hospital. Won't that be fun?"

"No."

"Go get killed then," he said dismissively. "Or come look at sick people. You said you used to be a doctor of some kind, I can't remember which variety. Frankly, I never believed you. I bet you five bucks right now that you don't know how to deal with a busted toe." He looked me over and shook his head. "Know anything about splinters? I mean for realsies? The difference between a wart and a mole? How to get a bean out of some kid's nose? What to do when someone gets a lightbulb stuck up their—"

"I'm calling the police," I interrupted. "They'll get rid of those guys, and then I can get the hell out of here." It was all I could think of. Clarence laughed.

123

"Them boys have PhDs in deception, Simon! They're probably smarter than you are too. You call the police, you take a hit for impersonating an officer. I'm not sure if they go extra hard on you if you fake at being a crazy cop. Dummy. But I bet you'd go over great in county. Those clothes? That magnetic personality? Your fur condition? Make all kinds of new big boy daddy friends in the first night. Now you got me all jealous and shit. Let me get you with some eye shadow, maybe a little lip gloss before you dial."

I stared at him. He exuded beatific satisfaction.

"You trapped me," I said. I could hear the wonder in my voice. I'd spoken the thought as it came to me, which is something I never did, even at my very worst. My ex-wife had listed lack of spontaneity as one of my many character flaws.

"Aw, you so smart, Simon." He puckered and blew me a kiss.

"You trapped me," I said again, more firmly. His smile faded, and his eyes changed. His jaw hardened a little. Something in him shifted for the second time that day, and I caught a glimpse of something beyond what he referred to as Tay Tay Farrow. His trail through time had been a long one, I realized. In that flash of an instant I realized that in every way that mattered, Clarence Farrow was far, far older than I was, even though I'd been born more than a decade before his parents even met.

"Let's go look at sick people," he said softly. "It may do something for you. To you. Sounds stupid, I know. But this is a stupefying situation."

———————————

The lobby of Saint Francis was littered with a comprehensive field of the damned. Every tattered vinyl sofa and every old plastic chair had a bleeding or otherwise damaged being on it, and there were more people on the floor. Nurses were buzzing around. People were crying, laughing, talking on cell phones, yelling at each other, and it smelled like sweat and hair and old building. Clarence inhaled deeply. So did I. I almost vomited.

He clapped me on the shoulder.

"Time to rumble," he purred. "Dicks hard. Gloves up. Let's go check in."

I followed his path as he wove through the patients to the Lexan-enclosed front desk. The fat black woman running the forward computer looked up and adjusted her glitter-framed glasses. She smiled.

"Tay Tay," she called. "My man with the magic. You bring me them pickles?"

"Two more weeks," Clarence replied. He tossed his thumb at me. "But I abducted a doctor. That good enough for today?"

"Two weeks my ass," she replied. She hit a button and a buzzer sounded. The battered door to the interior of Hades popped open. Clarence pulled me through, and it closed and locked behind us.

Inside it was . . . quiet. A wide corridor with an old black-and-white linoleum floor was lined with closed doors. There were a few patients sleeping on wheeled gurneys, the old kind that had come into service after the Korean War. The hallway split about fifty feet down. Clarence pointed at the office to our right.

"Go show your creds to Bernadette. She the big girl who bitched at me about the pickles, which we better actually put up this weekend. Don't even tell her we didn't, in case she asks. She'll print you up a tag. I'm gonna go suit up. Call me on my cell in an hour. And keep your fingers away from her mouth if she has a snack on her desk."

10

Public Knowledges

"SO WAS THAT CRAZY NEGRO, Tay Tay, full of shit, or do you have an actual degree in something more impressive than English? We could use that too, so don't feel bad if that's all you got. Just means you'll be on sweep and mop." Bernadette smelled like dollar store perfume, coconut oil, and flatulence. Her desk was a mess, and all five lines on her antique phone were blinking red. Her wide, greasy face was unlined, but she seemed like she may have been close to retirement. There was a small wad of tissue stuck in the bulging bra line of her florid muumuu. She cocked her head, skeptical.

"I'm Dr. Simon Resner, chief administrator at Sellwood. I came out of Oncology. UCLA."

"Wehehell." Bernadette crossed her heavy arms. "What brings you all the way to the far east, big shot?" Unimpressed. Her glasses were incredibly greasy.

"I gave Clarence a ride. He works at Sellwood, and we've become . . . he's . . . he's my houseguest. I'm not gay, if that's what you're wondering. It's a long story that—"

"Can wait," Bernadette interrupted. "We don't have time to give you a tour, Doctor. It's a busy day, as you can see. Nice to meet you, and thanks for getting my boy." She made to turn away.

127

"Wait," I said quickly. "Bernadette, right? Clarence said if you could get me a tag or a pass or whatever, maybe I could just look around. I have the rest of the day off." There was no way I was going to hang out in the lobby all afternoon. I was too fragile for anything that depressing.

Bernadette sized me up. I took out my wallet and showed her my credentials. Three minutes later, I had a day pass with my name scribbled on it and I was standing in the hallway. A nurse appeared, and then time . . . stopped.

The first sutures I'd done in more than seven years. I trafficked in a blur of burns, lesions, and undiagnosed ailments ranging from diabetes to skin cancer. A knife wound, a case of serious food poisoning, an allergic reaction. I lanced more than a dozen explosively infected boils, and then I realized five hours had passed. I realized it because Clarence suddenly appeared while I was examining a woman's sprained and possibly broken ankle. I'd just finished wheeling her into line for the single x-ray machine, which by then was only eleven patients deep. Clarence looked tired, but in a peaceful way.

"Talk of the town, Simon," he said. He cocked his head a little. "The high-speed Doctor Fixit from the other side of the tracks, gettin' all touchy-feely with the people's people."

"Clarence," I said. "You homosexual negro dipshit."

His huge eyes widened and sparkled with delight. "And you even learned a new word." He rolled his wide neck. "Quittin' time. Let's blow. I could use some pool time and a fancy bottle of wine. Maybe I'll add some pineapple to the salsa. Bring it right to the edge of hot, sweet confusion."

"I have to . . ." I stopped and considered. He put his giant hand on my shoulder.

"You have to go wash up and toss your whites in the basket in the staff room. Night shift is prepping. We need to get out of their way. I'll meet you by the car. Gonna smoke my daily ultralight." He turned to leave and then stopped himself. "You did good today, Simon. And by that I mean you used your hands to do good things. How'd that feel?"

I shook my head and smiled. "Like I should hit you over the head with something, except I know you'd just beat me up." We walked together toward the lobby. "But seriously, we need to talk on the way home. I saw a thousand ways this place could use help. There are all kinds of free things out there if you know the right reps. I should set up a meeting with the administrator. Who is he?"

"Bernadette," Clarence replied. "You two met earlier. She's the Saint Francis version of you. Just, well, she's compassionate, deceptively bright, she has principles, inhuman motivation, she probably went to a better university than you did, and on a scholarship no less, plus she—"

"I get it," I said, cutting him off. "Meet you out at the car in five. Check the street to make sure your friends aren't still out there."

Clarence laughed. We both knew they were long gone. He went out through the hell gate. I spun off to the side, into the staff room, to toss my whites and look at myself in the mirror of the men's room, to see if I appeared sane in any way.

The staff room was small, with a row of battered lockers, a scarred-up old table surrounded by more than a dozen folding metal chairs, and a desk with a coffeepot and Styrofoam cups. Men's and women's restrooms. The men's room had two stalls, a trough urinal, and seven sinks, all of it circa 1960.

The first phase of the night shift was rotating through. Maybe fifteen people, all gossiping and laughing and suiting up. The mood was very different than the staff room at Sellwood, which was more like a spa. But there was more to it than that. Many of the people seemed actually happy to be getting to work. Some of them were quiet and thoughtful looking. A few seemed sad about whatever was going on in their lives. The emotional spectrum was less guarded than it was at Sellwood. These people had moods and personalities that they felt no compulsion to hide. At Sellwood, everyone wore a mask—the one I had given them.

One woman in particular stood out. A Mexican in her late twenties, maybe early thirties. It was hard to tell. Her long black hair reminded me of a raven's wing. Her hands were slim, with unpainted nails, and she wore no jewelry of any kind. She radiated something—a kind of warm, sad glow, a lonesome and complex aura I could easily associate with a bottle of red wine that was rare to the point that there was only a single bottle ever made, yet to be opened. Everyone's lockers were packed with clothes and snacks and various personal items, but hers was spare to the point of empty. I tossed my whites in the bin and then watched her for a moment. No one spoke to her, but there was a unanimous, fond deference to her personal space. Interesting. And she was painfully beautiful, so much so that I wondered why she was even working at a place like Saint Francis; the thought instantly made me feel ashamed.

On the way out, I stopped by Bernadette's desk. She was on the phone and held up a finger for me to pause. I waited. While I did, I looked around. She had three assistants, two laboring at the desks beyond her and one running the window. It was loud, with phones clanging, old computers hissing, and printers chattering. The printers were the small kind used by high school kids.

"Doctor Resner," Bernadette said finally, snapping me out of it. I focused. She had the phone cradled under her chins.

"Bernadette," I said, nodding. "Is it okay to call you Bernadette?"

"What the hell else would you call me? Jemima? Big old lady?" She cackled.

"Then call me Simon, please. I just wanted to . . . I had an agreeable afternoon. I just wanted to express that."

She snorted. "Come on by an' agree any time—long as it's volunteering. And get that lazy-ass Tay Tay to make them pickles. I know he's lying. Ain't even got 'em in a jar yet, has he?

Don't you fix to lie to me, boy. I see it. Oh, now you flummoxed. Tell that fool he busted."

She turned away, and I realized I'd been dismissed. Just like that. I went out of the front office and through the big metal door. The lobby was only half full, and nothing looked urgent. I felt a certain satisfaction at the sight of so many empty chairs. When I stepped out into the last part of the sunset, made so beautiful by what I knew to be the methane in the smog, I felt the lightness Clarence had planned for me to experience, and it made me wonder, for a moment, if the cosmos had a scale balancing the seemingly broken mechanics of existence. Tortured at the hands of a white, white woman in a white, White Palace, and then made to appreciate a smoggy sunset by a gay black man in a place of terrible darkness, where the only light came from a thing I'd closed the door on. I shook my head. It made no sense at all, but nothing truly worth thinking about ever did.

11

The Mirror, the Party

"WE GOT EVERYTHING?" I ASKED. Tay Tay nodded and turned on the radio. He casually ignored me while he drifted through the stations before finally settling on some old Ray Charles country. Wanda would never imagine me riding home in the BMW with a huge, gay black man or even listening to any kind of music at all. It was almost like I was in someone else's TV show, even to me.

"You mean the pineapple? In the crisper. Man, when was the last time you actually really looked in the refrigerator? I mean other than for the vodka you keep in the freezer?" He laughed and slipped out of his orthopedic shoes and wiggled his toes.

"Can't recall." Clarence had the same weird buzz going that I did. We drove like that for a while, decompressing and enjoying the postwork high. Gradually the landscape changed back to the LA freeway visuals I was accustomed to, and for the first time ever, I realized the absence of color, the comforting blandness. At the moment it didn't seem real.

Home to the White Palace. Home to the cotton place of blank paper and empty glass. That didn't seem real, either.

"What you thinkin' over there Simon? I can hear your hamster wheel pickin' up the pace."

"I don't know what I'm thinking. But I'm starting to think about something." I glanced at him. He was relaxed. Listening. Still amused. So I continued. "Why . . . why did Wanda insist that everything be painted white? Did you ever wonder?"

Clarence shook his head. "How the hell am I supposed to know? I never even met her. Is that what you were really thinking about, or are you just making conversation?"

"No! Well, sort of. Maybe it's the sunset. All that graffiti. I dunno."

"Whatever."

I agreed. Whatever. My torso felt buoyant. I realized I didn't really want to go home. Once again, I didn't want to sleep in the big bed where Wanda and I had slept, where we had made our thin version of love—which was quite possibly very bad, especially considering the photos I'd seen of Jack, who looked like the kind of man who lived off of oysters and aerobics and steak tartare and threw airplanes when their engines stalled. If sex had anything to do with art—as every movie, every song, every piece of literature, indeed, everything the act was ever mentioned in would lead us to suspect—then Wanda had definitely been faking it, and so had I. Jack could probably play piano while he painted a landscape with his feet. I imagined that a man like that could draw the locust out of the most barren soil with the vibration of his passage. Most of the time, I had trouble telling art from random disaster. The realization wasn't even particularly offensive, which represented a step forward. Whatever. And I didn't want to sleep on the patio again, either.

"Wanna stop for a drink?" I asked. Clarence had been watching the world pass. He roused himself.

"Where?"

I shrugged. "Someplace we've never been. Let's pick a place at random."

That got his attention. He sat up straighter and regarded me, his big eyes full of curiosity. "Random?"

"Yeah." I thought. "Someplace in Santa Monica, maybe.

Down by the beach, where all the shitty stuff is. The Strand. Get a few margaritas and people watch."

"People watch. At a random place. On the Strand. In Santa Monica, where all the shitty stuff is."

"Yeah? So?"

He shook his head, smiling what I thought was a private smile.

I took the exit and parked in a pay lot. When we got out, the sun was finally down and the night was warm, almost the perfect temperature. The leaves on the palm trees swayed gently in the breeze. Ripples of sand blown over the asphalt crunched beneath our feet. Clarence yawned and stretched, his wide face almost sleepy. In the near distance, the plastic-and-neon lights of the Strand spilled down the side street, carrying with them the sounds of laughter, overlapping music, and the smells of bad pizza, cotton candy, the ocean, and pretzels.

"Tourists in our own city," Clarence marveled. "Gotta love this."

We started walking. "I used to come here all the time when I was in college," I said. "There was this place, I can't remember the name . . . the King and Castle, or something corny like that. It had photos and paintings of sand castles all over the walls. Every winner from a competition in the seventies. Seashells everywhere. Fishing nets on the ceiling with starfish, and those big Japanese glass bulbs. The waitresses all wore jeans and denim shirts and straw hats . . ."

"Sounds dreamy."

"It was . . . it was." We rounded onto the Strand proper, a wide sidewalk lined with bars and restaurants on one side, interspersed evenly with T-shirt and sunglasses operations and an expanse of beach on the other. I led us to the right. "They had cheap fish and chips. Pretty good too. I had this serious crush on one of the waitresses."

"And? For how long? Was is painfully awkward? Did you get some? You *did* get some."

I frowned a little. "Just once. Couple times a week I ate there, just to see her. For two years, actually. That was before stalking was such a popular word. Anyway, I didn't think she ever noticed me. This one night though, through a random miracle or two, she got off early and we went for a walk, almost all the way to Venice. So it turned out she had noticed me, shyly eating my dinners alone and being a houseplant. It was late. Early fall, and that night the stars were out like they never are in LA. Some kind of Niño wind had blasted the stratosphere clean, and it seemed like it was just for us. We held hands, and I was so surprised. And it felt really, really good too. We talked on and on about everything, and we had so much in common, even the small stuff. I finally told her I ate at her place just to catch a few words with her every once in a while. She told me she always waited for me . . . that it made her night every time."

"And then you shagged her on the beach, mac daddy raw dog, boy Conan."

"Yep." I smiled at the memory. "Yes I did. Totally unusual for me, even in those days, as you can probably guess. Anyway, the weirdest thing happened."

"You got sand in your little dingus hole."

"No. Well, I probably did, but that wasn't it. No . . . no, I couldn't consummate the moment, if you see what I mean."

"Lost your wood? Pecker pooped out?"

"Nah, I couldn't . . . I couldn't . . ."

"Jizz? Spurt? Blow your load?"

"Yeah. I mean, no. I couldn't."

"Well that's fucking awful, Simon! What happened?"

"To her? Well, about—"

"No, no," Clarence interrupted. "I mean what happened to your junk?"

"Ah. That. Well, I guess after all that time courting her, at least in my mind, I guess I didn't want to just do it on the beach like that. I was afraid it would all end when I was done and I would never see her again, kinda like a dream or a song that was over. That wasn't what I wanted."

Clarence drew in a sucking breath through his teeth.

"Simon, that's just fucking weird. She not, like, what . . . she didn't wiggle just right? Couldn't trick it out of you?"

"Nope. And it wasn't for lack of trying either. She looked kind of skinny and small breasted, sort of wore baggy clothes, but naked she was . . . damn."

I stopped talking. We walked past a fortune-teller's booth, and something stirred in my memory. We were nowhere close to where the restaurant had been. It was at the south end, and we were on the northern edge. It probably wasn't even there anymore.

"You can keep talking," Clarence offered. He lightly clapped me on the back. "It ain't grossing me out all that bad."

"I'm glad." Up ahead was a raucous-looking bar with patio chairs, maybe the last one before we hit the big patch of sand between us and Venice. "There," I said. "Margaritas. Great big ones."

"For my powerful thirst," Clarence agreed. "So you were just getting to the postnaked part, right after your failure to unload your man cannon."

"Right. So that was right around the time I met Wanda. I was close to getting my first real work as a doctor. Wanda . . . she was Wanda. Brought me a cupcake one day. Laughed at all my jokes. Asked all kinds of questions about my work, where I was going with it. She was interested, and she didn't make any kind of secret out of it. She hunted me."

"And this other one didn't."

"Not even close. I called her all the time after the whole beach episode, but one night she told me she didn't like talking on the phone."

"Ouch."

"Ouch. I didn't quite know what to make of that. See, I worked really hard to become a doctor. All the long nights.

So much study, years and years and years of it. And I did it. Me. No help from my parents along the way. So right then I felt like it was time to move on to the next phase of my life in an orderly fashion. One step leads to the next. And the next was get married, buy a house, and have a couple of kids. And I really, really wanted to take that next step."

"How come?" We got to the bar and sat down at a table. Clarence ordered for us and then looked on expectantly, so I continued.

"It seemed right. It felt right. And I'm not talking about that American Dream bullshit either. I wanted to love that woman. I did love her, but I wanted it to last forever. I wanted to like, see her barefoot and pregnant, in our house. I wanted her to do shit like sing and make tea and all the rest of it. That night on the beach, we even talked about kids. She wanted them too, as bad as I did."

"Hmm." He steepled his fingers under his chin. "Hmm. So then what?"

"I started dating Wanda. I couldn't help it. But I kept thinking about Jane—that was her name, Jane. About five months after our last conversation, I sent her an e-mail. Something long and romantic. I spent hours trying to get the words just right. Anyway, she e-mailed me back about a week later. She was three months pregnant. Happy."

"Shitty," Clarence observed. "Must have been happy you dodged that bullet."

"Gary said the same thing. I almost became a sperm donor."

"And a rock solid ATM machine. Child support in your bracket is . . ." He whistled. "Nasty. And she waited until the exact right moment too. You tell her all that shit about how you worked so hard and how you were ready to enjoy the life you figured you earned?"

"I did."

"Chump. But my heart does go out to you."

"Yeah . . . So in the resulting emotional confusion, I married

Wanda. She was cold in comparison to Jane, I suppose, though they both had ice cubes for hearts. So I've had two freezers in a row. Anyway, you know the rest."

Our drinks came. For a while, we drank and listened to the people around us. Most of them were young college students in from Orange County. Talking about Jane and Wanda had cast some sort of shadow, and all I saw were spoiled little date rapists and their scheming and manipulating targets. A few locals were just getting off work and skimming drinks out of their neighborhood bars. A pod of skater kids rolled past. Then a few random people on Rollerblades. We ordered two more, both of us thoughtfully quiet, just enjoying the sound of the ocean and attempting to join in the general good cheer around us. The people watching and the giant drinks kept me from getting too burned about my freezer conclusion, which wasn't a new one, after all.

In hindsight, I would of course have definitely rather been the sperm donor, no matter what it cost in the end. Especially considering what happened instead. I wondered, for the millionth time, what had happened to Jane and who the guy had been. I'd heard conflicting rumors before I lost track of her altogether, most of them varying degrees of sad. Wondering made me wonder why I even bothered to tell anyone. Gary had been pretty drunk the night I told him about it—distracted by problems of his own that stemmed from having too many girlfriends at once—and he dismissed it as the kind of thing that happened to normal, lesser men all the time.

"You know what I've always wondered the most, Clarence? Especially after the divorce?"

"I can guess," he said soberly. He kept his eyes on his drink.

"I wonder if Jane had a dream too. Of her doctor coming home and picking up the kid. Of her making me do hippie things that I'd complain about but were good for my soul. Of being barefoot in a little house with a garden and making tea. What if . . . what if I blew it because I was a coward. Because

I let Wanda steamroller my ass. Because, see, that baby could have been mine."

He was quiet for a long time. I don't know why, but putting it into words made the empty part of me seem so much larger. Eventually he cleared his throat and leaned across the table and put his huge hand over mine. I didn't pull away.

"You'll never know that, Simon. You couldn't know it then, and you can't know it now. Faith like that is too much like gambling. But you got that close, man. For some people, that's more than they ever get. Love is rare, baby. It doesn't meet itself as much as it should. But I tell you, and I know it's true, those sad songs and the sad fuckers who sing them can all go to hell. Love makes you strong, even if it is a mess, even if it feels like an accident you just barely walked away from."

"The light that stays at the end of the tunnel," I said. I squinted at him to cover what I was feeling. "Are you trying to make me feel better, Clarence?"

He slapped my hand and picked up his drink. I prepared myself for some pithy rebuttal, some folksy gay wisdom tempered with his singular brand of antidepressant, but he didn't say anything, just looked out at the ocean.

"Clarence?" I cleared my throat. "What about you?"

He turned to me and narrowed his eyes. "What about me?"

"You ever been in love?"

"Of course I have." He smiled in a casually dismissive way that conveyed how stupid I was for asking. Clarence had a smile for every occasion. "Of course I have." His smile faded most of the way, and he sipped his drink. I thought that was all I was going to get, that the ban on explicit anything of any kind extended to that moment, even though I'd just broken the rules I'd set down about privacy and come close to crying about it. But he eventually continued.

"Met him at the gym," he said, swirling his drink and watching it, slowly shaking his head. "About eleven years ago, give or take. White man, big and strong like me. Big voice too, and lots to say with it. That man could laugh and it would shake the walls. . . . We had so much fun together, Simon. I guess in the end, he was a little like your Jane and I was sort of like you." He laughed. "I wanted to domesticate." He snapped the word out a second time. "Domesticate. Tay Tay."

"You're the most domesticated person I've ever met," I said incredulously, meaning it. "You're a fantastic cook. You run the house. You never get too drunk. Clarence, you're 'domesticated,' as you put it, whether you want to—"

"Not what I mean," he interrupted. "Simon . . . words, definitions, they're flexible, but only within the frames of the pictures they paint. I told him I wanted to settle down. Be a couple. Grow old together. Have cats. Maybe move someplace where there was snow in the winter, take our show off the road. See?"

I sat back. He kept his eyes on his drink.

"Yeah," I said finally. "I do. Domestic partnership, they called it then. You wanted the same thing as me."

"And I didn't get it. Your Jane and your Wanda weren't offering it in any way you could understand, and neither was Roy." He looked out over the water. "Roy. And that Roy wanted to party, party, partay! For all his worldly *this* and his sophisticated *that*, he never seemed to get it. There was always something he had to see and touch, to feel, and it was just right down that next road, in the next city over. He was sensual. So head over heels in love with life itself."

"Huh." I finished my drink. Clarence finished his, and we sat there, waiting for the check.

"So where is he now?"

Clarence shrugged. "Seeing and touching things. Round that corner and down that road of his, I guess. I don't know. I don't get a Christmas card."

I somehow couldn't imagine anything like that could happen to him, but evidently it had. He looked out at the black water again, and I watched him out of the corner of my eye. He didn't look depressed or sad; his expression was something I didn't have any words for. And then he took a deep breath and flashed me a grin.

"Simon, what is love? I mean, medically."

I considered. The biochemistry of affection was still an expanding field of research. In many ways it probably always would be, because beyond molecules, there was physics. I raised a hand and motioned for another round. We were going to need it if I was going to nerd out.

"The healing effects of love," I mused, back in my element. "Neuropeptides. Remember those? No? Oxytocin? Vasopressin?" I thought. "The messy methylation of receptor genes." I sighed. "Wolves fall in love, Clarence. Did you know that? Voles. I don't find that particularly encouraging. Anyway, love itself comes from the oldest part of the brain and then confuses the rest of it. Incompatible hardware. We have our dopamine and our endogenous opioids and a racy mélange of other neurochemicals, and all of it works together to form the kinds of bonds that give us our evolutionary edge. Love is possibly the ape's greatest power when you think about it, if you can with any kind of dynamic clarity, which is doubtful. Cognitive blinder."

"Of course," he said, smiling.

"So what is love. From a biological point of view, it's all of that, but its function is an evolutionary one, obviously. Some studies suggest that we can smell parts of a potential mate's DNA, and that plays a factor in initiating the oxytocin dance. Confusing in your case, but just as confusing in mine. Maybe more confusing, in fact."

"Maybe. Maybe not."

"Let's make some equations," I suggested. "The flowers, the walks on the beach? Dopamine and noradrenaline. The overpowering desire to, well, you know—become naked? Testosterone and estrogen. And the wedding ring? The wanting, the needing of a life with someone else? There you have your oxytocin and vasopressin." I shook my head, unsatisfied with my explanation. "Clarence, have you ever seen cats mating?"

"I have not watched cats actually gettin' down," he replied. "But I seen a cat in heat."

"Okay, when you see that, you can't help but think that it isn't even an animal anymore. It's so crippled by the need to reproduce that it can barely think. At that moment, the cat resembles a very complex plant. Now, that is entirely driven by chemistry. What we experience as love has a clear example there. Simply more complex, more lasting. More dangerous. More damaging."

Clarence laughed at my troubled expression. "Simon, that might be . . . you got mangled even worse than I thought. I'm not sure you're ever supposed to be that clinical about love. Man, do you really believe any of that?"

"Science is believable stuff, Clarence."

"And there it is! The root of all your problems, man. So what if it's believable stuff? Maybe all that's just the beginning, see? Maybe there's something more to all of it than just the raw facts and the undiscovered science. These two women of yours, they both wanted ATM machines, and they didn't really care what happed to them as long as they worked. Economics. That's banking, or a market infrastructure concept. But you loved one of them, right? And she hurt you. So you built the White Palace. You did! You did, and you paid for every white thing in it. You let Wanda into your life. And you're a smart man, Simon. You knew exactly what she was and what would happen next. What you didn't know was that she would eventually tire of her own reflection and leave you stranded in her mirror."

He sat back and the drinks arrived. It was clear that he had just put it together, and we were both stunned into silence. He sipped. Then I did. His looked of revelation eventually turned contemplative.

"I wonder," he began, mostly to himself, "I wonder if we all do that kind of thing." I leaned forward.

"Clarence, if the biological mechanisms of love, if, if all of it is just the foundation . . ." I waited expectantly for him to finish the thought.

"Then ultimately it's in the shape of the eyes," he said softly. "That's where it continues into nonsense for me. Somehow though, way in there—past all the chemical doors and the languages and all the music—it probably does wind its way back to your chemistry. Love is kinda painful all by itself, when you look at it or feel it all by itself. But it feels so big. And that makes everything feel bigger."

I sat back. We watched a small pack of skaters roll past, chirping their mating call. People were surprising me more and more in the last week, myself included.

"Maybe," I said thoughtfully, "there's anaerobic bacteria in my soil again. Growth is occurring. A root medium is forming."

Clarence snorted and shook his head. "Disgusting."

"Depends. You're the one who talks about weeds and seeds every morning."

I finished my drink and saluted with my empty glass. He mock scowled at me.

"There's no cure yet," I declared. "But the world of science is full of sociopaths, so I'm sure some people are looking."

He snorted. "Whatever man. You ain't gonna meet your next ex-wife sittin' around here with me. And frankly, you're blowing my chances of getting any phone numbers that might lead to cats or houseplants of my own. Let's boogie."

12

Folded of a Circle of Water

SUNRISE.

I woke up on the couch in my clothes. Clarence was singing softly in the kitchen, making coffee. I sat up and rubbed my face.

"Lookie there," Clarence sang. "Simon sleeping inside. Like a real person. Least like a big boy, anyway. And you didn't even get trashed, so you did it on purpose." He held up two mugs.

"We absolutely have to paint this place," I said. "One of the chairs. The inside of one of the cabinets." He came around the kitchen divider and handed me my cup. He was wearing his ridiculous Speedos and luminous green flip-flops.

"What color?" He arched an eyebrow.

"Who cares. You choose." I sipped and scratched my scalp.

"Good thinking."

I rubbed my neck. Clarence blew on his coffee and stared out at the pool.

"Long fucking day coming up," he said, like it was just another thing. "I really have to make them pickles this weekend. The stress is killing me."

"Saint Francis again?"

"Yep. Only seven hours, but Bernadette's gonna be on my ass all day long less I bring her something. I should have never

145

brought that woman the special Tay Tay's Spicy Cajuns. Spend three years—an' I'm talking an obsessive three years—just getting the recipe perfect, and look what I get. Bunch of angry fans." He shook his head. "It ain't easy being famous, Simon. You just watch out."

"Maybe I'll go with you," I offered. "Keep you out of trouble."

"Really?" He glanced at me, skeptical.

"Sure. Why not. I actually had an interesting time yesterday. Sellwood has a ton of stuff in storage. Useful stuff. If I could shuffle some of it off to Saint Francis, I could use it as a tax write-off."

"Huh." He looked back out at the pool. I got up.

"I'm gonna get ready."

I went into the master bedroom, closed the door, and then looked at myself in the floor-to-ceiling mirror doors on the walk-in closet. Mine was on the left, Wanda's on the right. As far as I knew, all of her clothes were still in there. A fortune of clothes. On impulse, I opened her door.

Rows and rows of garments, coded in a complex system of color and function. I turned on the closet light and stood there.

All of her stuff from our trip to London was in a neat section starting on the right. She'd worn them only there, and it had taken her the first two days of the trip to pick it all out. I stepped in and ran my hand over them. Wool. They were wool, earthy tones, with odd dashes of scarlet and burnt orange. So unlike her. Next came Mexico, much more in keeping with her taste in things. Vivid turquoise and robin's egg, lacy gold and rust, and of course white. I looked down at the rows and rows of shoes, and then I turned out the light.

The smell, there in the darkness, was instantly familiar. It was Wanda's scent, her perfume—what she smelled like when she woke up in the morning, what trailed behind her when she passed. It was the smell that rose up when she was in my arms, when I was holding her to my chest and feeling her heart beat on my sternum. Wanda smelled just like a dark closet full of incredibly extravagant waste.

"My God," I whispered.

I staggered backward and fell out of the closet and then sat there looking into it. A confusing horror rose up and stuck hard in my throat, and I could feel my pulse in my face. An inconceivable, wild desire to commit arson swept through me, and I shuddered. I shook with something close to madness, something I knew in some part of me that I shouldn't be feeling, something dangerous and deeply wrong, something no one should feel. A giggle escaped me, and I caught my breath. White spots danced in the whiteness at the edges of my vision.

"Oh my God," I whispered again.

I slowly got up and went into the shower and turned it on. After the water had run over me for a few minutes, I took my clothes off and left them on the shower floor. I stood there for so long that Clarence finally knocked on my door.

"Simon!" I heard him shout over the water. "I made French toast! Hurry the fuck up!"

We were both quiet on the drive to the hospital. Clarence made small adjustments to his appearance, like touching up his eyelashes and inspecting his molars from various angles. I'd passed through some kind of episode and was trying not to think about it. It wasn't until we got past the security at the front gate that Clarence started to lecture me.

"You're quiet this morning, Simon," he began. "Quiet isn't good. It means you're either thinking about bad shit or you're trying not to think about bad shit. It's always the same with you."

"Clarence," I began. He didn't let me finish.

"We're going into a hospital, Simon. And it's not just any hospital. It's where poor people go for some kind of mercy. Now you shut up and let me finish. Your head has to be in the game. This ain't Sellwood, not by a long shot. Yesterday you were good. You went in there and rolled straight up healing machine. But you can't go in there with a long face. Everyone does that. Half the people who work in there, more than half, some part of them got worn down and they turned off. Couldn't help it. Now you, you go in there and show them some shit. Smile. Get that groove back on. I've seen you do it. These people need to be inspired. Not all of them, because in there are some people . . . the kind of people I've never even seen before. And I've seen all kinds of people. All the rest of them? These patients? They need more than the whole Tay Tay Human Prozac routine. You get me? You're on my team now, and on my team we inspire the people we work with so we can help the motherfuckers who come through that door. This is America at its worst. Right in there." Some little bit of drill instructor was in this tone, in the set of his shoulders, his expression. His eyes held mine, and they wouldn't let go.

"I . . . I understand," I said. I shook off the weird mood, and somehow it was easier than I thought it would be. Clarence was right. There were more than patients in that building; there were the people who were trying to help them. And they were losing, because the broken flood would never end. I'd seen it with my own eyes. I smiled with grim resolve and widened my eyes into Clarence's clear and appraising gaze. What he saw made him smile back.

"Then let's go," he said.

"Dicks hard. Gloves up."

13

Designed for Hard Bedlam

"WHERE DOES IT HURT?"

"What were you doing when this happened?"

"How long? I see. Can you move it?"

"If you ever do this again, you will die. I'm serious."

"We can't undo the restraints until you—"

"What year is it?"

"Walk with me. No, she was DOA. Was there a purse? Did she come in with—"

"The calcaneus. Now, let's immobilize this and—"

"This will help with the pain."

"Here, let me do that."

"Pulmonary fibrosis. Again. Let's get her signed up."

"Just lie back. We have you."

Four hours later, I found Clarence in the staff room. He was alone, sitting at the table with his shoes off, rubbing his feet. He glanced up and smiled.

"Simon." He sighed. "I need to get some kind of arch support. Either that or I need to paint my toenails."

I crashed down into a chair. Clarence chuckled.

"Some of these people are crazy," I said. He cocked his head.

"Everyone is crazy, sweetums. Every last person on earth."

"You seem happy about that, Clarence. Not that I disagree with you. And please, don't ever call me sweetums again. Toenail polish . . . bright green to go with your flip-flops? Do they even make that?"

"Yeah." He flexed and his big toe popped loudly. "So you got a real weirdo? You got that young man who ate a dozen sponges, didn't you? Or the lady who swallowed all the Barbie heads?"

"No. I was talking about me, actually. But . . . is there some patient here today with doll heads in her intestines? You can't see—"

"Simon, did you have some kind of episode this morning?" He pulled one of his shoes back on, playing indifferent.

"Sort of."

"Bound to happen. Lot of change for you this last day or two. You came out of your doctor shell. Slept inside your own house. Didn't get drunk last night. Told me a long sob story without crying."

"I took a shower this morning with my clothes on."

"Happens," he said easily. He put his other shoe on. "Why? I mean, do you know?"

"I looked in Wanda's closet."

He arched a plucked eyebrow. "And?"

"It just freaked me out is all."

"Freaked you out." He gave me one of his motherly looks, all eyes and pursed lips. "Let me ask you a question. How much of the stuff in that house is yours?"

"Mine?" The question surprised me. "All of it. It's my house. I own it."

He shook his head. "Not what I meant. I mean how much of it is *yours*? You know, like your furniture from college. Knick knacks. Shit like childhood pictures. Your rock collection. The crap you found on the beach. The key to your first car. That kind of stuff."

He watched me think. Wanda hadn't liked any clutter. I didn't have the kind of objects he was referring to. They were

150

all long gone, in tidy boxes in an untidy landfill, and I'd never bothered to accrue any more. When I didn't say anything, he blew out a deep breath.

"Simon, you're camping in your own life. You did it by accident, true. You did it for love—or whatever kind of mutant poon sorcery the white lady threw down on you—also true. But you have to stop now, and you know you do. And in some ways, you already have. You started with just about the most precious thing in the world."

"And that is?" I must have looked like someone expecting a miracle, because he beamed with true delight and clapped me on the shoulder.

"Me!"

I didn't know what to say, so I didn't say anything. Clarence stood and straightened his uniform.

"Enjoy the rest of your break," he said. "I got a whole list of shit to do. I'm on the short end of the stick today. Goddamned pickle fiasco is kicking my ass, irate big-tittied woman. Coffee's on the card table. Don't drink any."

The door closed behind him, and I was alone. I sat back and let the tension flow out of me. It was the first time I'd sat since Clarence and I got out of my car. He was right, once again, and that was frustrating on some level. Wanda had thrown away my old life, almost like it reminded her that I'd existed before she'd met me, like whoever that person had been was not good enough to know or for me to remember. That what she made of me after she entered my life was somehow more valid, more real, than whatever I had been before. I shook my head.

Why hadn't it been more obvious? Why had I just gone along with the program? Like a disgracefully obedient child. Like someone who was lost enough to walk toward any kind of light, even if it was impossibly distant, as it turned out to be—and the light coming through a glacier as well. I'd been fine before. Lonely, to be sure, and searching for something I didn't have much confidence in finding, but I'd been okay. I'd been sane then. I hadn't lived in a white house where I'd been sleeping outside for months. I never took showers in my clothes in those days. And my best friend had been a clothing entrepreneur instead of a gay black combat chef nurse. My hobby had been miniature golf. I ate seafood and daydreamed about a barefoot and pregnant woman who listened to Simon & Garfunkel and did things like bake cookies. I'd even selected my own clothes back then.

The door opened, and the Mexican woman I'd noticed the day before came in. She smiled briefly and went to her locker. Idly, I watched her from behind. She was thin, in a way that was part athletic and part genetic, with a hint of the ascetic. Long legs, long hair, long fingers, and a slender neck. Beautiful. Extraordinarily so. Maybe she could feel me watching, because after she opened her locker, she turned and smiled again.

"Hi," I said. My heart was beating a little faster. She smelled like berries. And soap. And what I imagined honey might smell like if it was warm, on a spoon, in the sun, at a café where the buildings were old and full of memories.

"You're the new doctor," she said, still smiling.

"Volunteer," I clarified. "A friend of mine works here."

"Tay Tay," she said. "He's one of my very best friends in the world."

"Yes," I said, awkwardly. That was good news. "Clarence. You just missed him, actually."

"Clarence." She sat down across from me and tied her hair in a ponytail. "He mentioned that you call him that."

"Did he," I said. "And what else did he mention?"

"Not much, Doctor . . ."

"Simon," I said.

"Not much, Doctor Simon. You two work at some other hospital? He said the food there is good. It's a shame about the benefits and the lousy pay. I don't know why he doesn't come on here full time. Bernadette offered him a good position last month. He's so good with the patients, and he brings joy wherever he goes."

"I, uh . . . I couldn't say."

"It's depressing, even for people like Tay Tay, though he's never said so. Happiness isn't as infectious as it should be."

By then I was nervous. I was powerfully attracted to her, of course; I couldn't imagine any man who wouldn't be. But I was Clarence's boss, the very person behind his poverty-level wages and his health care jeopardy. I'd done it all so I could fit myself, along with everything else of mine, down Wanda's garbage disposal. And it was just possible that I was responsible for him staying at Sellwood.

"Clarence and I are having a party," I said abruptly. My mouth was suddenly dry, and my hands were tingling. I felt lightheaded. "Are you free this week?"

"You mean Thursday?" The day after tomorrow. "It's my only day off."

"Thursday," I said, nodding. "Exactly. You absolutely have to come. We're having an open bar, of course. Lots of food. He's cooking."

She nodded. "I wonder when he was going to tell me."

"We just decided this morning," I lied quickly. "On the drive to work. Spur of the moment, really. Last of the good nights for barbecue, he was saying. It's a good chance to meet new people and all that."

"Ah." She lowered her head a little, her eyes still on me, and her smile grew almost sly. "So, Tay Tay's new friend."

"No," I gushed. "I mean yes, but not . . . not—"

She laughed. "I know, that's not what I mean. He said he made a new friend at his other job and moved in, but he was even quicker than you to clarify exactly what kind of friend." Again with the laugh, a wonderful, throaty thing. "You aren't even close to his type. He likes lumberjacks. No, I mean, he's such a personality. You must be an interesting person, Dr. Simon."

I winced. "Yeah, well . . . I . . ."

"I'll be there. He had the greatest dinner parties when he was with poor Roy. I guess that was five or six years ago now. Hard to imagine. They had the cutest little house. We had to close the street off more than once. Such a shame. Roy had the greatest strawberry garden in the history of the San Fernando Valley."

Poor Roy. A cute little house. Such a shame.

She rose. I did too. I had to stop from wringing my hands. I caught her aura again, powerfully in that instant, almost as if she was glowing. She held her hand out, and we shook. Some kind of current flowed from her.

"My name is Maria."

14

The Incubation Code

"YOU REALLY ARE FUCKIN' CRAZY." Clarence jetted smoke through his nostrils. "I was just kidding earlier about everyone being a nut job. You got enough to go around. I mean . . ." He smacked his forehead. "Simon!"

We were standing in the Saint Francis parking lot. An otherwise beautiful sunset was lost on both of us at the moment. I was frantic, partly because Clarence seemed genuinely angry. I wondered if I really was crazy, but more importantly, I wondered if he had just figured that out.

"I didn't know," I said, which was true. "How was I to know that this was going to get around this fast? I mean, it was just an idea, but—"

"Simon, we got almost a hundred people coming over! The day after tomorrow! And I was the last one to find out, man! And I'm doing all the cooking!" He took another furious drag. His eyes were wide, menacing. I held my hands out in surrender.

"I'll pay you," I said. It was all I could think of. "Five hundred bucks. If you want, we can even have it catered. I know a ton of great—"

"Now you fixin' to really piss me off," he said in a low voice, visibly suppressing a swelling thunder. "You think that I, Tay

155

Tay, would have a party with catering? Catering? Like some kind of rich, trashy, dumbass dipshit with an iPhone instead of an apron, just to—"

"Wait," I interrupted. "We can just cancel it. I don't know what I was thinking, really, I mean—"

"You motherfucker," he growled, looming over me. "You think that I, Tay Tay, would cancel a dinner party just because my cohost is a total piece of dry pussy? Is that what you think?"

"Clarence, I only mean that—"

He cut me off by taking a final quick step forward, and all of the sudden I was staring up into his wide face. Even his head was big.

"You think Tay Tay is going to fail?" he whispered.

I made a small noise.

"Simon, you best find religion, because you need to be thankin' some kind of higher power that I have tomorrow off. Which means you do too, 'cause you, little white man, are my servant. My house nigga blanco. My pet slave. You will be chopping. You will be peeling. You will be shopping, running errands, watching timers, stirring pots, lighting candles, and anything else I can think of. And when you're done, we'll get started on the hard part. Nod once if you understand me, but do not speak."

I nodded mutely. He put his hand on my shoulder. It was hot and weighed twenty pounds, not including the wrist.

"That's good Simon, that's real fuckin' good." And then he smiled, and the setting sun flashed across his eyes. He crowed with delight and shook me. "This is going to be the party of all motherfuckin' year and the years on either side, baby!" He howled again. I laughed, and some rubber band around the nervous wad in my chest twanged and shot away. Clarence was in charge. Everything was going to be all right.

―――――――――――

"Get up an' swim, you nauseating beast."

I opened my eyes. I'd slept on the couch again. The sun was

156

shining in through the giant windows, and giant Clarence was standing over me in his Speedos, holding two cups of coffee, beaming. I sat up.

"Morning."

"Good guess," he said indulgently. I took the coffee cup. "But not just any morning."

"Right." I sipped. "Tomorrow is party day. And I'm a servant."

"Yes you are. A servant. My servant. So the first thing you need to do this morning is go get your trunks on. You gotta swim for a minute. And you can't go naked 'cause I value my eyesight too much to go blind this young, and you can't swim in the underwear you slept in 'cause that's too much like yesterday. Hear?"

"I don't know how to swim," I objected. He tsked and went to the sliding door.

"Liar liar, kitchen's on fire. Two minutes."

I watched as he sat his coffee down, saluted the morning, and dove in. I rubbed my eyes. I didn't even know if I had a swimsuit. It was time to find out, though; getting Clarence started in a bad direction first thing would give him some kind of playful grudge to torture me with all day long.

The suit was in the top drawer of what I referred to as the men's dresser. Socks and underwear, always neatly folded, in the top left drawer. Color-coded leisure wear I'd never seen before in the middle drawer, ranging from designer T-shirts with matching shorts to three tracksuits—white, blue, and black—evidently made by Germans. In the last drawer, five white swimsuits and some kind of blousy shirt thing that reminded me of baby clothes, probably to be worn in the pool to contain my hair and cover up my paunch. I took one of the suits out and changed. The door to Wanda's closet was still ajar, but I kept my eyes averted, like I was trying not to look at someone else's suffering patient. I wanted to, but it would be an intrusion . . . on what, I didn't know.

157

"White on white," Clarence sang as I emerged onto the patio. He wiped water from his face, treading in the center of the pool. "Need some sun on you, Simon. Some sun and some rain and some wind. Come on then. I'll catch you." He spread his arms and nodded encouragingly.

I ignored him. The sunrise was a fantastic explosion of golds and yellows and pinks. I looked at it, just as he had. A party. A party at the White Palace. I was going to blow off work and spend the entire day cooking with the black man laughing in the pool. All to impress the most impressive woman I'd ever met, whom I knew next to nothing about, who glowed with a quality I'd never experienced before. And I was thinking about it all while I was watching the sunrise.

I dove in, and the night-cool water, the storm of bubbles, and then the sudden quiet enveloped me. I twisted in the dive's momentum, and my open eyes took in the blurred sky, now shot through with brilliant white crescents of light on the surface. I exhaled and watched my breath rise, and then I pushed off the bottom and broke free into the air.

"Wonderful to be alive!" Clarence cried, spinning slowly with his head back. He crowed like a 250-pound rooster.

"Let's try not to wake the neighbors," I said, but I realized I didn't care. I might have entered a new pattern, I thought an instant later. A luminous iteration cycle. My day had begun with water instead of tranquilizers. I liked it. It felt good. Dreams were afoot, and they weren't lingering nightmares. I wanted more.

"Fuck 'em," Clarence declared joyfully.

"Indeed." I fell into an easy backstroke and made for the far side of the pool. Clarence struck out in a lazy circle, talking as he did.

"Simon, you know, the reason it's so hard to figure out why people do things is because most of the time they don't know themselves."

I reached the far edge and pushed off. He continued.

"I mean, look around. Here we are, swimmin'. Just swimmin'. Now I know why we're doing this. It's fun. It feels good. It's the brand-new start of the brand-new day."

"I was just thinking the same thing."

"Good man. Which brings us to the party. Know why people come to a party?"

"No idea. Why?"

"Who can say? I don't think a single one of them knows, and I'm talkin' about any party, anywhere, ever. It just don't make any sense at all, not when you really think about it."

"True enough. I usually hate parties."

"Figures you'd have one, what with the weirdo streak an' all. You know what makes a party great instead of just good? Makes it worth going to?" He spit water into the air like a fountain.

"Again, no idea." I reached the other side.

"They gotta find out why they came! See, a good party, you have a good time. Might even get laid. But a *great* party—well, that's a whole different thing."

I wiped water off my face and hooked my elbows on the edge of the pool. Clarence floated on his back, looking up. I looked up too. I thought about how nice it was going to be to blow off Sellwood for a few days. I thought about having a gathering of strangers in my house. I thought about calling Gary, just to be polite.

"See, everyone confronted with that same mystery at the same time, that's what puts the fresh into tired souls. Because you wonder why you do anything right then. A great party, Simon, is when you know that you do what you do because you're alive."

I thought about that. There was such joy in his voice, but I somehow wondered if he was talking a little bit about this Roy he'd apparently lied about. If so, his joy was a more evolved joy than I had ever known. I thought about the kind of will that could fuel such a thing. And of course, I thought about Maria.

"**Clarence, I think** I sprained something in my hippocampus. I can't remember anything you just said, and I just forgot that I was concentrating on trying to remember it. What did I just say? Jesus."

"Shut it, you big baby," he scolded. He was pushing the cart. People were staring. I was wearing a suit, which was normal enough, but in the grocery store—the third grocery store of the morning, no less—it made me look like Clarence's lawyer, or maybe his PR rep. He was wearing tight purple shorts, a form-fitting yellow T-shirt, a checkered, Middle Eastern bandanna, and his dayglow green flip-flops. And makeup, of course. Normally, his color ensemble was more thoughtful, even at its most triumphantly gay, but this was his idea of punishment, and he was enjoying every minute of it.

"Are we almost done? Just please, please say yes."

"No way, raw daddy." Totally sassy. And loud. A prim yuppie woman in a power suit with a basket full of fruit and melba crackers glanced our way, but she didn't have the courage to scowl. She was briefly transfixed by Clarence's huge painted toenails, and then her face closed like a phone book slamming shut.

"What possible . . . no live animals, Clarence. No skywriting, no dyeing the pool fuchsia, no cannons, no—"

"Run that mouth, little white serving man," he said loudly. "Run it up and down and all around." He made a broad circling gesture with his hand and snapped his fingers, cocked his NFL butt out, and stared at me, bug-eyed. The entire grocery store paused. I deflated. He cackled.

"Maybe I'll wait in the car," I suggested. I handed him my wallet.

"You better call that motherfuckin' florist," he scolded, snapping it out of my hand. "And call your friend Gary. And check on the glasses. And while you're just sitting in the parking lot like some big dummy done flunked doggy school, you get on that wine order. And don't you *even* forget to check an' see if they got some mariachi operation we can put up on a stage. I want midgets, Simon." He said "midgets" extremely loud. I started backing away. "A midget. Mariachi. Band." Louder still.

Once outside, I immediately wished that I smoked cigarettes. It would have been an ideal time to light one. A flask would have come in handy. Even gum. Instead, I walked over to the car and stood there. It was a bright, beautiful day. The smog wasn't too bad. The breeze was perfect. We were almost done with the shopping.

I took my phone out for the tenth time and scrolled to Gary's personal cell number. For some reason, I'd been afraid to call it. What I'd been worried about was I'd find that it wasn't his number anymore, that I'd call and a secretary would answer and I'd discover that he'd moved on to a different, more powerful, more exclusive number, and that my name would be taken by an overly polite woman and appear at some point on a sheet with a thousand other names and numbers, the type of paper he'd glance at and then hand back to whomever had given it to him. I dialed, made brave for the moment by the grim specter of a midget mariachi band.

"BCH Records and Freestyle and all the rest of my crazy shit," the recording blared. Gary had a California surfer radio announcer vibe. "Leave your name and your zodiac data at the squibble, and remember that the most important thing you do today will be to—" Beep. Funny.

"Yeah, hi, Gary," I began. "It's Simon. So hey, man, I'm having a party. I know. Me." I laughed, and it came out nervous. "So yeah, anyway, it's tomorrow night. Short notice, and I don't even know if you're in town right now, but God, it's been so crazy. So it's mostly people from . . . these people from this other hospital I've been doing some volunteer work at. Sort of a long story there, but see, my roommate, Clarence, he ah . . . oh yeah, I have a roommate, you might have met him. Long story again. So yeah! Bring a date! Bring two! Hell, I don't care." Nervous laugh again. "Anyway, lots of great food. Bye now."

161

I disconnected and stood there, blank, and that's how I remained until Clarence rolled up with a cart loaded with half of the grocery store. A clerk was following him with a neat stack of Styrofoam coolers.

"Simon, you loafin' on duty," Clarence began in a chastising tone. "Now you help this other little white man load the car while mamma calls in a delivery." He tossed me my wallet. "Tip him, 'cause there's a ton of shit here."

"Hey," I said to the clerk. He glanced back and forth between Clarence and me and smiled. The expression vanished when Clarence glared at him and scowled.

"Sir." The clerk actually stood at attention. I opened the trunk, and he got to work loading the groceries. I took the coolers and put them into the backseat. Clarence oversaw the entire operation while he placed a wine order in a sugary voice, so sweetly that it wouldn't have surprised me if we didn't get everything for free. By the time he was done, he'd made a new friend for life with whomever had taken the order, the clerk was gone with a crisp new ten-dollar bill, and I was wishing I'd brought sunglasses. Clarence tapped around to the passenger side of the car like he was wearing high heels and waited for me to open the door for him. He'd been doing it all morning.

"If you can please not refer to yourself as 'mamma' anymore, Clarence, I would be especially grateful. And the mariachi band is going to have to go the way of the Doors cover band, mostly because I suspect they're just friends of yours, and the sound violation problem is—"

"Get in the car and drive, you fool," he said primly. "Mamma needs to fix brunch and go swimming. Need me a mimosa and some pool time. Shopping done wore me down."

I closed the door, rolling my eyes. I was actually having a pretty good time, and Clarence knew it.

"I called Gary," I said as we pulled out. "Left a message on his voice mail."

"You call the florist too?"

"When we get home."

"When we get home, we eat, catch a buzz, swim—I mean, at least I do—and then we peel shrimp, set some marinade, and do the dressings. Make jalapeno corn bread. Be an afternoon. And then we bust a bottle of wine, screw around with the preparations, and maybe, just maybe, if you real fuckin' good, we catch a movie on cable. I get to pick."

"Deal." And what a deal, I thought. A morning with the Clarence Show, an afternoon of peeling potatoes and stirring pots, an evening of vodka and a kung fu movie, and a house full of strangers the next day. All for an evening in the company of Maria. It was the bargain of the year.

15

News of the Speed of Sound

PARTY NIGHT.

Clarence and I were both awake at dawn, swimming. I'd slept on the floor in the dining room because he'd taken the couch. We were both exhausted after the insane day of party preparations, but I felt alert, rested, and prepared for anything. Clarence was oddly quiet, but I knew he was just mentally fixated on details. Eventually he spoke.

"Do you think we should get more limes?"

"What, for the ceviche? We made a giant vat of it. We're good."

"Cucumbers?"

"In cooler number four."

"We have enough chairs. I know we do." He sounded confident.

"We ordered an even hundred. Sixteen tables. They'll be here at ten. When do we take the mignons out of the pomegranate juice?"

"Whenever."

"The keg and the wine is at two."

"I think we have it all," he said. "The menu is a tiny bit

165

elaborate for chitchat fare, but the boys can handle it." Clarence had hired three young men he knew from God knows where to act as servers. They would be under his command, each running a station. One on meats, from the barbecue we'd rented: marinated filet mignons, bone-in chicken breasts stuffed with mushrooms and grilled radicchio and roasted garlic, pork ribs, shrimp, and steamed oysters. Another would be assigned to the asparagus, fingerlings braised in rosemary and duck fat, and the skewers of cherry tomatoes, zucchini, and balsamic-marinated fennel bulb, as well as the four variations of salad, to be ferried out onto the patio from the kitchen. The third would be on the curried goat stew, eggplant, breads, and desserts. Then all three would move to refilling drinks until everyone was properly bloated and loaded, as Clarence described it.

"I need to call Gary again," I said.

"Your buddy? The clothes guy?"

"The very same."

"Tell him to bring a date. We certainly made enough food. Maybe he should bring two." Clarence paused by the edge of the pool to sip his coffee.

"He could. You, ah, you invite someone special?"

"Nah. You?"

I couldn't tell him that I'd impulsively gotten us into the entire thing because I'd developed a spontaneous crush on one of his friends. But I could tell him that feeling something was a sign. I could tell him that Maria radiated some rare and regal magic.

"Nah."

"Boy," he chided, like he could tell I was lying about something, but he didn't chase it down. "Then we got some time to kill. People start coming at around five. Until then, I say we eat breakfast, put on some music, fuck with the rental guys, and catch a decent buzz."

"I like the way you think, Clarence." I lolled along the pool's edge in the direction of my coffee cup.

"You invite anyone from Sellwood?"

"No. You?" The idea hadn't even occurred to me.

"Couldn't think of anyone," he replied. "Couple cool cats over in my department, but I thought it would freak you out. It's all Saint Francis people."

"Probably." I saw my opening. "So who's on the list?"

"Pretty much everyone who isn't working and all their significant others. Bunch of people."

"Bernadette?" Tossing out a false trail.

"Probably get here late. Steal a bunch of cheese."

"Good. That guy Tony? From x-ray?"

"Both Tonys and Barbara."

"Huh. Who else did I meet . . . What about the one lady . . . long black hair? Friend of yours, she said."

"Maria?"

"Yeah, her. She wanted to talk about that tax shuffle on Sellwood's equipment."

"Then she'll be here." He pushed back into the water. I tried to think of a way to keep him talking about her, but nothing came to mind.

"Maybe I should make a list for her."

"Make it for Bernadette tomorrow. For now, let's just follow the plan. Eggs Benedict and mimosas."

"Okay." I pushed back out into the water and floated. The sunrise was perfect, once again. I couldn't believe I'd missed it so many times. "Why Bernadette? Isn't she overworked already?"

"Yeah. But Maria's leaving next week."

Shit. "How come?"

"Long story," he said dismissively. And that was it, I knew. Any more and he'd be on to me. I had no idea what Clarence would do if he found out I'd thrown a party and made him both the chef and the host just so I could talk to a woman for a few minutes. He might just laugh, and then again he might be tremendously disgusted, but either way it would reinforce the crazy. I knew it would, because I thought I was crazy for doing it. And in my own estimation, I was too crazy to determine who was crazy in the first place.

The sun broke free of the cliffs on the far side of the canyon. The cars sounded a little louder. I submerged and stroked through the underwater silence to the far side. When I broke the surface, Clarence was already out and toweling off.

"I'm gonna get breakfast goin'," he said. "You be in charge of the mimosas."

"Got it."

"What are you wearing? You can't wear a suit."

"Why not?"

He tsked. "Wear something casual, Simon. Not jeans. You know, like chinos. Flip-flops. Short sleeves."

I thought. "I'm not sure I have anything like that. Wanda had this—"

"And no more talking about her. Jesus. Just go look. You still have time to run over to the mall." He carefully folded his towel and stretched and then went inside.

There was nothing in the way of leisurewear in the bedroom. Suits, the dresser selection, which I didn't like in the least, and my swimsuit, which was wet. I took a shower, and after a moment of frowning and cursing I selected a pair of knee-length tan shorts and the matching shirt. The shirt was button up and it had a black collar. No flip-flops or sandals, so I decided to go barefoot. I examined myself in the mirror and sucked my gut in. Wanda had dressed me for my first real party, where I would speak with a lovely Mexican woman. Unbelievable.

"Now we're talking," Clarence crooned. "Like, you look normal, man!"

"I don't always look normal?" I instantly regretted asking.

"Simon. Shame on you. But I don't either, so don't feel bad." He flipped the ham and started whisking the hollandaise. I went to the refrigerator and took out a bottle of champagne and the orange juice. The refrigerator was absolutely stuffed with party supplies, forming a nearly solid wall. It had taken Clarence more than a half hour just to fit everything in. I popped the bottle and poured.

"I'm going to need to zip down and get some skewers for the shrimp. I knew we were forgetting something." He checked the poaching eggs.

"Take the other car," I offered. I set his mimosa by the stove and sat down on a stool in front of the island.

"Okay." Slow and even. He didn't look up.

"It just sits there. If no one ever drives it, something will gum up. Bad for the resale value." It was a rationalization, I knew, and so did he. Somehow Clarence driving the car would make it less . . . something. His talk about crap, about the knick-knacks and the seashells and whatnot had made me realize that I had, in fact, accrued a bunch of sentimental objects that were in desperate need of losing that value. One of the closets in my bedroom was full of it. So was half of my garage.

"Breakfast." He put my plate down in front of me. Two perfectly poached eggs, ham, English muffin, hollandaise with fresh dill, cantaloupe, and a strawberry. He sat his down on the counter and dug in. No strawberry, I noticed.

"Gotta hit the gym," he said around a mouthful of ham. "Wanna go?"

"Nope."

"Shit-ton of calories here."

"I'm a doctor, Clarence. I know."

A few minutes later, he left. I heard Wanda's car start on the first try, the garage door open, and then, very faint, Stevie Wonder on the radio. I stood in the kitchen and finished my drink. Then I went into the bedroom.

The bed was some kind of English thing, with an irregular mattress. Shorter and wider than a normal king and supposedly superior in every way because of it. I'd always thought it was too firm and somehow off because of its odd dimensions. I'd never mentioned it, of course. I stared at it. The thin white comforter looked puffy, like a giant bandage from the burn unit. I wondered what it smelled like. I wondered what it would feel like under my feet if I walked on it. I wondered what kind of sweatshop it had come from. What kind of creepy little Swede with tiny wire-rimmed glasses was behind the company label.

I lay down on the right side. My side. I looked up at my side of the ceiling. Then I scooched over into the center of the bed. Maybe it was nothing more than the subtle change in the angle of the shadows, or something different in the depression in the bed, or having my body on some new part of the once-familiar surface. And maybe it was because some piece of the whiteness around me was in motion, moving away with music of its own. Whatever it was, I took a nap.

"The old fool! And my car still had a whole blond man in the trunk!" Bernadette spread her heavy arms wide as she finished her tale. "Cop gave me ten bucks for gas. True story!" Laughter.

The party was unlike anything my neighborhood had ever seen, so much so that I had no doubt my neighbors were in hiding, many of them placing emergency calls to therapists and Homeland Security. East LA had come, and they had brought their friends, pets, children, and enough beer to fill the swimming pool, which had more than twenty people in it playing an invented game called "Pogo," or possibly "Pepe"—I couldn't be sure.

I was sitting by the barbecue, watching as Clarence's "staff" finished serving and geared up to pass out more beer and wine. They were, of course, the young criminals from the taco truck episode. The three of them he'd selected looked ridiculous in what they considered waiter garb: white T-shirts, baggy black jeans, and dollar store flip-flops. With their heavily tattooed skinny arms and slicked-back hair, they looked almost artificial, like paintings of extremely dangerous angels made 3-D.

Clarence was having a ball, swanning through the crowd and petting dogs, blasting a smile turned to maximum radiation, hefting children, and generally behaving like a cross between an extremely charismatic mayor and everyone's eccentric twin. Dozens of conversations were going on in small groups, and he visited them one by one while I watched contently from the sidelines. Eventually, his one-man performance came to a pause in front of me.

"Simon, we have ourselves a hit here. Get enough to eat?"

I patted my stomach. "Too full to drink."

"Me too. Nice to have you holding your shit together. All kinds of new things going on in that round melon of yours, what with throwing parties and napping in your own bed."

"Yeah," I said easily. I was enjoying myself, I had to admit.

"Mingle," he suggested. "Play with those kids out in the front yard. They brought some Frisbees."

"Frisbees," I repeated. "I haven't thrown a Frisbee in twenty years."

"Like riding a bike."

Bernadette called to him, inviting him into her story about a carjacking gone horribly wrong and the aftermath in the Saint Francis waiting room, which involved Clarence doing a wild verbal bongo impression. Clarence winked at me and spun off in her direction, pumping out a beat. I got out of my chair and went through the house to the front yard. There were five little barefoot Mexican boys and one little girl playing a game with two Frisbees, where group one tossed and the opposite group tried to hit the Frisbee midair. A third Frisbee was already on the roof, and I watched as an errant shot bounced off the side of the house. I waited for a minute.

"You kids are doing this all wrong," I said eventually, loud enough to stop them. They froze, instantly guilty. "Give me those."

One little boy reluctantly brought the two Frisbees over to me. His hair was a little sweaty. I took them and paired them together.

"Okay. You kids line up. I toss them both at the same time.

See, they'll split apart midair, and no one will know where they're going until about halfway through. Here, watch." I made to throw. They lined up reluctantly. "Get back a little." They did, and I threw.

The two Frisbees made a beautiful, heavy arc. About twenty feet out, they split—the lighter one lofting up on its spin, the heavier one beelining right into them. They scrambled, shrieking, and caught them both. Then they tossed them back, excited now. The second toss I arced high, and the Frisbees curved in on the breeze, neatly landing in the wild cluster of them. And so on. We were playing hard and fast when Maria showed up, and I was so involved in perfecting a new twin downward floater that at first I didn't notice her, standing off to the side, smiling, her arms crossed.

"Catch!" I tossed her a Frisbee. She neatly caught it and shot it into the mob of kids. I fired mine in right after hers.

"Glad you could make it," I said. She nodded, watching the children. "Everyone's in back. Tons of great food and lots to drink."

She said something in rapid Spanish, too fast to follow even if I could speak it. The children ran howling back into the house, pausing to wipe their feet. We watched them, and once again I was struck by her presence, its volume. She turned her eyes on me and smiled, shy, wise, and quiet in some way that seemed remote, that made me feel like I was looking at her through someone else's glasses. I blinked.

"Tay Tay said you have a very interesting home."

It was the first I'd heard of it. "It, ah . . . well . . . c'mon. I'll give you the tour."

I was already stammering, and I could feel a bloom of nervous sweat on my back and between my butt cheeks. I'm sure my face was red. She followed me inside. A few people were in the kitchen talking by the bar Clarence had put together on the island, but we were otherwise alone. I made a sweeping gesture at the huge living room, with its white grand piano, bleached-bone leather furniture, the Clorox carpet, the white-and-crystal chandelier. She took it all in, and I was surprised that she appeared mildly shocked. It seemed completely out of character for someone I had already pegged as extremely reserved.

"Surprised?" I offered, shooting for world-weary. She turned her expression on me.

"Do you believe in signs, Dr. Simon?" It came out hushed, like she was in a church or a library.

"No. Why?"

"I do."

She walked over to the piano and stared down at it without touching the keys. I watched her, confused. It wasn't going very well so far, I reflected. She'd only just entered the White Palace, and it was like she'd seen a ghost. Abruptly, her head snapped in my direction. Her wide eyes looked almost black. I made a tittering sound.

"Barbecue out back." My voice was high and squeaky. She continued to stare. "Do you . . . do you play piano?"

Abruptly the spell was broken. "Not yet." She took a deep breath. "A drink?"

"Drinks! Right! Right this way."

I led us into the kitchen. Clarence had insisted that we rent a few hundred wine glasses, so I took two out of the box and poured myself some red. She took the glass I offered and poured herself some sparkling water, and right then I knew I didn't stand a chance. It wasn't the water that signaled my doom. It wasn't even the piano. It was her. She was thinking about something else. I had no idea what it was, but it clearly wasn't the single feather I had in my bird-of-paradise plume, which was obvious wealth, even if its display was colorless. I'd failed, and it astonished me that I was actually relieved, so much so that I gulped my wine and sighed. She noticed and looked around the kitchen.

"Simon is actually my first name," I said easily. "Simon Resner. Just call me Simon."

173

"Why white?" She seemed genuinely mystified, but not in a judging way.

I shrugged.

"You don't know."

"Absolutely no idea."

She nodded, as if it made perfect sense.

"So the piano. You said 'not yet.' Exactly what does that mean?"

The smile again. "Absolutely no idea."

"Hmm." We stood in companionable silence. Eventually she sipped her sparkling water, and I noted her long, slender hand again. She'd make a fine pianist.

"Tay Tay is watching us," she said. I looked out at the patio. Clarence was talking to a small cluster of people, but every now and then his eyes lifted and scanned us. I nodded at him, but he pretended not to notice.

"Clarence is very mothering," I said. "He's doing it to the entire party right now. Maybe he wants to talk to you."

"Maybe," she said. "I'm actually here to talk to you. Is there somewhere we can sit down? Somewhere private?"

I'd be lying if I said my heart didn't skip a beat. I was more certain than ever that I didn't have a chance of spending an eternity of happiness with this exotic, singular person, but I didn't care. I'd misjudged the situation in some comical way that would have been tragic in the past. I had no more in common with her than beagles had with the rings of Saturn. But I was certainly enjoying talking to her. I had never talked to people like her, at least not for a long time. She reminded me of Clarence. Of Bernadette. Of the kind of person I'd read about in the better books in college, or the figures that came into my dreams. I led her back into the living room, and we sat in the west corner.

"You mentioned redundancies in the operating infrastructure of Sellwood Hospital. Can you elaborate on that?"

I was in my element. "Of course. For the last few years, I've attended every conference and every convention I could find.

Part of it was to get away from this place"—I gestured at the white—"and part of it was because it's my job and I had the time. We have equipment that's still in the plastic, and I have a line on almost every other thing Saint Francis might be able to use in a comprehensive upgrade. So much of this is trail related, so we're talking contract loans with specific research requirements that . . ."

For the next few hours I rambled and she nodded, occasionally offering a comment or posing a question. She was incredibly aware of everything I had seen at Saint Francis, and also, possibly because of Clarence, she keenly understood what Sellwood had to offer. It was rare that I actually enjoyed talking about imaging systems and chemistry, regulations and trail conditions, but I did with her.

"I'll mention all of this to Bernadette," she said eventually. "You two should have a meeting."

"More than one," I replied. She nodded.

Our drinks were long empty. I didn't want any more wine. The sun had set, and Clarence had turned on all the patio lights and lit the tiki lawn torches we'd picked up at Home Depot. I looked out at the collection of happy faces, lit by blue and flickering yellow. So did she.

"Why do you work at Saint Francis?" I asked eventually. "You could be a rep for any of these companies. You have more than enough background."

"I work at Saint Francis for the same reason you do," she said simply. And I understood. I leaned forward.

"This . . . this is going to sound awkward, but . . . listen. I really do want to help. If there is ever anything I can do for you, just let me know."

She nodded but said nothing. If I had only known where that statement, that promise, would lead. If I had only known.

She handed her glass back to me, and with a quiet thank-you she departed. I realized she'd never even eaten anything or ventured into the back and said her hellos. I watched the front door close behind her. After a minute, I looked at the piano. I can't say how it happened, but looking at it and thinking about the music I'd heard come from it—the soulless tones that had come from the white thing, there in my white house—suddenly seemed like a grain of sand to me. A grain of sand on a beach I hadn't walked on for years, next to an ocean I had lost the bravery to swim in.

It was the money. Wanda had so wanted money, so adored it, so breathed it, that to live in her world was to fall utterly under its spell. There was no dreaming of anything else in the presence of something that immense. The overwhelming power of that vision had swallowed me whole, and the stomach of it was white and soft and safe and stale. As empty as the small talk, as tasteless as the kale, as absent of feeling as the piano's only song, as artificial as the smell in the second closet in my bedroom, and as barren as my inner landscape had become in that long and terrible drought, the signs of which were all around me. I looked up and then out the front window. Maria had left something in my eyes, and it was like I was looking through the window for the very first time.

The manicured lawns, the perfect houses with their perfect cars, the clean and prosperous people who were my neighbors— we all lived in a bubble, created for us and engineered for our safety. None of it was real. And the white house, where no one had ever truly lived, was entirely in keeping with the locale. It looked different because I had just been sitting across from someone who actually couldn't even see it. The obvious magnitude of my bank account and the environs it had generated were invisible to a creature like Maria. She hadn't seen the same thing as me when she took in all that was the White Palace; she had seen a sign.

I was studying the keys, thinking about nothing, when Clarence appeared.

"Simon. What the hell were you talking about in here with my lovely and talented friend?" He sat down where Maria had

176

been sitting. He crossed his legs and leaned back, smiling and casual, but interested.

"Medicine," I said simply.

"For two hours? Figures. Kinda strange, but it figures." He glanced at the door. His expressive face went from curious to a little troubled and then to something else. It was the same look he'd had when we were drinking at the little bar on the Strand, when he was talking about loss and the mystery of how it had changed him.

"What's up?"

He sighed, his eyes still focused on something far away. "Maria. So much going on with that gal."

"How do you mean?" I sat forward. He frowned.

"About a month ago, I don't know . . . she changed. I've known her for years. She's . . . well, she is what she is. Sort of magicky, if you see what I mean." I nodded, and he continued. "This guy. Ambulance brought him in. Head wound, ribs, back, basic full-body mangle job. When he woke up, he didn't know who he was or where he was. Total amnesia."

"Unstable situation," I said. "Complete breakdown?" People usually did a lot of crying when that happened. Disorientation and severe depression, terrible paranoia. Clarence shook his head.

"Not this time. This fucking maniac woke up on fire. Never seen anything like it. He wanted out, and even though he couldn't walk and only one arm worked, he kept trying to escape. The police came around and cuffed him, but not because he was trying to crawl out of Saint Francis into the ghetto. Whatever had messed him up that bad had gotten him into some kind of trouble. They didn't talk about it, and neither did he. Happens all the time at Francis. Convicts. People out on bail. Persons of interest."

"I see."

"No, you don't. This guy . . . he starts to remember who he is right about the time the FBI comes around, which was a little

177

too convenient, if you ask me. Anyway, Maria spent day after day with him after her shift ended. There he was, all shackled in place, but what a fuckin' charmer." He shook his head, remembering. "She laughed, which is something she never did a lot of after her sister died. Anyway, she washed his hair one night. Then she started feeding him. The poor guy had been wasting away for the first few days. The two docs who looked at him right after he was brought in, well, he wasn't expected to pull through. He started to get better—and I mean fast, like you wouldn't even believe—and the FBI started coming around more and more. When they did, he always went back to amnesia and this lunatic 'fuck with me at your own risk' attitude. Dude was so smooth about it too. For a little while there, it was like we had our own TV show."

"Jesus. So what happened?"

Clarence shook his head. Then he looked around, conspiratorially, and leaned in close.

"Maria told me she was in love with him. I couldn't believe it. That's what her whole 'glow' is about. So one afternoon, when it was all quiet—which is almost never—I brought in a wheelchair and cut him free, gave him a few bucks for a cab. The FBI had just called and told Bernadette to prep him for transport. They were taking that little guy away, God only knows where. Bernadette watched the front door, and I watched the parking lot and the street for as long as I could. He wheeled himself out and took a left and . . . vanished. I don't know if he ever got that cab or if the ghetto outside Francis ate him alive, but I somehow suspect he made it. Never got to say good-bye to Maria, but at least he got away. FBI guys were furious when they showed up a few hours later. Police too. I'm a terrible liar, but Bernadette shut them down something fierce while I waited in her car. She loved that little man. I guess we all did in the end."

"Damn."

"Yeah." Clarence looked distant as he played it all over in his mind. "You know, Simon? That was a strange time for all of us at Saint Francis, even me. Maybe especially me." He shook his head. "The day the guy comes to? Out of his coma? The first day—Jesus. He didn't even know who the president was. Nothing. He fell asleep for a few hours, and when he woke up again, I asked him if he knew where he was. Nothing, just those eyes. Fierce, busted up. Then I asked him, 'Do you know why you're here?' I will never forget in this life what he said. He looked at me like I'd asked a different question, not if he knew why he was in the hospital. No. He had no idea who he was, where he was, how he got there, any of it. No, he thought I meant why was he *here*. On earth. I could see it in his face when he thought about it. He was that fucked-up."

"What did he say?"

Clarence sat up a little and looked into his glass. "He actually said something that changed my life. Maybe yours too, now that I think of it. He looked at me, all wild and somewhere else, and he said, 'I'm here to do good things.' Just like that. Like it was the most obvious thing in the world. Like it was a question that shouldn't need asking or answering. Just . . . pure. That was what was in his soul. And then he squinted at me with that one eye, suspicious and dangerous all of a sudden, and asked, 'Exactly what the fuck are you doing here, big boy?'" Tay Tay laughed softly. "I don't know. It sort of freed me somehow. I can't even say why."

I thought about that. It made my throat feel tight. "Did he ever remember his name?"

"Oh yeah. He remembered everything. His name is Knottspeed."

Part 3

16

Transportations

WHEN I PICKED UP THAT goddamned albino at the airport, I had no idea I was about to get him into the exact kind of trouble he was looking for, even thirsting for, filled as he was with divine lust and premonitions and the howl of some beast years wild, deep in the bright cream of escape from zooery. I had no idea I was about to learn about the nature of orange fire under the bones of the head, or what some of the most songish of songs were never about, or about how the true nature of moonlight could only be seen when reflected in the water of someone else's eyes. My fare that day was just a scrawny gringo in a wheelchair, with crazed-on-messy blond hair and giant sunglasses that made him look as uniquely strange as I was soon to discover him to be. The United Airlines kid pushing his chair was laughing at something he was using his hands to tell, and I should have taken that as a sign. The man didn't have any luggage, either. If I drive a cab for another twenty years, I'll never pick up that combo ever again. Some things you can't survive learning more than once.

United wheeled him up, and the stick man wobbled to his feet with help from the cane that had been hanging from the back of his big blue chair. I popped the trunk, but United closed

183

it; evidently the wheelchair was airport property. United opened the door, and the wraith of a poltergeist fell into the backseat. A rolling carnival of his recent history spilled off of him, one of gin and women's perfume and basements and blood, airplanes and old tools. A diseased dog was just under the surface of it all.

"Hola, vato. Me llamo Knottspeedo." He tossed his cane on the seat next to him. It looked discount and a little bent and scuffed, like he'd been hitting stuff with it. "I fucking love LA. I just wanted you to know that right away."

"What's not to love?" It was an amicable enough start. His skill in deception hinged on his every word being entirely possible, I was soon to learn. Everything he said was always true, but he was never, ever talking about what you thought he was. I pulled out into the slow traffic. "Smog. We got guns. Palm trees. Sunshine every day of the year, except on the day you move. Where to?"

"The ocean," Knottspeed replied. "The ocean first. Then I'll pick out a hotel based on a visual assessment of the balcony situation. I need a view. The right shade of curtains. A certain kind of lobby."

"Santa Monica? It's a straight shot." And a decent fare. The hotels were good.

"Santa Monica," he said wistfully. His face was pointed at the passing Long Beach airport to our right. "I bought a skateboard there once. I donated it to needful thieves a few weeks ago. You are actually a Mexican dude, right? The real deal?"

"Jose Ramirez," I confirmed. "Mexican American transportation technician, at your service. So Santa Monica? On the strip by the beach?"

"S'fine." Knottspeed glanced out the window to his left. I looked back a few times, but it was hard to tell if he'd passed out or not with his shades on. I decided to keep him talking. I never do that anymore.

"What brings you to LA?"

He roused himself and winced, shifted a little, adjusted his glasses.

"Fate." He said it like it was obvious, like that was what took people anywhere.

I laughed. "The movie business! No, no wait. There are no good movies anymore. No, I sense in you the great depth of cable television."

"I don't watch movies or television, and I certainly wouldn't work for them. No, it's more of—first place we pass that has smokes, pull us in. I left mine somewhere in the rain with my wheelchair."

"Smokes," I repeated. There was a convenience store I went to almost every day a few blocks down to the right; I pulled in there. The lot was almost empty, so I pulled up right in front and put the blinkers on. When I looked back, he was struggling with his cane and the door handle.

"You want me to go get 'em for you?" I offered.

"Yep." He leaned to the side and dug his bulging wallet out and then passed me a fifty. "Get me some booze too. Vodka— nothing fancy, but not the cheapest kind either. Nothing with green on the label."

"How much?"

"I don't have any luggage yet, so I guess a pint. I can smuggle that into the hotel or wherever I wind up. And I need a lighter. Nothing with letters or naked women."

I took the fifty and left him there with the cab running. He didn't look like he was in any shape to steal anything. I made so many mistakes evaluating that one ride that I'm permanently shaken. Everyone is suspect now—but especially extremely white people with canes and huge sunglasses. And Mexican men over fifty, with stupid mustaches and droopy eyes and worried gardens; they are simply too ignorant to trust if they remind me of myself.

Toby the clerk was a fat, sweaty white boy. He stood at parade slouch behind the register and kept a lazy eye on some hobo who was inspecting the Fritos. I got a Coke from the back and went up to the glass. Toby smiled at me.

"'Sup, Tobe," I said. I nodded out at my cab. "Fuckin' albino in the back, and he's waaaasted. No luggage, but he's loaded. Whattya think?"

Toby peered out at my cab. He shrugged.

"I'd say FBI. Maybe CIA. Cirque du Soleil."

"Yeah. Pack of smokes, and . . . lemme see. Gimme one of those pints of vodka with the red Russian shit on the label."

"What kind of smokes?" Toby took the vodka down and ran it past the scanner and then scanned my Coke while I considered.

"I could go back out and ask, but that would probably cut into my tip. So I gotta wing it." I looked back at the cab. The Knottspeed guy had his head out the window, his face turned up toward the sun. He'd taken his glasses off, which was a bad thing in that hard light. His right eye was a scabby, swollen mess. He was perfectly motionless, like a fake plant in an attic. I turned back to Toby. "Lucky Strikes, no filters. Matches. And a lighter with no writing on it. And a pack of Kools, full flavor."

"My guess exactly," Toby said, taking them down. He rang it all up and glanced back out. "Sunscreen?"

"Suggestive overkill. You white boys get so white about your whiteness."

"Sombrero?"

I picked up the bag. "Mañana, Tobe. Your hobo just lifted some cheese."

I walked back out. My fare was still in place, head out the window. I stopped and looked at him, since I could. His eyes were closed, and some kind of tranquilizer was in him. It was more than booze. It didn't even look like a drug. I heard on NPR one time about a shrink who had a patient who thought she was a tree. He decided to be a tree with her and make a forest. I don't know why I did it, but I turned and put my face up to the sun. Los Angeles sunlight. Hot. Hazy. Blue through my eyelids. It felt good, and the soda in the bag was cold and good pressing on my taco gut. And right then and there, right when I'd felt a

186

second of peace for the first time in three months, the mother-fucker started talking.

"Juan Julio," the creature Knottspeed called to me. "Saints and sinners and fifty-dollar bills all have something in common. Give me that bag, and I'll tell you all about it."

"Jose Ramirez," I corrected. Normally I might have been offended by his make-believe Mexican name, but there was some kind of simple joy in the way he talked. Like my grandmother, who had the Alzheimer's. "No smoking in the cab." I put my hand on his door to open it, and he withdrew into the interior. I passed him the bag through the window and opened the door. "Just kinda hang out and smoke one. I'll stop the meter. Got me a cola, so I owe you a buck."

Knottspeed looked into the bag I'd handed him and passed me the soda. His knuckles looked like whoever gave him the eye wasn't much better off than he was. His hand actually looked broken, like the pinkie had been snapped and then set by feel. He inspected both packs of smokes and then tapped down the Lucky Strikes. I watched as he peeled back the cellophane and the foil and shook one out. He pocketed the garbage rather than tossing it into the lot and then fired one up with the matches. He took in a deep lungful and then jetted it out through his nose, which was a pussy move in my book. Starlets on the black-and-white TV. Again, so impossibly wrong.

"Carlo," he began, "the pleasures of tobacco are almost exactly the same as the pleasures of a European party girl. I like them so very much, and I'm easily tempted to fabricate a fiction, like this Lucky has vitamins and minerals not found in normal food. Micronutrients, like in expensive dog food or seaweed. Mackerel." He'd said "mackerel" with crackling, spitty diction.

"I don't eat any of those," I said casually. I watched as he spun the top on the vodka and took a good lip-smacking pull of it. It made me thirsty, so I cracked my Coke and drained about half of it. I could nurse the rest of it for an hour if I set it right in front of the AC vent.

"I went to Vegas with this gal one time," he continued. He grabbed onto one of his pant legs on the thigh and lifted it over the other, crossing his legs. Still not the most masculine thing I'd ever seen. "Talked to this cab dude, fresh out of the airport, just like I am now. He knew where to get the goods. North Vegas, some Aztec place with a name so fucked-up I can't even remember it. There was a wedding going on that night. We just sort of snuck in. The food was unbelievable. Margaritas the size of my head. Those little tiny jungle elves were the best sort of people, Juan. The spirit of the rainforest was strong in them."

"Vegas," I replied, mostly just to keep him going. He nodded and sighed vodka fumes and smoke.

"Yep. I got married there once. Also got into a bad fight with a big black dude who wanted me to hire some poon. Really forceful salesman, and there I was hip deep in little love gone sideways. Check this out." He peeled back his lower lip with one finger of his bruised, scabbed hand. I peered into his mouth. His teeth were perfect. "See 'at?" he managed.

"No man," I said. "Your teeth are as white as your fucking hair, homie."

He spit. "Well, he cracked one. Just a tiny shard. I always kinda wondered if anyone could see it."

I shrugged. He took another long drag and exhaled, and then he inspected the cigarette.

"Nazi's fucked these smokes up, my new Mexican friend. Know how?"

"What. Lucky Strikes?"

"Yep. I know they did. Had something to do with the labels. They went from red to green and back again. Something to do with bombs. Can't say I remember, exactly. See this fuckin' thing?" He ran his finger along his bruised eye and destroyed eyebrow and over the top of his scalp. I looked closely. There was a fading purple line there. I suddenly wondered about the bone under that white skin, and what was under the bone. His soft, pink brain. He must have seen the small domino of speculation on my face. Even the 'stache can't hide my train of thought. Expression is a curse I got from my mother's side of the family.

"Yeah, yeah. Stop looking if it freaks you out, you big baby. So I remember this and that. It's like my inner librarian lost his glasses and has to wander around and find the books by feeling the spines. Thing is, right here, right now, I'm okay. But I don't remember my birthday or who the president is. Concussion combined with rampant alcohol abuse is a fantastic way to focus. Clears out all messy shit on the sides."

"Pills?" I asked. He shook his head.

"Nah. 'Cept on disco night, which I don't ever fuckin' do. Know what 'pill' means in Whitey?" He took another drag. I somehow knew he wasn't making fun of me. He was talking to himself a little, including me as an audience. The way children talk to adults.

"I do not, esse, but please, go on." The parking lot was getting hot. Pickups at ten in the morning were not bad unless they went all the way through noon or too far inland. We'd be fighting the AC either way in about a half hour. He took another nip of vodka and rubbed his scalp as it burned through him.

"Pill, in Blancoese, means two things. One, some intrusive thing you swallow to fuck around with how you feel. Two, a vague bummer of a human. Note the similarity. A pill could take pills to try to be less of a pill. Think about that long enough and you'll hook a hose to your exhaust pipe and wink out listening to Sting. So I don't take pills."

"Fuuuuck." It was over right then. I never liked Sting. I don't even like the people who are supposed to be better than Sting. My fare took one last drag and shot his smoke far out into the parking lot.

"Let's blow," he said, abruptly all business. "We have to make some stops. Keep the change as long as I can smoke in your cab. I'll pony up on the meter when we get to wherever the fuck we're going. This next part will be very confusing for you, but I want you to know how well you're doing so far."

189

I was already up almost thirty bucks. That actually was doing well.

"Keep the windows down," I said. I walked around and got in. While I was fastening my seat belt, he told me a little bit more of his Iliad, which was far from the last page.

"I just came from a freezing place that smelled like wet dogs had died on my entire body," he said. "This smog is like air candy. You people."

"We people?"

"Angelinos." He dutifully blew fresh smoke out the window as we pulled out of the lot. "I don't give a shit where you come from—the weather is always bad there. You were probably just thinking about how it is getting hot."

"I was."

"Human condition." He was back to breezy. The vodka was mixing in with the gin. "We project. I went to an island once that was perfect. Off the coast of Spain. The water a blue I've never seen before or since. Swaybacked, whitewashed buildings, terra-cotta tiles. There was this little cactus in the cracks in a tile outside my hotel room window. I would have stayed there and just done what I do, but there was a woman involved. She sorta kinda needed a no-stay-in-Spain guy. Massive error in judgment there, Paco. You can tell everything you need to know about someone by measuring their willingness to be happy. Takes about as long as this cab ride has so far."

He was blessedly quiet for a minute, as he no doubt thought about that place and time, which might have been a month or a decade ago. I look in the rearview a lot—a personal safety habit. This time I was watching for fun, which was rare enough. Usually when this happened, it was a really old person who had captured my interest. They sometimes overflowed in the same way, like cups filled to the brim.

"Extra twenty in it for you if you help me out, Carlos," he said. "I need a briefcase or some kind of flea market duffel bag. Maybe a suitcase, as long as it has wheels. Bermuda shorts, a few shirts. General shit. No carpets—don't you dare fuck with me like that. And I need a suit. Black, with a white shirt. No tie. And I need some black flip-flops."

"This is the confusing part?"

"The beginning of it. It won't end, trust me."

"The wardrobe change is for your cover," I concluded. "The coastal hotel with the view."

"Bingo."

"No problemo. We got a Ross coming up. The outlet mall. There's one of those parking lot crap sale places about a mile down. You need a wheelchair?"

"No wheelchair. I almost have this. But I do need a more fashionable cane. And no malls. I just couldn't take that. And I'm starving too. So if you have Mexican cab driver powers like the Vegas guy did, let's stop for lunch. On me. Someplace with oysters."

"I know some good taco stands," I offered.

"Thank God," he said. He took another nip of vodka and then lit one of the Luckys. I rolled the rest of the windows down and let the warm wind suck the smoke out.

"So you never did say what brings you to LA. Fate? Which one?" Now that we were going to be having lunch together at my cousin's, we'd gone from driver and fare to acquaintances, even though he couldn't seem to remember my name.

"Right. The whole fate thing. It's actually kinda over-whelming, Juan. Let's save it for the taco place. I'll puke if I have to go into my whole Gordian scissors thing on a stomach full of coffee and gin and three sips of potato fire."

"Parking lot junk-and-crap coming up. We in?" I looked back. His thin face was set for go. He nodded grimly.

The parking lot bazaar was one of those mini flea markets that had cropped up all over LA ten years back. You never knew what was in them. Mostly Chinese and Korean, Zeppelin shirts, boxes of Hello Kitty socks, bandannas. The entire fence was draped with fake zebra rugs and flowing Hawaiian muumuus. I glanced again in the rearview as he put his shades back on.

"Get us in as close as you can and leave the meter on. You'll have to come with me in case my legs give out."

"Your dime," I replied. I pulled into the edge of the loading zone and put my hazard lights on. But I turned the meter off.

"Adventure," he breathed. "Be prepared for the worst, Juan Julio."

I drank the rest of my Coke and got out, and then I helped him out of the back seat. He was taller than I'd thought, about my size, right around five foot eight. But even under the heavy coat he was wearing, I could tell I had a hundred pounds on him. Whatever had happened to his face had happened to the rest of him in a serious way, more than once in recent history. I held his skinny arm while he steadied himself.

"Okay," he said. He took a deep breath. "The best way to shop in situations like this is to go in with no plan at all. Like bodysurfing. We just go where the wave takes us and watch out for rocks."

"Wise," I said, nodding. It sounded perfectly stupid, though I was later to learn that improvisation was to Knottspeed what the piano was to Mozart in his final years, when he had gone deaf and had lead poisoning.

"Good. Then we roll. Don't walk too fast. If my legs start to go, I'll hopefully wobble for a few seconds first. Just don't let me fall on my head. Push me into something softer than concrete if it looks like that's going to happen."

"Right. Can't catch, push toward soft. Much like dealing with more than one little boy."

We went through the wide gate into the gypsy crap bazaar. There were about twelve vendors, selling everything, almost all of it low-end knockoff junk they probably got in weekly boxes from relatives overseas. Knottspeed veered toward some tracksuits. There were dozens of them, all either black or blue or bright yellow.

"Now we're talking," he said appreciatively. He took a bright-yellow one off the rack. It had the Nike swish, but there was no way it was real. Ten bucks. "This," he said, handing it to me. I draped it over my arm like an attentive Mexican. He wandered over to a fifty-gallon cardboard barrel of flip-flops and selected a pair of lurid red ones with thick straps and black soles. No emblem, two bucks. He dug around in the pocket opposite his wallet and came out with a roll of big bills, very untidy. He used his thin lips to peel out a twenty and gestured with his head for me to pluck it from his mouth. I did. He was growing on me.

"Pay that dude," he said. "Leg time is hovering somewhere between thirty seconds and maybe way longer. Just FYI."

I left him standing, stock still, leaning hard on his cane and staring at the ground with an intense expression. The tiny Cambodian man made change for the purchase out of a battered tin box and then scowled over at my albino. For some reason, it pissed me off.

"Tú hablas Inglés?" I murmured to him, my voice low and scratchy. He cocked his head. Little fucker gave me a stare like he had a hatchet in each hand.

"No refundo." He spat a slimy stringer with lazy contempt and made a shooing motion. His hard little eyes were dead, dirty mirrors, all full of jungle and boredom and rice moonshine. I spit myself, a string of mucous off to the side, hard old vato.

"Puta," I said. "Means bad fish. Like in the pussy kind of way."

I had no idea why I was talking like that. None. I have no temper. The 'Bodi didn't either, to the point where he had no reaction at all. I turned and discovered the albino was moving, headed toward a towering booth of gym bags and purses. His legs had bowed a little, and his wobble was getting freaky, like he had some kind of spaz coming on. I rushed up behind him and tucked my arm under his, opposite his cane. Up that close, I could smell the pond-water-leper-dog stink in the hard shine coming up from under his coat. He also smelled a little like Band-Aids and raw hamburger.

"I know," he said. "I'm a complicated smell. The result of sponge baths and medical shit, plus my pet Indian couldn't get the dog out of the air. He tried, bless his big soul."

"You had a soulful pet Indian giving you sponge baths?"

"No." He nodded at a black suitcase with an aluminum handle and little plastic wheels. "I'll take that one. And a briefcase."

I checked out the price tag. It came to almost forty dollars. Robbery. East LA or Compton, maybe twelve bucks. Knottspeed eyed them as well and pulled another fifty out of his wallet. I flicked an eye that way as he did. It was stuffed full of big bills. The messy wad in his pocket must have been for twenties and smaller.

"You see anything that looks like underwear?" he asked while I paid the man. "My eyes don't work too well."

I got the change and squinted around. It was getting hotter. "Eh. Swimsuits over at the other end. Think you can make it?"

"Nah. Find me a chair or something, and then go get me some. My tailbone is bleeding just a little bit, so nothing white."

There was a bench for sale in front of a rebuilt yard crap place. I guided him over to it. The old fat lady manning the place gave me a sharp look. I inspected a chipped garden gnome.

"He's going to test it," I said, smiling and nodding. "We might get it on the way out."

"Test," she repeated. There was no telling if she was dark Polish or Ecuadorian. Her face was a raisin, and her shapeless dress could have been from Nepal. Knottspeed didn't wait for me to find out.

"For my front yard, woman. Juan Julio, get on with it while I haggle. Hurry up, before I fall in love."

I had to smile at this, as did the old fat lady, who suddenly looked motherly, even grandmotherly. I left them talking softly. Behind me, a dozen steps later, I heard her tittering laugh. Some of the other vendors glanced over, as if the chunky little ancient thing didn't make the sound too often. I realized I was having fun.

I estimated that Knottspeed's legs were as long as mine but that his wasted waist size was around twenty-seven inches, give or take. I found a pair of black slacks and a black belt that I thought suited him. There was a large barrel of men's briefs, all in either canary yellow or Scottish plaid. I got a three-pack of plaid. I skipped the swimsuits altogether. To swim would be certain death for him, though I was getting the impression that he was a hard thing to kill.

I'd paused in front of a stand selling a wide and unrelated assortment of items, ranging from lawn furniture to the socks I was inspecting, when my cell phone rang. I shifted my items and took it out and squinted at the number. My oldest son, Raul. He ditched on the third ring, before I could even pick up. Butt dial. Typical.

When I returned with the goods, Knottspeed held them up for the old woman's inspection. She gave me the evil eye over the underwear, and I scowled in return, but everything else met her grudging approval. She particularly approved of the belt and tapped it a few times, nodding.

"Good work, Juan," Knottspeed said, wobbling to his feet. "I wish I could just change right here, but . . ." He winked at the old woman, who winked back. "Later." Then to me. "Let's roll."

"Where to next?" I asked as we slowly made our way back to my cab.

"Let's get a couple suits," he said. "I'm going to do a multiple clothing upgrade, Paco. I smell too bad to check into the kind of hotel I need for all the shit I'm doing to work. So I have to change into the flea market outfit for the time being, then we continue. I'll be in good enough shape at that point to buy some real suits. We can use the bags and whatnot as distractions at check-in time."

"That's a shit-ton of work to go through, hombre."

"Almost everything is." I opened the door for him, and he tumbled into the back and went about adjusting his legs. I put the bags in beside him and got in and pulled out of the parking lot. I eyed him in the rearview as he began emptying his pockets. He actually was going to shamelessly strip in my cab.

"I can't stay in just any old hotel, dude," he continued. "The first part of this trip is all business, so I have staffing issues." He struggled out of his coat and his shirt and then threw them out the window. His naked torso was covered in bruises ranging in age from about a month old up to yesterday. He was impossibly thin, his unbruised skin as white as milk.

"Maybe just put the used stuff on the floor," I suggested. "I can get a fine for you throwing shit out of my cab, if you can believe that."

"Figures," he growled. "Always after the little guy. What other kinds of bullshit tickets do they stick you with?" He started struggling out of his pants, visibly in agony. In a moment, I'd have a completely naked man in the back of my cab. I'd heard of such a thing happening, but it had never happened to me. I began steering toward a parking lot.

"So staffing issues, you were saying?" I asked nervously, changing the subject.

He held a shoe up, inspected the inside, dropped it. I pulled into the lot and stopped well away from any other cars. He closed his eyes and struggled into the underwear, gasping once, and then spent a tortuous minute on the pants.

"Staffing," he managed, panting. "For the big job."

"You . . . you're employed?"

"Not . . ." Yank. Gasp. He shuddered. "Not yet."

"Ah." I wanted to help him, but something made me think he might bite me if I tried. He took a few deep breaths, then took the shirt and pulled it on, struggling with his broken hand as he buttoned it, glaring down through one eye.

"Juan?"

"Yes?"

"Get this shit out of here. Let's leave that fucking dog on the pavement, where it belongs. I'm going to drink and smoke for a minute. If I pass out, it isn't the booze, it's . . ."

"The pain?"

"Then on to your buddy's taco shack or whatever." He lit a

cigarette and smoothed his hair back, held the bottle up to his lips, and took a moderate nip. "I'm a tiny bit disappointed that you're so obviously squandering my hard-won cash on some friend's salmonella operation."

"It's my cousin's taco place, actually. It's my nature. Keep it in the family if you can." Knottspeed nodded, as if he understood perfectly. "Do you have a preference on a suit store, or can I continue with my squandering?"

He drank and glared out the window. I got out and opened the back door, picked his old clothes up, and carried them over to the nearest shopping basket. The dog smell was powerful, and there was dried blood on the inside of the shirt. I paused by the basket, then dropped the clothes and stared at the little pile for a moment. It was fascinating in a way, like the skin of a molting snake. When I got back, he was visibly more composed. I got in and looked back.

"Let's just take it low and slow toward some kind of idiot hipster territory," he said. He took another nip of vodka and shifted painfully. "What we're looking for will be a smaller kind of place. Tasteful. A mall of any kind will get us both arrested, because I'd just freak out at the horror of it all. I think I already mentioned that."

"You did, and I certainly believe you." I wheeled out and headed for the ocean. Behind me, Knottspeed fired up another cigarette. Menthol this time.

"I need some fucking Advil too," he continued. "And a disposable cell phone. Maybe a hundred minutes on it. That's probably all I need."

"Another convenience store it is." I glanced at him in the rearview. "Are you a criminal, Mr. Knottspeed, to need such a phone?" I was joking a little, but he didn't laugh, just smoked and stared out the window.

"Just Knottspeed," he replied finally. "And in answer to your question, of course I am. Everyone is. Capitalism is just the official terminology for the concept, Jose. There are varying

197

degrees, of course, but the social history of crime is an evolving flower—just to bring you into the loop."

I admit I laughed. When again he didn't, I stopped.

"So," I said slowly, "by conventional standards, in the parlance of the common man, exactly what do you do?"

"Whipping out the big words isn't necessary, dude. But what I do is this—I solve puzzles. You have a problem? I might be able to find the solution. Got a vintage car you need to get rid of, but it's in Dallas? I can find a way. No title and it's not yours? More expensive, and I can still find a way. Et cetera."

"Is that . . . is that what happened to you? Your injuries, I mean."

"Was I stealing a car in Dallas? No. No, I wasn't. I was in LA selling shitty landscape paintings to a hotel. Some dipshit hit me with his car and knocked me over the edge of a freeway overpass. I was walking and trying to figure out how to text on what was then my new phone, which I guess makes you a target in some places. Most recently, I fell in a parking lot, wiped out in front of a junk shop for Jesus minors, fell out of a window at one point, and don't take this personally, but I've been in a series of spirited scuffles with cab drivers. In fact, even the cab driver that took me to the airport."

"Sounds like bad luck." And it did. I glanced back to gauge his reaction. He cocked his head.

"Not really," he replied. "Every aspect of this entire debacle is key. The reason I'm back is a complicated one, but in other ways, maybe it isn't. Hard to say."

"I see." Even though I didn't. "Too much in life is this way."

He snorted. "Not for me, sadly. But things are different now. Different in a most unusual way."

"Ah." Still no idea.

"Yeah. Now I'm solving a puzzle designed just for me."

"A puzzle for the mirror. There's a song in there somewhere."

"There!" he cried, suddenly animated. He pointed and I looked. Aldercamp's Haberdashery. A mini palace for albino

198

snobbery. I pulled into the space right in front. Behind me, Knottspeed breathed a sigh of relief.

"Thank the forces that be," he said, tossing his cigarette. "Yoda, Jesus, and the fat guy all. Leave the meter running, hombre—you're coming with me. We have to make this fast, because I need those tacos and I'm going to pass out soon. Ready?"

"Ready." The meter was getting close to one hundred. I turned it off again. I'll never know why.

I followed as he wobbled at top speed across the sidewalk to the door, carrying the vodka with him. When he stopped and just stood there, I thought for a heartbeat that he had looked through the glass and changed his mind. Then I realized he was waiting for me to open it.

"I'll get it," I said, pulling the heavy thing open. He wobbled through and fell heavily into the chair next to the door. I entered and, unsure of what to do, just stood there.

Aldercamp's was mostly vintage, with hundreds of suits, rows of shoes, and cases of everything ranging from bow ties to watches, handkerchiefs to bowler hats. The attendant, if that's what you called him, looked up from the antique desk and frowned a small, extremely polite, shitty kind of frown. He was too young to be as bald as he was, and his blue eyes were too bored and boring for any face of any age. I disliked him instantly. So, evidently, did Knottspeed, who held up a hundred-dollar bill in his busted hand.

"Even bill just to get us started, turtle egg. I need two suits, two shirts, a cane, a cool lighter of some kind, a watch, and some shoes. And I need it all in less than ten minutes."

"Ah, sir," the turtle egg began. "First and foremost, there's absolutely no drinking—"

"Miguel!" Knottspeed said sharply. "My new socks from the car! The one's I'm wearing smell like a dead dog, and there's dried blood on them."

"Sir," I said crisply, "yes, sir!" I snapped to attention and spun on my heel. Fucking with the snob guy was the high point in a very dull week. I hurried; I didn't want to miss any of what came next. It was certain to be better than anything on the radio.

"—thing green, you moron," Knottspeed was scolding the already red-faced boy-man holding a suit in front of him. "You went to Yale, and this is what they did to you? Look at me! Look at my hair! My fucking face! Do you want people to think I'm already fucking dead? Blue or black. And no fucking collar on the shirt. Nine minutes. Miguel! My new socks." He held his hand out without looking.

"Sir!" I slapped them into his open palm. The attendant scurried off, and I noticed that the hundred-dollar bill was gone. Knottspeed was free to abuse him, and he was doing just that. He looked up at me and winked. I stifled a grin and tried to project somber. I wished I had one of the little dangling white wires that high-end security had coming from their ears.

"Fucking people these days," Knottspeed muttered. "I swear, if we learn that the concept of bribing idiots to berate them has been restricted to the government and the corporate world, I will cut my own pinkie off and shove it up that dummy's ass."

"Brilliant, sir. Your blade stands ready."

Six hundred dollars and eleven minutes later, we left with everything Knottspeed had requested. To my great disappointment, he didn't want back any of his efficiency bribe. Pushing the attendant to the edge of a nervous breakdown seemed to have invigorated him. He flopped into the back of my cab and tossed his new cane on the seat next to him. It was a dark, polished wood, very hard looking, with a brass tip. A weapons upgrade. I was carrying all of his purchases in three large bags, so I walked around to put them in the trunk. When I got behind the wheel, he was just finishing the vodka, which he had been forced to carry in the open to the cab, and smoking again. He dropped the empty out the window. Since it was plastic, it failed to shatter, which deflated him for an instant.

"Tacos?" I inquired. He nodded.

"Tacos. To go. And then I have to take a long bath and soak

the dog and all the rest of this shit off of me, including whatever else I manage to splatter all over myself in the meantime. Onward. And let's get that phone and some beer on the way."

"Phone, beer, tacos, hotel," I repeated. I pulled into traffic and glanced back again. Knottspeed had instantly reentered his own thoughts. His expensive new glasses were vaguely insectile. Other than the cane, he had refused to touch or much less try on any of the new items. There was a small spot of blood soaking through the fabric on the upper left part of his chest. He still smelled, though less powerfully bad. Somehow I didn't mind, and as the heat of noon washed through the car it seemed to wash him too.

"That was fun though, right?" He didn't seem overly concerned with my opinion. "I mean, where the fuck did that guy come from? A mental institution? There was a Yale diploma behind the desk. Might have been the owner's, but his natural contempt had a breeding quality. Maybe I should have robbed the place."

"It's early," I said sympathetically. "Maybe he was just a man with soft hands and small wrists."

"Jesus." Knottspeed leaned forward, even though it clearly hurt to do so. "Are you actually trying to guilt-trip me? Really?"

"No," I said, laughing at his genuine concern. "I found your performance completely—"

"Performance!" he interrupted, slumping back. "From guilt to insults in one breath. And here I thought that was restricted to white people and Muslims. Just focus on the phone."

"And the Advil. And of course we can't forget the beer."

Knottspeed blew smoke out the window, watching his internal movie again. It was difficult to tell from his expression if he was in one of the action sequences, but if I had to guess, I'd say he was in some kind of mushy part. I pulled into the parking lot of a 7-Eleven advertising disposable phones and reeled off the price to him. He passed me a hundred without looking.

"Don't forget the beer," he said absently. "And get yourself another Coke. It's hot as fuck out here with the windows down."

17

Hotel Florez

GETTING KNOTTSPEED INTO AN upscale hotel was easier than I thought. Once we reached the Santa Monica Pier, we headed north. Traffic was bad, so it was slow going. He smoked and drank and surveyed the hotels as we passed, preparing for the performance to come.

"Close," he said, gesturing at one. "See those potted palms? Quality plastic. Shake those things just before dawn, and rats will fall out. They hide up in the phony leaves by day."

"I see."

"There," he said, pointing. "But don't pull in! Just slow way down. Give me the phone now, but unwrap it for me. My—"

"I got it." I unwrapped the phone and entered the activation digits and then passed it back. He'd poured two beers into a Big Gulp cup I'd furnished him with and was slurping away as he dialed. There was an answer. I almost held my breath.

"Hi, yes. I need a room for one, something with a view? Availability?" Pause. "Great. That's great. I'll take it." Pause. "Okay, hang on just a sec." He dug his wallet out and gave her his credit card number. I was a little amazed he even had one. "Smith. Anderson Smith, right. But I'll be paying in cash." So no credit card after all. "Okay then, I'll see you in a few, Becky.

Thank you so much." He hung up and sipped for a moment and then looked back at the phone, checking the time. "Okay. Let's do this. Just follow my lead."

I pulled up and parked in the covered drop-off area. Knottspeed got out and drew himself completely upright. He seemed somehow more like an alien when he did, but whatever he was radiating drew less attention to his overall state of poorly disguised filth and bodily damage. He must have used the same trick to get onto whatever airplane had landed him in Long Beach. I grabbed the bags out of the trunk and caught up to him just as he went through the wide front doorway, still leaning on his cane though not quite as hard.

The marble-tiled lobby was twenty degrees cooler. Swank. Spendy. Polished brass and huge, glittering chandeliers that spilled buttery light on the rich and foreign guests. There was absolutely no way we were going to make it. I unconsciously clutched the bags tighter.

Knottspeed approached the front desk at a speed I had no idea he was capable of, obscuring the lower half of his body as quickly as he could. The beautiful Asian woman at the check-in terminal looked up, and though I could not see Knottspeed's face, whatever was on it made her smile. I stood off to the side, following his lead and holding the expensive-looking bags emblazoned with the Aldercamp's name and odd logo—a stylized top hat—in front of my faded work shirt.

"Anderson Smith," Knottspeed said, "reporting for a room with a view."

"Mr. Smith," the woman said brightly. "Welcome to the Florez."

"Thank you so much," Knottspeed replied. "I'm so happy to be here. My ex-girlfriend swears by this place. Does a guy named Jaxifer still work here?"

"The concierge? Yes, but he's actually out right now."

"No matter. She just insisted I say hello and ask him about some tickets I need. I'll call down later." He thwacked the credit card down on the surface in front of him, and she took it. I was amazed. I was amazed again when the card seemed to work.

"All right, we have you in Room 311. It has a magnificent view. Just sign here . . ." A printer chattered, and she returned the card and then put a paper and pen next to it. Knottspeed made a bold swish of a signature with an elegant, eccentric grace and speed that made it almost impossible to see the state of his hand. He palmed the card in the same motion. His legs were beginning to shake, but it was just a tremor.

"All right." She smiled, and Knottspeed beamed back and then abruptly whipped his cell phone out and whispered into it, flashing a polite smile at the woman while he pretended to listen. While he spun off to the side, she finished everything and slipped his room card into an envelope. As soon as she was done, he ended his call and swept up the envelope.

"Thank you," he said brightly, and then to me, "Help me with the bags, Miguel." With a final nod, we were off to the elevators. I used the bags and my own body to try to shield him from the direct view of any oncoming employee.

"Jaxifer?" I inquired as we walked.

"Nameplate on the concierge desk," he replied. "God, I hope they have an honorless bar."

"Anderson Smith?"

"Ah. An alias I created for a . . . friend a few years ago. I use it myself sometimes. Especially now. Come to think of it, I may let the charge ride, just to screw up the profile."

"I see," I said, blind again.

"Yeah. He was a nice enough guy. Used to come around for the dinner parties, et cetera. Book collector. He stole one of my favorite Sheckley collections while I was in a coma and everyone thought I was bound for the next new world. My antique radio too."

"Bummer." We hit the elevator, and I shifted the bags to hit the button. The doors opened immediately, and we entered. I hit three, and the doors closed.

"Yeah. I wish I had more time for vengeance, but I don't. Confusion will have to suffice, plus paranoia. Deep, freakish paranoia is an excellent weapon, maybe the best ever devised. Its access path is so perfectly natural."

"Of course. The eyes. The ears."

"The rumors. The lies. The suspicion that you're being followed."

"All culminating in disaster, and with no direct participation. I like the way you think, Knottspeed." The doors opened.

"Me too," he said immodestly, but he said it in a way that implied that he was used to bragging. I can't trust a man who never brags. For me it means they're hiding something, that they're afraid of scrutiny, of testing. I followed the wobbly white man, drifting along in his dog wake, suppressing a smile. By far the most interesting fare of the month. I should have never felt that moment of faith in him; that is how most disasters begin, with the purchase of a ticket on a train bound into the unknown.

"Here we are," he said, "and just in time." He slotted the room card and pushed the door open. "Just in fucking time." And then he fell through the doorway.

The room was huge, with a king bed, a desk area, and a giant balcony with potted rat trees. The mirrors were gilded. It was all very tasteful. I stepped over Knottspeed and walked to the bed to set the bags down.

"This carpet smells like a brand-new wig," he announced, his voice slightly muffled. I carried the taco bag over to the table.

"I won't ask how you know that," I replied. Behind me, he struggled and flipped over and wiggled so that the door would close. With a grunt, he got to his feet and crashed down into the chair across from me as I set the tacos out. We'd gotten five lenguas and five pastors, plus four rellenos and four sauces.

"Well, I guess I wouldn't ask about my wig episode, either. France was involved."

"I have no doubt." I sat down across from him. He took a pastor, tore the waxed paper off, and ate half the taco in one bite, panting slightly through his nostrils. He ate like a starved madman. I took the lids off the sauces and went after a pair of rellenos.

"Good," he managed and then swallowed. He looked around. "Does that balcony actually look out on the ocean?"

"I think so," I replied. I glanced over. "Either that or the back parking lot."

"In Malibu, I noticed that they build with a great view of the neighbor's roof."

"The canyons too. It makes you wonder if rich people think they have something in common with birds."

That made Knottspeed squint a little. He slowed his chewing, and then he selected a lengua and dumped some of the fiery red sauce on it. He chewed through it, still squinting at me, before he spoke.

"Kind of a weirdo, aren't you, Miguel."

I shrugged and took a taco.

"Whatever," he concluded. He took the other two rellenos and smothered them with the green sauce. "Want a Coke?"

The honorless bar, as he called it, was over by the huge flat screen TV.

"Sure," I replied, rising. "I'll grab it. Beer?"

"Yep. And some kind of scotch. Maybe tequila."

I walked over to the bar and opened the door. The Coke was probably five or six bucks, but I didn't care, and whoever Anderson Smith was would go on record as having begun racking up what was sure to be an impressive bar bill with a Coke, which lent an air of mystery considering Knottspeed's beverage preferences. So in a way, I was doing him a favor. I looked at the vast array of little bottles and beers.

"Tequila and a Corona?" Another twenty bucks, minimum. The little refrigerator had sensors in it, I knew, so that nothing could be replaced.

"Sure," he called, his mouth full of relleno. I took the drinks out and rejoined him.

"Ocean," I reported. "Right out front. Balcony faces west."

"Good."

We ate and drank in silence after that. I realized I was hungry after the busy morning. Knottspeed ate six tacos and two rellenos, outdoing me. When we finished, I gathered up all the trash and tossed it and then wiped my hands on my pants. Knottspeed was paid up, and my tip had come out to sixty-eight dollars and lunch and three Cokes, so it had been a good day so far.

"I'm having a dinner party tonight," Knottspeed said. "Eight o'clock. A place called Santiago's. Know it?"

"Venice?"

"Yep. Bring a guest. And leave your number and take mine. I sometimes require emergency cab services."

"Okay," I said affably. There was no way I was going to be joining him for two meals in one day, or even a month, or a decade. I wrote my number down anyway, because he tipped so well, and wrote his down on a cab card just to be polite. He lit up a smoke in the nonsmoking room and used the already empty beer bottle as an ashtray. He watched the smoke curl up to the ceiling for a moment, and then he rose and wobbled over to the balcony and opened the sliding glass doors.

"See ya," I called. "Thanks for the tip."

"Eight," he said. I could sense that he was already deep in thought about whatever it was that preoccupied him at every turn. I left him that way—staring out into the west, framed against the blue sky and the flow of white curtains in the ocean breeze.

In the elevator, my cell phone rang again. Raul, my oldest boy. This time it wasn't a butt dial.

"I'm working," I answered. "I'm actually in an elevator. The strangest thing happened today—"

"He's back." There was a terrible despair in his voice, edged with desperation, tinged with shame at being the bearer of such awful news. My mouth went dry and my heart skipped a beat. I lowered the phone and stared at my warped reflection in the polished elevator doors. I was almost as white as Knottspeed.

Knottspeed.

18

Santiago

I WENT INTO SANTIAGO'S ALONE just before eight, dressed in slacks, my good shoes, and my white shirt with all of the buttons. I'd punched in Knottspeed's number a few times as the tension in my house escalated over the long afternoon, but for some reason I'd always stalled when it came to the last digit. A deal with the devil could only be made in person.

Knottspeed sat transformed at the head of the Santiago's only banquet table, a fifteen-seat stretch with only two empty seats. The upscale restaurant had a low-light, fruity cha-cha thing going for it that made him glow like an ivory domino in a bowl of Tic Tacs. His white hair was clean and slicked back over his skull, and his blue eyes shone brightly. Scabs had been replaced with pink, and the hands curled around his drink and his cane tip were less swollen, with manicured nails. He'd selected the blue suit, which looked tailored and twice as expensive as it had been. His eyes flicked to me and registered no surprise. In that instant, I had the unsettling feeling that he'd read my mind, maybe even before I came through the door. He rose.

"Ladies and gentlemen, may I introduce Jose Ramirez, my wheels for the duration of my visit." So he knew my name after all. Every head at the table turned to me. Some of them,

I already recognized. Most of them, I didn't. But all of them nodded, and there was genuine curiosity in those faces. The devil's wheelman. Someone he trusted. Someone who might know more about him than they did. He continued.

"Senior Ramirez, may I introduce you to Lila Fan"—he gestured to the desk clerk who had checked us in—"and Jaxifer Sloan." A small man in a tuxedo with the tie undone nodded and raised his drink. He continued to the fat woman from the gypsy place where we'd bought his first set of clothes. "Consuela Magrine." And then, with a sweeping gesture to one side, he announced, "The rubes and art homos from the gallery I was shamelessly fleecing before my accident, in order, are Peter, Dwayne, Bobby, Dave, Gary, Ron, and Mr. Percy. The man who will be sitting next to you is Carl Crogan, an actor and sometimes bellhop in charge of bandages and assorted errands for Jaxifer. And of course Mary Tegali, my new manicurist and an aspiring massage therapist. Did you bring a companion?"

I shook my head. Knottspeed nodded.

"If everyone will excuse us for a moment? Senior Ramirez and I have to briefly catch up on developments in my itinerary." Everyone gave me polite smiles and returned to their drinks and the conversation. Knottspeed came around the table and tapped along, leaning less heavily on his cane, refreshed and noticeably stronger. The fat gypsy wanted to be his mother. The Asian desk lady and the manicurist wanted to see him naked. All of them watched his passage for at least a second. They all wanted something from him, every last one of them. I could tell, and I felt suddenly ashamed.

"Relax," he said, taking my arm and pointing me toward the bar. "Tell me what happened."

"What?"

"Jose. May I call you Jose?" He continued without waiting for an answer. "There is only one thing that could have brought you here tonight after spending the morning with me. Something bad has happened in your world. You have a puzzle. You need a key. Bla bla. Get on with it."

"I . . . I," I stammered. Knottspeed held up two fingers at the bartender, who poured us each a tequila. Knottspeed picked up his drink and toasted.

"To Anderson," he said, "who will soon discover how much those books meant to me. Drink up. Brace yourself, and then tell me the truth. Don't lie, because I'll know. And keep it short. We're about to start the appetizers." Then he stared at me. I picked up my glass and drained it. I never did care for tequila.

"All right. My daughter, Laura, she's beautiful, the youngest of my four children and my only girl. Sixteen now." I looked down. "Less than a year ago, she began dating a local drug dealer on the rise, one Ignacio Medrano. He's twenty-one, and he just finished doing sixty days in county. We thought he was gone for good. He isn't." I paused. Knottspeed blasted the bartender with two fingers again and motioned for me to continue. I sipped this time. I could already tell he wasn't interested. My story needed meat. Maybe it needed to be vastly more complicated. Maybe there needed to be money involved.

"Medrano graduated from slinging weed to coke. Then he rolled both and became a player by adding pills of every kind, speed . . . You name it, he sells it—and he likes to use my Laura as one of his mules. She runs point on his deals, and it's set up for her to take the fall, which for her is two years, until she's eighteen. Medrano just leans back and takes the money, especially now after his last jolt. He's roped her back in already, and she's gone off to run for him. That life, with the cars and the dresses and the all night on fast-forward. If my other two boys find out, they'll get themselves killed. My oldest boy is on the verge of it as we speak."

"Stop," Knottspeed instructed. He took a deep breath and looked down into his empty glass. Then he sighed, and when he spoke, it was barely loud enough to hear over the people around us. "Money. Drugs. The ambitious scumbag, new to the big time. It's not my normal type of deal, but . . . I can work with this. I need his phone number and a location on him. Plus, a picture of your daughter. I'll be done in forty-eight hours." He looked up, and his eyes burned into mine, completely frightening. "My fee, Jose, is this. You drive me around tomorrow and the next day. I keep everything that shakes loose. You get your kid back. And you don't ask questions."

"Deal." We clinked our glasses together. I felt light-headed all of a sudden. The lights seemed a little dimmer, shadowing parts of the white man's face.

"Call your oldest boy, and tell him you've got it handled." Knottspeed brightened with that suddenness of his and clapped me on the shoulder. "We'll talk more later. Don't get too wasted tonight—you're my ride home."

"The desk lady looks like she might not mind." I had tried for lightness myself, but my voice cracked. "She's been eyeing us. The manicure woman too. The fat lady is scowling at them."

"I'm . . . spoken for," Knottspeed said. He flickered from focused to distant and then back again. "C'mon." He tossed his head at the table, setting back. I followed, taking the second-to-last chair. A moment later the appetizers arrived, ceviche. I methodically devoured mine without tasting it or making conversation with anyone around me. Then I excused myself and stepped out into the parking lot, patting myself down along the way for the cigarettes I didn't have. As soon as I was outside, I dialed Raul.

"Papa," he answered, his voice grim.

"Hola, boy. I took care of it."

"How?" Like he didn't believe me. I rolled my eyes.

"I hired a man I know. He's, well, he's not . . . he isn't . . . he's hard to describe. But Medrano has an appointment with the very most unusual thing he will ever meet."

"Papa, what the fuck are you talking—"

"Don't get in the way, Raul," I snapped. "It's too late! He knows about Medrano now! He has my phone number, and I feel sure he knows my license plate. He knows all about me! It's too late! We can't go back!" I was screaming as quietly as a quiet and desperate scream could be at the end. I drew a deep breath. I'd never yelled at Raul in all his life.

"Papa, what have you done?" It was a whisper.

"I need Medrano's phone number, or an address. Tonight if you can."

"Papa."

"It's too late," I whispered again.

My breath stopped as Knottspeed reached around me and plucked the phone out of my hand. He held it up to his ear.

"Raul Ramirez," he said softly, "my name is Knottspeed, and your father is correct. It is too late. Do as he says. And you and your brothers stay far away after that." He hung up and handed the phone back to me. He didn't smile.

"Dinner is served."

A massive bill slammed into the Anderson alias in the form of round after round of drinks, platter after platter of seafood, braised beef in chilies, sopaipillas, enchiladas, lamb in garlic and wine, beans, rice, and wine with more wine. Laughter rang all along the table. Throughout the night, Knottspeed tended his audience well, regaling us with ridiculous stories that caused smaller conversations to form along the table, then taking carefully orchestrated breaks to have a few private conversations of his own. I realized he was already working on my problem when his fat new mother glanced at me and scowled, when the dapper concierge Jaxifer shot a look my way and then gave Knottspeed a shrug with his eyebrows.

And all the while, I wondered what I had done. Most of all, I wondered why I was so utterly afraid of the future. I knew Knottspeed was not an evil man. He was, however, something I could not understand. For years I had been a great reader of books, of people, of the small prophesies in the contrails out by the airport, and I listened closely to the voices at the edge of the wind. There were signs in the flowers in my yard, flowers that were so hard to grow. Maybe it was the tequila. Maybe it was the way that a man with a cane had appeared behind me silently in a parking lot and spoken to my oldest child. Then again, maybe I was just transfixed with his very whiteness. But something momentous, large and shadowed and minded, was peeking through the veil of tomorrow, watching for our arrival.

No two people can agree on the color cyan. Some see more of the grass in it, some see more evening blue. The same can be said of how we feel about everything, and I—a cab driver, a widower, and a father—well, I had my own ideas about everything. About half of them were only half right, and the other half were only half wrong. But my inner consensus was that I had traded one trouble for another, or possibly had just given my problem to someone else without reading the microscopic writing at the bottom of the contract. I was pondering this when I felt someone looking at me. My eyes rose from my plate.

"Señor Ramirez?" It was the actor/bellhop Carl Crogan, who had been sitting next to me all along while I ate in silence, brooding. I nodded at him and gave him a polite smile.

"Jose, please."

Carl was a little drunk, but professionally so, still in control. "So you're Mr. Knottspeed's driver?"

"Yeah. And I think it's just Knottspeed."

"Huh." Carl forked up some of the pork on his plate and ran it through the red sauce. "So you've known him for how long?"

"Just met him this morning, actually. Picked him up at the airport."

"Right on." He ate and talked. "He called from the phone in his bathroom and requested a bellhop. I came to the door, and he yelled for me to come in. It took us a few minutes to realize he was trapped in the bathtub. Jaxifer let me in, and we pried him out and helped him around until he got dressed."

"He does that kind of thing," I said. I looked down at my food. I'd spooned up two enchiladas when the plate passed without even realizing it. I'd eaten half of one already.

"Yeah. So what the hell is it exactly that he's doing here in LA? I mean, I know about the art thing, but one of them told me that they met him through a guy who sold high-end goat soap. Maybe it was cheese. I can't remember."

"Interesting." I wished he would stop talking. I drank some ice water and then helped myself to some passing seafood stew. Carl did too.

"Yeah. So I'm an actor, right? Theater mostly, but I'm trying to break into TV. People are doing really well in commercials right now. Fuckin' great time to be in Hollywood, man. You do anything other than drive around cool out-of-towners?"

"I do," I said. I could just picture him on TV, which blurred things that already had a funhouse mirror element. I sighed.

"Like what?" He seemed genuinely bored with me all of the sudden, but he did his best to try to hide it. Like most actors, many of whom I had driven from one dead end to another, their primary goal in socializing was to ascertain what you could do for them. If the answer was nothing, you became invisible.

"Today I've been bartering with forces I can't understand to engage a terrible evil that is attempting to consume the soul of my daughter. At the same time, I'm trying to keep her brothers from committing suicide, plus I'm the wheelman for our host. Those are my current hobbies. I drink sodas by day, beer by night. Sort of like Batman. But also like Batman, I can't drink too much, because a DUI would ruin me. I hallucinate sometimes, especially in my garden. I read too much, if such a thing is possible, and I consider myself contaminated by the works of Isabel Allende. I don't get laid very often."

"Huh." That pretty much did him in. I wondered as he turned away to carry his game across the table what he thought Knottspeed could do for him. If I had known his role in the coming opera, I would have advised the poor bellhop to run screaming into the night, back to the farmlands of his family, to change his hair and change his name. But his fate had become entangled with my own already, though I couldn't see how. It was too late, for better or worse. The signs, weak as they were when they came to me, had become as invisible as I was in the glare of the beacon Knottspeed.

The evening rambled on like that. I switched to Pepsi to rinse the three drinks away, and gradually, one by one, the table emptied. Knottspeed had a private conversation with each of them before they left. Some of them glanced my way; some of them didn't. Whatever his plan was, it had formed fully by the time we were finally alone. Once he'd paid with the Anderson identity, we went outside. He lit a cigarette with his new lighter. The snap of it was as clean and crisp as his next words.

"You're wondering exactly what the hell I'm doing, aren't you, Jose?" He tapped slowly in the direction of my cab. I walked alongside him. The evening air was filled with the ocean. "Trying to get a bead on things? Contribute in some way, so you don't completely lose control?"

"I am."

"Don't. It won't make any difference, and it might irritate me. But I will say this. I knew, I absolutely knew, that some kind of problem was going to crop up, some kind of thing I had to solve before I could get to the next phase of my existence. I find it fitting that it came in the form of you, the very first person I met outside of the airport. Let me ask you a question, my new friend. Exactly why the fuck do you even live in LA? This place sucks."

I shrugged. "It's home. And I thought you said you love LA."

"That's a piss-poor excuse for an answer, and don't feed me my own fiction. I watched you sitting there brooding all night, and I thought that maybe you were wondering. But no. Jose Ramirez—armchair philosopher, cab driver, dipshit. Why did you shut our bellhop slash actor kid down like that?"

"He was acting."

Knottspeed chuckled and jetted smoke. "Don't be so harsh, amigo."

"Exactly what does he want from you?" I asked.

"Same shit they always do. Give me their head shot, try to turn me into a pimp. He's about to come in handy, so the next time you see him, why don't you mind your fucking manners."

We got into the cab. This time Knottspeed rode in front, next to me.

"Where to?" I glanced over at him. He stared out at the restaurant, which had powered down to running lights. It was getting late.

"Compton. The night is young."

19

Horn Cannon

IT WAS HARD TO BELIEVE, but Knottspeed did, in fact, have a long-term memory under all the scar tissue on his head. I witnessed it in action when he dialed a number without looking at a piece of paper or insisting that someone find it for him. Whoever it was answered on the first ring.

"It's me. I'm back. Let's hook up, but not in a sexual way because you're gross and your ass is too round and you'd just bounce off of me again." Pause. "Yes, yes. Of course you are. If we had a baby, it would be like you giving birth to a taco. Speaking of which, my ride is a real live Mexican, so don't shoot him. This is sort of a cash transaction." Pause. "No dummy. I said don't shoot him. Jesus Christ, what the hell have you been drinking?" Pause. "Save me some." Pause. Knottspeed turned to me. "ETA?"

"Fifteen," I said. Traffic was light.

"Twenty minutes," he said. Pause. "No. He'll stay in the cab." Pause. "Because he's the cab driver." Knottspeed rolled his eyes. "I'll tell you in person." He hung up.

"What are we doing?" It didn't sound good at all.

"Going to meet a friend of mine. She's fantastic. Artist, mostly graffiti, but some acrylic on cardboard. Radical departure

219

on the violin as well, and even her mother can't guess where that came from—or where she got the violins, for that matter. I do know where she got one of them, anyway. That's how we met. She's the finest burglar I've ever known, really otherworldly. She's also, unfortunately, kind of bipolar. Maybe just psycho . . . I dunno. But stay in the car."

"How, uh, exactly how do you know this person? A stolen violin?"

"None of your fucking business, but I'll tell you anyway. She robbed a guy, he hired me, I wound up siding with her. She needed the violin—like *need* need, like birds need air. He didn't. He played it on Sundays in his study, bad little Kleenex riffs of Chopin. She could use it to tear a black hole in space. We had a really, really sordid relationship in the aftermath, but it didn't work out. But we did become friends."

"She robbed you? Or the violin guy?"

"Oh yeah, both of us. It's what she does for a living. She and her . . . friends."

"Why did you pause?"

He was silent for a long moment. "She doesn't really have friends. Some people are just that way. And what the fuck do you not get about the no questions part of our deal?"

I followed his directions as soon as we hit the edge of the war grounds, where blacks and Mexicans clashed over real estate. The Mexicans were winning, as we do when we aren't busy killing each other. Knottspeed directed me to a street I would have never driven down, a street lined with black houses filled with heavily armed black people who were mostly asleep. A lone woman stood under the lone streetlight. She was, of course, black, with braided cornrows, and she was wearing boots, black jeans, and a black T-shirt. She looked very young and very dangerous. Knottspeed whacked me lightly on the shoulder with the back of his hand at the end of the street, about five houses down from her.

"Just hang back right here," he instructed. "There's a chance she'll attack me. I'd say an even chance. If she does, and now that I think about it, she probably will, don't freak out and do anything stupid. Just hold your position. If everything goes completely to hell, then blow and leave me here."

"That was my plan," I confessed.

"Traitor," he said, disgusted. "We'll make something out of you yet, vato. I perceive that common sense may have finally released you rather than digging in deeper. You might escape after all." When I had no reply, Knottspeed got out and started walking.

It was hard to imagine what Knottspeed walked like when his spine wasn't healing from some kind of injury, when his body was free of scabs and bruises. Even with a cane, he looked like an elegant scarecrow, tapping along smartly with a slow and sinister grace. I anticipated total disaster, and my hand hovered over the ignition. His arrogant strut was sure to provoke a bad reaction, and maybe that was his intention. I'll never be sure. If it was, it worked.

Knottspeed stopped under the streetlamp a few paces from her. She cocked her head and spat some invective at him. He laughed. A knife appeared in her hand and she took a slashing swipe at him, tagging his hand. There was a bright spray of blood, and then his cane whistled up into the side of her neck. They crashed into each other and fell, and then both were still. I didn't start the engine, and I didn't go help either. I just sat there, frozen by the sudden violence.

Knottspeed eventually sat up. He took a handkerchief out of his suit coat and wrapped it around his hand. She sat up and rubbed the back of her head and then said something that made both of them laugh. She scuttled over to him in a slow crab, and he held his hand out for her to examine. She sniffed it. Then he rubbed the top of her head with his good hand and she passed him his cane. They rose and, arm in arm, went into the nearest house.

Over an hour passed. When Knottspeed finally emerged, he was wobbling dangerously, and so was she. They were both finally drunk, it appeared. Under the streetlight, he examined the top of her head one last time. There was something passing between them then, a type of sibling affection. It would have been sweet in a totally different context, with totally different people, on a completely different night, far away, somewhere else, and with another kind of witness. They actually hugged, which was truly scary. Knottspeed made for the cab, all grace lost. Behind him, the young psychopath staggered back into what I hoped was her house. Seconds later, Knottspeed managed to get the cab door open, the back this time, and fell headlong across the seat on top of his cane.

"Let's get the fuck out of here," he managed, "before she changes my mind again."

I started the engine and did a tight three-point turn. Behind me Knottspeed groaned. For the thousandth time, I looked at my watch. It was almost four in the morning.

"I think I learned something important, driver," he continued. "Moonshine and whatever else I was drinking tonight makes you hurt all over. Have you ever freebased Drano?"

"The hotel?" It came out as a prayer.

"Yep. No choice. The rest of my miniature race war will have to wait."

I couldn't speak.

"Turn the radio down," he slurred. "I can't stand mariachi music, especially at this hour. You should see the inside of my head. I think it's on fire."

The radio wasn't on. Abruptly, he struggled into an upright position and lit a cigarette. His hair was once again a crazy mess, but the blood from his hand had amazingly missed his suit, at least from what I could see. He briefly studied his hand in the strobe of the passing lights, squinting through one slitted eye.

"That gianna cut my hand open pretty good," he observed, "but her stitch work is decent, even if it is dental floss. Most of the blood missed my new suit, in case you were wondering."

"I was. You should do something about your hair before we get to the hotel." He smelled like the woman's perfume, a mix of cocoa butter and rose water.

222

"Up yours." He smoothed it back as best he could, the cigarette dangling between his lips. I knew I wasn't supposed to ask
questions, but I decided to anyway.

"What the fuck was that about?"

"Well," he began slowly, drawing that single word out for
as long as he could, "it's about the complex art of social judo,
if you must know. In situations like this, you want to use preex-
isting momentum as much as possible. Those crazy women are
worse than your little what's his name, and they'll certainly find
a creative use for whatever they yank out of this score. The cash
is mine."

"I see."

"You almost certainly do not," he replied. "But if you shut
up for long enough, you might."

I zipped it.

"I know you've never had a dream, Jose. You know why?
A dream is different than a goal, or even an agenda, and the
word 'dream' has been misappropriated in general. In this
context, I mean a dream that is the product of both a goal
and an agenda. Not something like riding a unicorn. Something more like fashioning a monohorn, building a cannon for
it, finding a white horse, stealing it, and shooting it in the head.
Following me?"

"Well, see——"

"You aren't," he interrupted dismissively. "I know you aren't.
Don't even bother trying to lie your way out of it, either."

"Fuck you," I said. It was like he didn't hear me.

"The world needs people like me because of people like you,
dildo. You made me. I sometimes wonder what I'd be, what the
fuck I would actually look like, if people had imagination. If the
concept itself were universally assigned. You know what I would
do if I had four kids and one of them had a monster behind
her? I don't either. But for now, for right now, you're borrowing
a part of me that I'm sick of lending out. Because people never
give it back, for one thing. So pretty soon we'll see what you

would do, because I'm going to do it for you. And this is the last fucking time too. I'm sick of this shit."

That gave me pause.

"This is exactly why the government rapes everyone, why people shop at Walmart, and I'm absolutely certain it's responsible for obesity itself. Don't get me wrong. The reason I'm doing this isn't for you, or for me. I can't help myself any more than you can, apparently, but at least I have a dream." He shook his head. "A real fucking dream. For myself. Pitiful shitheads like you just gave me something to practice on so it could even be possible."

We were both silent for the rest of the drive. When we finally pulled up in front of the hotel, I turned back to him. He was on his third cigarette, his ten-mile stare fixed in place.

"You're a mean drunk," I stated.

"Meet me here at noon." Still disgusted.

"And then what?" I watched his eyes in the mirror. He never even looked at me. Instead, he shot his cigarette out into the gutter and opened the door.

"Then I keep going." And then, almost as an after-thought, he asked, "Has Ignacio Medrano ever seen you?"

"Medrano? Never."

There was a little blood in Knottspeed's teeth when he grinned.

"How could I have guessed." He got out and slammed the door.

20

The Bright Red Undomestication

I WAS TIRED WHEN I pulled up in front of the hotel ten minutes before noon, and it was potently irritating to find Knottspeed lounging out front wearing the black suit, looking fresh and well rested, drinking coffee from a paper cup, and shooting the shit with Carl the bellhop/actor. Carl waved at me cheerfully. I forced a smile and waved back. Knottspeed ambled over to the cab and got in the back, lighter on his cane by the day.

"Got a number for me?" he asked brightly. I handed back an envelope.

"Two phone numbers and an address. And the photo of my daughter."

"Fucking excellent. Your boys out of the way?"

"I sent them all to my mother's to paint the house. They know something's up, but only Raul knows about Medrano. I told them Laura was at her friend Mari's and that she was going to be doing some night work at dispatch."

"Good." Knottspeed looked out the window. "Good."

"Where to?" I couldn't keep the irritation out of my voice.

He sighed. "Don't be pissed at me. That little cuckoo bird almost cut my hand off. And she made me drink that horrible moonshine, which tasted like creamed corn mixed with solvents. I'm still burping it up. Did I charge you extra for that? No. Am I being mean about it? Of course I am. I mean, last night was just nasty. But—"

It was my turn to sigh, which made him stop talking. For a moment.

"Back to the taco stand," he continued. "I have to get this horrible corn polish out of my mouth. And then . . ."

I glanced in the rearview.

"And then back to the place where I got my suits. Let's bring the dickhead a few tacos too. Pork?"

I drove.

The same guy was at the desk at Aldercamp's Haberdashery reading the *New York Times* and sipping a latte. He turned scarlet in one heartbeat when we came through the door. Knottspeed crashed down into the same chair as last time. I walked over to the desk and dropped a greasy bag of four pastor tacos on it.

Knottspeed produced the Anderson credit card. "We need a suit for my man Carlo here. Sinister, not banker. Shoes, socks, belt, a red tie, a cool watch, and some cologne, because he smells like my cigarettes."

I glanced at Knottspeed as though he had finally gone truly mad and lost sight of his plan. His gaze remained fixed on turtle egg.

"Do you need it . . . fast?"

"You can eat your lunch after we leave," Knottspeed said firmly.

Fifteen minutes later, I emerged from Aldercamp's in a black suit with a red tie, some kind of fancy watch, buffed wing tips, the whole nine yards. I was the best-dressed cab driver in all of LA, and I knew it. As I shot my cuffs and adjusted my tie in front of the place, I began to perceive where some of Knottspeed's power came from. Naked, he would certainly still be formidable, but that suit, it made me feel great.

"Sharp," Knottspeed said. He'd picked up a black bowler hat with a little red feather for himself. We studied our reflections in the Aldercamp's window. We looked like successful criminals.

"We're going to set up an appointment with Medrano, aren't we." It wasn't a question.

"As soon as we get another disposable phone."

"7-Eleven right around the corner."

Knottspeed adjusted the brim of his hat and put his sunglasses on. I put on my new shades too.

"Let's roll." He fired up a smoke. "Tacos erased the corn, so let's get some beer and a soda."

I grimaced at my new, empowered reflection. Maybe I'd get something more like Perrier. We got in the cab, and this time Knottspeed rode in front again. He lit a cigarette and snapped the lighter closed. He was even considerate enough to roll the window down a little. I left mine up to catch the AC.

"So what do I tell him?"

Knottspeed considered. "What he wants to hear. You're a friend. You want to see him. Et cetera."

"And that will actually work?" It didn't sound like it. He shrugged.

"Course it will. If you're a cop, he has to find out if you're the beginning of some kind of hassle. If you're a rival, he needs to know how big you are. If you have cash, he'll want it."

I glanced over at him.

"So am I a cop, a rival, or a customer?"

Knottspeed remained silent.

21

Medrano Igni

AFTER WE PICKED UP ANOTHER phone at 7-Eleven, Knottspeed gave me a pep talk. It was predictably unusual, but it unfortunately made sense at the same time. It was more than slightly abrasive, for which he apologized even before he began.

"I'm sorry for what I'm about to say, but it's true, so we'll just have to move past it. Agreed?"

We were standing out in front of the store, Knottspeed smoking furiously and drinking beer out of a Big Gulp cup and me sipping the Perrier that was in keeping with my costume. I gave him the fierce glare that came with the suit, but it was, of course, lost on him.

"Mexicans all have one thing in common when it comes to drug deals. Racist? No. Fact. I'll toss in some Asians to reduce the blunt force trauma. The reason the cartels exist is the same reason the triads do and why so few of them wind up where lesser versions of the same game cool their jets. It's stone-cold, deep-rooted paranoia. The reason I point this out to you is because it's a continuation of the lecture I gave you last night. You're not paranoid enough to make a decent criminal, Jose, much less a Mexican one. That's why you're in this mess."

229

I scowled. He took a deep drag and continued, on a roll now that I was irritated again.

"I can see that you understand. That's good. Now in order to think like Medrano, at least for the time being, I want you to alter the parameters of your otherwise bland and nondynamic personality. This is no time to be a thoughtful cabbie, roaming the streets and listening to the radio and wondering why gravity makes rain, you fucking dummy. No. That's over for now. Right now, I need you to be pushy. Manipulative. Calculating. Guess where he's going and then guess again. Anticipate every problem as far in advance as possible and then multiply it by five. Imagine yourself as the head of a small empire that could be decapitated with a single well-directed sneeze or that you're playing chess with a drunk Russian who has a grenade, and you can't tell if you're supposed to win or lose—or if you can even do either—because the rules change with every move. But at the same time, never for an instant give the slightest hint of capitulation or even thoughtful consideration, for that matter, because that brings us right back to the cartel and triad psychology. They just don't do that."

He paused to sip. I sucked in my gut a little. He noticed my posture and nodded.

"All right then. Call that little scumbag, and let's get this show on the road. We got something for free, just giving it away. We're from Seattle—that's in Washington."

"How did we get his name?"

"From Ortiz."

"Who's Ortiz?"

Knottspeed shrugged. "If he probes too deep, get pushy, then paranoid." He shook his head in disgust. "Just follow the drill."

I took the paper out and dialed. It went straight to voice mail. "Medrano. You know what to do." Beep.

"Medrano. I am Señor Nochezo. Ortiz sent me your way. *The* Ortiz. Call me now, or I call the next number on this list." And then I hung up. I turned to Knottspeed, who looked at his watch.

"And . . ." He held up a finger and then put his hand down. The phone rang.

"Hola," I answered.

"Who the fuck is this?" A woman.

"Who the fuck is asking?" I shot back.

"You got the wrong number, esse." She sounded high, irritated, and young. She was also chewing gum.

"No, I don't." Knottspeed was listening, head cocked. He could hear everything she said because she was obnoxiously loud. He mouthed the words "hang up." I did. "Now what?"

Knottspeed dropped his cigarette and ground his foot over it. "Now we go to his house. He's going to call in a few minutes. Freak the fuck out of him if we're right outside."

"Huh." We walked over to the cab. "What if my daughter's there?"

"By the time it matters, she won't be."

Too smooth. That's when it hit me—Knottspeed was making a lot of things up as he went along. He didn't seem concerned at all, which made me far more nervous than I already was. I realized I was actually his hostage in more ways than one. It was the only way it could be, and it had started the moment he'd been wheeled up to my cab.

22

Kleptorubicon Rojo

MEDRANO CALLED WHEN WE were still five minutes from his house.

"Speak," I answered, following Knottspeed's instructions.

"Ortiz. Yo, I'm calling for Ortiz." Medrano sounded like he smoked too much, like his hair was slicked back, like he had a suit on and was sipping expensive booze with a snake in his lap. I scowled.

"He's in fucking D Block," I growled, following the script. "He sends a gift. Or I send it with his blessing. Or I have a gift for you. Whatever."

"Naw, man. I don't need no 'gifts.' They always bad." There was a rustle.

"I'm in town for one day," I continued. "I'm here on business, but my meeting didn't go well. Ortiz, he tells me things. So we're back to the gift."

It could only be drugs. I could almost hear him thinking. I finished the rest of Knottspeed's drama, after which I was going solo improv.

"I'm from up north. Cold as fuck. Snows all the fucking time, esse."

"I got that," Medrano replied. "Too much snow is way fucked-up, man."

"S'why I'm here." Knottspeed had been listening in. He pointed at a shabby strip mall with a hair salon, a tattoo shop, a pet store, some kind of Korean mini-mart, and a pitiful burrito hovel called Muchachos.

"I'm at a place called Muchachos. Drinking, not eating."

"You alone? No chica?"

"I brought my pet white guy. He's all beat to shit, and he was dumb to begin with." Knottspeed nodded approvingly. "I'll be here for as long as it takes me to drink a couple beers."

"Enjoy." He hung up. I turned to Knottspeed.

"Now what?"

"We drink beer," he said cheerfully. "I act stupid. You set yourself up to get ripped off."

"I . . . what the fuck kind of plan is that?" I pulled into the parking lot.

"You feel confused and paranoid? More than a little desperate?"

"Yes," I said evenly.

Knottspeed clapped me on the shoulder. "The kind of plan that's working perfectly. Just stay with your current vibe."

"Christ," I snarled. He got out and started toward Muchachos. With a final curse, I followed. He gave me one final, sorrowful smile before he took his sunglasses off and visibly shifted into character. In an instant, the irritatingly bright luminosity, the grating self-assuredness, the cursed centrism, even the deplorably smug cheer—all of it left him. In its place was a pale Swiss toy with dead eyes and terrible injuries, motivated by plague, and sworn to the lunatic machinery of damnation. The thing he had become opened the door for me, and I almost cringed as I passed.

"Beer," Knottspeed snapped, to no one in particular. There were four people seated at the booths that ringed the walls, one saggy waitress, and one fat, unsweaty cook peering through the window under the heat lamp. I scowled at all of them and sat down across from Knottspeed in the booth nearest the door. No one looked happy to see us.

234

The waitress reluctantly approached, clutching two menus. I regarded her without expression. Knottspeed hissed ever so softly, and she shuddered.

"Beer," I reiterated. "Now."

"Coors or Bud? We also have—"

"Coors," Knottspeed snapped. "Cold glasses."

"Keep the menus." I almost felt bad, but the place was the kind of dump where only chunky white people would eat, so the waitress was something of a hustler in my book. It evened out somewhere.

"Now what?" I was picking up Knottspeed's vibe, and it came out cold and toneless. He fixed his mask on me.

"They'll be here in less than twenty minutes—long enough to make us wonder if they're arranging the playing field out there, but not long enough to blow the possibility of a freebie."

"Irritating."

"Predictable. Kat gave me a sample bag last night. We pass it off and set up a big thing for later. I'll watch how everything goes and feed you your lines. It will look to them like I'm your advisor, which will be easy enough, since it's true."

"Irritating again."

"Keeping you guessing is part of the way this works, dumb ass. Your face, that ridiculous mustache, the whole picture . . . keep your sunglasses on, for God's sake. I'm using your talent for projection as part of this."

I looked at my hands. I wanted to punch him. Knottspeed was facing the door and the dirty windows, so I watched him. Our beers came, and he drank his. Then he drank mine. Then he ordered another round and kept drinking. I didn't notice any change in his expression when the door opened behind me. He didn't telegraph Medrano's entrance in any way, so I was almost surprised when he sat down next to me.

"FBI? Locals?" Medrano was shorter and slimmer than I expected. I looked at him and kept my face carefully disdainful, which was easy. He flicked me with his serpent stare and then locked his eyes on Knottspeed.

"No. You?" I shifted so I was facing him.

"Fuck this guy," Knottspeed whispered. Medrano's eyebrows went up and he laughed, an ugly, oily sound.

"The gringo thinks everyone is a Fed," I said. "He's never right. No one gives a shit about anything these days."

"So." Medrano turned to me. I had his full attention. "Why the fuck did you call me? And how the fuck did you get my number? And who is Ortiz?"

"Who are the five guys in the parking lot?" Knottspeed countered. "And why the fuck do you have some brainstem answering your digits? And why don't you know anyone and they all know you?" Knottspeed looked at me. "Small time. Look at the suit. Fuckin' kid just got out of juvie."

Medrano's hard eyes went junkyard dog. "Tell the white boy to shut up."

"Shut up," I said. Knottspeed sneered and held up his beer and snapped his fingers for attention. Behind him, the waitress responded with a doomed expression.

"Good," Medrano said. "Now, what? Why the fuck am I here? I'll tell you why I'm here. I want to know who the fuck you are. You're kinda in my hood, esse."

I didn't say anything. I just looked at him, watching Knottspeed out of the corner of my eye, waiting for a signal. Medrano looked back, bored.

"Lot of a certain kind of shipping up in Seattle. I'm in the import business. Chinese crap. Stuffed animals, psycho porn, crappy electronics. . . . Too much to get rid of, and my website is always down. So I set up a meet with a seriously greedy motherfucker here in LA. Hence the way my white boy looks. You get the picture."

"Shame he didn't get a different mouth out of the deal," Medrano said. "You were right about him being stupid."

"You have no idea."

The beers came. The waitress scurried away at speed. Medrano didn't touch his. I didn't touch mine. Knottspeed left his standing.

"So what? You want me to hook you up with some junk stand where they sell Chinagarbage? Who the fuck told you I do that? I sell cars, man. I thought you wanted a custom ride. LA style." He laughed and made a steering motion with his hands. "Vroom vroom."

Knottspeed cleared his throat. We both looked at him.

"The boss here won't let me do the talking," he began. "I'm going to get the fuck out of here and let you guys talk about whatever the hell he wants to talk about. I'll say hi to your boys for you."

Knottspeed slid out of the booth and grabbed up his cane. Medrano looked up at his skeletal face and shook his head.

"I wouldn't advise the lip," Medrano said. "My friends out there woke up grumpy. Too much at the dogfight; not enough rain."

When Medrano shifted back to me, Knottspeed tapped his watch and flashed me two fingers. Two minutes to make the criminal scumbag take the bait.

"Hard to hire good people these days," I said.

"I deal mostly with family. I sometimes like to employ the young and the poor." He said it easily, like he actually was doing something good.

"The corporate environment touches everything," I observed. "If you can't learn from the rich people at the top, the street just eats you alive. Nature of the zoo." The top of exactly what was open to interpretation. Medrano's reply was telling. I hated him for what he said then, more than I already did.

"Only better hustlers in the game than Medrano are fucking Walmart and the prison system." His smile had gold in the back.

"You're on the bright side, Medrano." What he'd said was true. It made me sick. It made him happy as a well-fed, three-eyed baby hippo, cavorting in the mud. I wanted to wash my hands. I wanted to pull his teeth out before I did.

"Only one way to age gracefully." His eyes narrowed. "So you were here on business, and it fell through. White boy has messy shit written all over him."

I took my sunglasses off. Knottspeed had prepped me perfectly. I was confused. I was desperate. I was out of my element to the point that I was a tourist in my own city, and now I was furious and filled with a desire to murder by gasoline.

"You ever dream about spiders?"

Medrano didn't reply, but his hard eyes went dirty broken glass and his fine nostrils flared, so I continued.

"I dream about them all night long. I talk to them, and all they ever tell me is lies and lies and bullshit about my only daughter."

"I dream about chickens," he said softly. "No heads. Jumping out of trash cans, just mad-level crazy."

"They have Band-Aids on 'em?"

"No," he whispered.

"We both need help, esse." Knottspeed would have been delighted. Medrano nodded, once.

"Call me tonight," I said. "Your kids have a sample. We'll work out a deal. Goes good, we roll month to month until one of us dies or gets greedy."

Medrano just stared at me, silent. Not even a nod.

We got out of the booth, and I tossed a fifty on the table to cover the beer. It wasn't my money, so I didn't wait for the change. We both put our shades on as we went out the door. Medrano's muscle waited in his ride; four hard-looking kids too young to grow facial hair but old enough to carry a gun. Knottspeed was nowhere to be seen.

"Tonight," I said.

Medrano looked me up and down and then got in the passenger side of the car. The stereo instantly rose to deafening, some kind of hip-hop kill kill. I watched as they drove away. A moment later, Knottspeed appeared at my side.

"I tossed the junk bag in the car," he said. "Waited in the pet store. You?"

"I talked about spiders. He has dreams about headless chickens and trash cans."

We thought about that. Or at least I did.

"We both played our parts like we were made for them," he said. "Which we were. I'm going to miss that part."

23

Gun Fighting in the Cemetery

"I WOULD TOTALLY REDO MY reel if I could use this as footage," the bellhop/actor Carl Crogan droned. He'd been talking nonstop for over an hour. Knottspeed was lost in his own dimension, staring out the window, gone to that place he went to, leaving me alone with Carl. "Real life, I mean really real, it just never happens! How the hell am I ever supposed to—"

The phone rang. The 7-Eleven burner.

Carl gasped. I sat up straighter and looked at Knottspeed. Knottspeed looked at the phone. It rang again. And again.

"Answer," Knottspeed said. "You know what to say."

"Speak," I said into the phone.

Music, more of the interchangeable ghetto grind. Wind. Static. Then Medrano spoke.

"You know who it is, old man. I tested your computer for viruses. It's clean."

"Good," I replied. He liked Knottspeed's sample of China White. "How much you want for looking at it?"

"It has a seventy K click in the hard drive." I did the math. He wanted two kilos.

"Whatever. I'll send my boy over to look, then we can meet

241

after. He just wants to make sure about the seventy before I squeeze my fat ass into a car."

Medrano laughed. "Maybe you just cut back on the donuts, vato. Eat more pussy." Laughter in the background. "So where for the surprise inspection?"

"Your place, fifteen minutes."

Pause. "Okay," he said slowly. "How the fuck you know where I live?"

"Same way I know where I parked. I keep track of valuables."

"Role on up. Soft as shit, homie, see what I'm sayin'."

"I'm at my hotel. Sending the white boy."

"Not the white white boy, one with the mouth. Him I see—"

"Different one. He can count as long as he isn't talking. Fifteen." I hung up. Knottspeed looked at Carl and nodded encouragingly.

"Break a leg," he said. Carl nodded, excited. Then he squared his shoulders and firmed into character. A method man.

"Right, boss." Not bad. He nodded, grim, and we watched him go. When the door closed, I turned to Knottspeed, who sat down in Carl's chair.

"Hope he lives," I said. Knottspeed nodded and lit a cigarette.

"I give him better than a sixty percent chance. He's going in with no money and no drugs. They don't have any reason to spring their trap just yet. This is really good for him. Dreamy."

"Hmm. So how, uh . . . why are you so sure they're going to rip us off?"

Knottspeed shrugged. "Common sense."

"And exactly how do we not get killed when they do this?"

"Because I have a plan, Jose. We had a deal about questions."

"We did, but this is actually super important, as in I need to know the odds. I mean, should I leave a note? Call my boys, in case we don't make it?"

Knottspeed gave me a long stare and then looked at his cigarette. He could have been tired, but with him it was impossible to tell. He did seem pensive in some way, like he was about to eat somewhere he'd been too many times, or he was getting ready to see a movie he'd seen before on a plane. He sighed.

"Jose, this is sort of the end of a long, strange game for me here, and it's longer and bigger and infinitely more complicated than you know. Years in the making. It almost seems like a simulation at this point."

"Far from encouraging." I couldn't help but be honest.

"I imagine so. Look. I have lots of scars, as you can see. I've even been recently wounded. So you have every right to be skeptical about your personal well-being in the immediate future. I mouthed off to the skuzzwad to draw his fire if it comes down to that, so that gives you an extra few seconds. But all I can guarantee is that within six hours, Medrano will meet the fate I've designed for him. And I'll meet the one that is the consequence of my existence. No matter how it turns out for you, your daughter will be safe, at least for the moment. Medrano will be occupied with something so strange, he won't even notice she's gone. And when that's done, I'll be gone, and you'll never see me again."

"So why won't you tell me what's about to happen?" I didn't like the finality in his voice. If he was having some kind of premonition, I wanted to hear it. He shook his head.

"You might blow it. Everything you need to know is in your head right now. As shitty as it is, you just have to trust me."

I'd quit smoking twenty-three years ago. I silently took his pack of cigarettes off the table and tapped one out. Menthol. I put it between my lips and looked at Knottspeed.

He lit it for me.

———————

The 7-Eleven burner phone rang at 9:31. Knottspeed looked at it and then looked at me. It was a bad sign. Carl was supposed to call one of Knottspeed's other phones. I picked it up and clicked the green button.

"Where the fuck is my white boy," I growled. Medrano laughed. Knottspeed could hear it, and his eyes narrowed.

"He's right here," Medrano said. "You want to talk to him?"

"I want him standing in front of me in twenty minutes, or I'm calling someone else," I improvised. "And you know who I'm calling, Medrano. Your competition. So that represents a power shift in your little business community." Knottspeed nodded and made a stabbing motion, then cut his throat with his index finger. "So kill the messenger. I'll make sure the word gets out that you're still a small-time nobody with lint in his pockets and shit for brains." I hung up. Knottspeed was aghast.

"What the fuck are you doing?" he demanded.

"Interpreting your fucking sign language!" I shot back. He smacked his forehead.

"Jesus. One actor down. Poor Carl, kid just wanted some life experience. Why the hell would you—"

"Stop!" I leveled my finger at his face. "This is your fault! What in the world were you thinking with all the paranoid bullshit and the 'act crazy' speech and the stabbing thing! The neck thing! And why did you even bother—"

One of the other phones rang. Knottspeed whipped it out of his pocket, looked at the number, and then visibly relaxed. "Thank God, he's still alive. Jesus, Jose." And then he smirked at me and blew me a kiss. I threw up my hands.

"What up, dog," he answered, holding the phone a little ways from his ear so I could hear.

"Holy shit that was intense!" Carl shouted. "Holy shit! Holy shit!"

"Easy," Knottspeed said. "Calm down, man. Are you in your car, driving away?"

"Yes! I got away! Holy shit! They told me to roll, and I am way fucking rolling!"

"You're almost certainly being followed," Knottspeed said calmly. "Get on the freeway and head north. Stay in the slow lane. Try to find out who's trailing you, but don't lose them. I repeat, do not lose them."

"What th—are . . . are you serious?" He sounded terrified.

"I am serious," Knottspeed said. "Don't worry, it's all part of the plan. Now, what did you see? Tell me everything."

"Jesus. Ten guys, maybe twelve. Lots of guns. Three or four chicks, one of 'em from the picture you showed me. Place is a dump. I mean, expensive furniture, but it's messy in a nasty trash kind of way. There was a dog and—"

"Did they have the money?"

"Oh yeah. They had lots of money. The main guy, what's-his-name, didn't let me count it, but they had an actual briefcase full of money."

"How much? Just guess."

"I don't have any fucking idea how to guess how much! I mean, okay, more than a little bit. Like, a lot."

"Like seventy thousand? A thousand bucks in hundreds is about half as thick as your pinkie. It's thin."

"Naw, looked like mostly twenties. Twenties."

"About as thick as your thumb, maybe thicker if they were old."

"Shit. Shit. It filled up a briefcase. Standard briefcase, you know the kind. The bills were old . . . I don't know. A lot."

"Just a sec." Knottspeed covered the phone.

"It's on. They probably have less than fifty grand rounded up, so they actually have to rip us off now. They have to give that money back to whoever loaned it to them, with interest."

"You did this on purpose," I exclaimed. "This whole last-minute shit!"

"Of course I did," he snapped. "If we gave them an entire twenty-four hours, they might have actually come up with the whole thing, Jose! Fucking pay attention. Christ. Messy means they've been in there holed up since we first called them. They're clumped together, so now we drain the pad."

"You dick. You—"

"Whatever, man. Everyone who works for Medrano is going to be seriously busy in just a few minutes." He took his hand off the phone.

"Carl? Yeah. You see a tail?"

"Weird news, man!" Carl sounded frantic. "I can't tell. Two cars back there. I . . . I . . ." he stammered and trailed away.

"Carl, get the fuck back into character. Now!"

"Looks loose back there, boss. Got a couple lane drifters, nothing too hot. I'm gonna slow lane granny the fuck out of 'em an' see what stands out." He sounded smooth and collected.

"That's my boy," Knottspeed said encouragingly. "Method, baby, method. Keep it real. You win an Academy Award, you remember me and Jose." He hung up. "Medrano should call any second. Give your inner child some cough syrup and snap out of it, Jose."

Knottspeed started putting things into his pockets, getting ready to leave. I smashed my cigarette out, and as I drew my hand away from the ashtray the burner rang. Medrano.

"We're good," I said. "I want to get back north tonight, so tell me where. When is a half hour."

"Warehouse off of Ronelle, 66112, close to the restaurant where we had those beers, right by the canal. You know it?" he asked.

Knottspeed nodded.

"I'll find it. Thirty."

"Come alone, and pull all the way around back," he said. "I don't want any kind of amateur hour, so you keep it cool, homie."

I laughed. "Right. I'm bringing the mouthy white guy. Can't leave him alone or he'll eat his tail. You keep your guy in your ride. And heads up, I roll the opposite of flashy. Cops are paid to never look at cabs."

"And we all set the tone for a bright future, right here, right now." Medrano sounded confident, and I knew right then that everything Knottspeed had said was true—about the paranoia, the pushing, the guess and guess again. There was no way Medrano would be so confident if he wasn't planning something terrible.

"Deal," I whispered. I hung up. Knottspeed stood and leaned on his cane. He put his sunglasses on.

"See?"

I stood. "I see."

"Then let's go."

On the drive over, neither of us said a word. Knottspeed stared out the window, dreaming again, calm. I clutched the wheel, my heart pounding, sweat boiling out of my armpits, trying to control my breath. We wheeled into the empty parking lot of the warehouse and pulled slowly around the back. The rear parking lot was just as empty, except for the car at the far end by the fence. Medrano stood in the dark center of the half acre of asphalt, holding a briefcase. I stopped. Knottspeed took out a phone I hadn't seen him use and hit a preloaded number. It rang once and clicked.

"Now," he said and then hung up. Nothing happened. He turned to me.

"I'll get the two kilos of baking powder out of the trunk. When I have them, we'll walk slowly to Medrano. His boys are all hiding in the canal over on the other side of that fence, so keep your hands away from your body."

I swallowed.

Knottspeed got out and walked around to the back, and I popped the trunk. A moment later, he closed it and walked down my side of the car. He opened my door for me, and I got out and stood next to him and straightened my tie. We started walking. Medrano slowly held his own arms out as we approached.

"We're going to die," I whispered.

"Maybe," Knottspeed breathed back. "Maybe not."

We stopped four feet away from the drug-dealing killer who had my daughter. This close, I could see his handsome grin. His eyes sparkled wetly. So did his hair.

"My friends," Medrano purred quietly.

"Medrano," I replied. "Where's your other guy?"

Medrano tossed his head at his ride. "Back in the car. Just chillin'."

"Good. Money?"

Medrano held out the briefcase, his smile never wavering. Beside me, Knottspeed slowly coiled and shifted. He put the paper bag with the two kilos down and stepped back. I followed his lead. Two steps back, he stopped and turned to me.

"Briefcase?" Knottspeed asked. I nodded.

Knottspeed raised his hands and slowly walked to Medrano. Medrano carefully skirted around him to position himself over the bag and then picked the bag up at the same instant he let go of the briefcase.

"Smooth," Knottspeed said. "Now we count—you test."

Knottspeed rejoined me and handed me the case. I set it down in front of me, squatted, and opened it. Just as he'd predicted, it was full of cash, random bills, which would take longer to count than it would take to get a reaction in the chemical test vial Medrano was using to check for purity. We had about two minutes. Right then is when it started.

My phone rang. My phone. My actual cell. I looked at Knottspeed, who looked concerned. He nodded that I should answer it. Medrano looked up from his delicate vial, paused in shaking it. I answered.

"Papa?" It was Laura, my daughter.

"Baby? Is that you?" A terrible fear, much more powerful than what I already felt, raced through me. I caught my breath.

"Papa, I'm in trouble!" She was crying. "I was at my friend's house, and these people took me, Papa! I'm in the trunk of a car! You have to he—" The line went dead. The phone fell from my hand.

"They have my daughter," I whispered. Then I screamed. "They have my daughter!"

"Easy, señor," Knottspeed whispered, clutching my arm. "She's safe. I needed you to scream convincingly so that—"

Medrano's phone rang. His eyes were wide, and he was backing away with the heroin, still shaking the vial. His backup guy got out of the car. Medrano answered, listened for a second, and then howled in rage.

"Everyone back to the crib!" he bellowed. "I'm getting robbed! Everyone back!"

Medrano started running back to his car. Knottspeed still had my arm. He dragged me with one hand and kept ahold of the briefcase with the other, cane forgotten behind us.

"Laura," I gasped.

"Kat has her," Knottspeed managed. "She's fine, so hurry the fuck up! We have to get the fuck out of here before—"

The first bullet hit Knottspeed just above the knee. He staggered, and I grabbed on to him and dragged him in a half lurching run. The second bullet went right through his side and blew blood all over me. He screamed, and behind us the headlights to Medrano's ride flicked on. A third and fourth bullet either hit Knottspeed or kept going, I couldn't tell, but he spasmed each time. We got to the cab, and I tore the door open and crashed into the driver seat, pulling Knottspeed across my lap. A bullet hit the top of the cab as I hit the gas in reverse and fishtailed wildly. Men were running out of the canal, shouting. Medrano was waving his gun, shouting too. It was chaos. I rounded the corner of the warehouse in reverse and slewed around, rammed it in drive, and peeled out. When we hit the street, I gunned it into the light traffic and tried to keep my heart from bursting. Knottspeed moaned and tried to sit up. I reached over and pushed his legs off onto the floorboards on the passenger side, and he righted himself the rest of the way.

"Okay," he managed.

"You're okay?" I almost screamed.

"No, Jose. No."

He pressed his hand into his side and coughed. It sounded ragged, awful. He gasped.

"Cigarette," he choked.

I grabbed a stray pack off the dash and stabbed in the car's lighter. My hands were shaking so badly, I could barely light the tip after the red knob popped. I passed it to him, and he took it with a scarlet hand.

"Top pocket," he said quietly. "My suit. Paper."

"Take it out?"

He nodded.

I reached over and patted his thin chest, found the paper in the breast pocket, and took it out, unfolding it with fingers that barely worked. It was an address in East LA, not far from where we were.

"Go there," he bubbled. "Nurse."

"A nurse! You need a hospital!"

"Fugitive," he breathed and then hissed. "Maria." His hand fell from his side. His white face was splattered with blood; there was blood everywhere. I couldn't hear any sound from him. No moan. No shuddering breath. No breathing. He was still clutching the briefcase, the prize he somehow couldn't let go of, even then.

24

One Petal, Ancient Flower Hurts the Autumn

I STOPPED IN FRONT OF the tiny house on Pennelton Street. The light was off on the deep porch, and the well-tended garden in the front was black and sculpted by shadow and the past. A light was on inside, just in one window. It looked lonely, too tidy, but in the way an old woman worked at order, left wild just at the edges as a reminder of everything in all the wide world.

I looked over at my still and grizzly package. The cigarette was still smoldering between his lips, stuck there like some horrific prank on a Halloween prop. I just looked at him, his skeletal features lit hard bluish-white in the streetlight, his face relaxed, splattered, finally tired at rest. I never knew where he came from or what he was really doing, why he knew so little and so much at the same time, what he'd been watching when he looked into that world he saw so often, the private one that consumed him. A raw feeling—a description of something sad and far into the distant cold of the unexpected—moved like music from my stomach into my throat, and a sob, a single jerk of alien sound, left me.

Knottspeed's eyes flicked open. He spit the cigarette out and turned to me.

"We better be there, Miguel," he rasped, just a whisper. "I lost my canoe, so you'll have to carry me. If you drop me in the water . . . I'll probably die." He tried to smile, and his face warped as a wave of pain rolled through him. He drew an uneven breath. "Better. Hurry."

"Unfuckingbelievable." I didn't know whether to hug him or punch him in one of his bullet holes. His head lolled to the side so his face was pointed at me. This time he did manage a smile and a tiny pucker, like he was blowing a kiss.

"How's my hair?" He mouthed the words with almost no breath behind them.

I got out and rushed around to the passenger side and lifted him out. Maybe it was the adrenaline, or maybe it was his dietary regime, but he weighed as much as a bag of cat food. I held him tight to my chest so he wouldn't slip; he was so slick with gore. He wouldn't let go of the briefcase, just pulled it over his chest and blinked in pain with all the movement. I ran up the steps and kicked at the door of the small house. The porch light turned on, and I heard feet approach. There was a pause as someone looked through the peephole. Knottspeed heard it too and waved, barely able to hold up his bandaged hand. He even managed a red smile.

The door opened. A stunningly beautiful young Mexican woman in a faded pink robe stood there, staring at Knottspeed, her expression wild. Her reaction was instant. She stripped Knottspeed from my arms and carried him inside. I followed, in shock.

"I'm sorry I didn't say good-bye. I was kind of in a hurry. But I did save the better half of a really good story for you." Knottspeed spoke softly.

"I knew you would," Maria replied. She laid him on her kitchen table and ripped his shirt back and applied pressure to his side. "Is your favorite part better than winter?"

"Trick question," he whispered. "You already know."

He reached up, and Maria braided the fingers of her free hand through his.

KNOTTSPEED

"He's been shot," I said. My hands and feet were cold and numb.

"It happens to him." She quickly began assessing the rest of his injuries. I looked away. The room was clean and bare like most of the house. There was an open book and a mug of something steaming by the sofa. She'd been reading. Maria quickly looked him over, clucking to herself. She ripped away the rest of his suit with a surprising strength born of desperation.

"Get towels from the bathroom," she instructed. "Quickly! And bring me my phone! Move!"

I ran into the bathroom and grabbed the towel off the rack and returned to her just as fast.

"Hold your hand over the wound on his side," she instructed. "When I take my hand away, you will replace it with yours without pause."

"Oh God," I managed. She took her hand away and instantly grabbed mine and pressed it over the bullet hole. I couldn't look. While she was ripping the towel up, she went quickly to the couch and got her phone.

"We'll switch," she instructed. "Bind the wound on his leg tight, then hold the rest on his side. Press hard so it seals the back." I did. She dialed with one hand.

"Tay Tay! Maria. I'm coming to your house." Tiny pause. "Yes. Tell Dr. Resner that I'm bringing him someone." Another tiny beat. "Knottspeed. I'm bringing him to the White Palace. He needs a doctor, and you know why we can't—" Beat. "Right." She hung up and turned to me. The leg was bound.

"Let's go. We'll ride in back." And she picked him up and swept through the door. I grabbed the briefcase and followed. Somehow it seemed important, after all we'd gone through to get it, after Knottspeed clutching it in what I had thought was his final moment. It was part of the giant plan, the one I didn't know the beginning of, or the end.

253

I drove without really thinking, on cab driver autopilot. My daughter was safe, though in the hands of a maniac who had slashed up the man in the backseat only last night and had presumably just robbed a midlevel drug dealer while his entire posse had been busy following our decoy, Carl the bellhop/actor, or shooting at us. The gunfire had been temporarily restrained by the confusion brought on by my screaming at my daughter's apparent abduction—well played on her part—the echoes of which were just fading as Medrano learned he was being robbed. For a moment, he'd thought whoever was doing it had hit us both. Brilliant. Or almost brilliant. I glanced into the back.

"How long?" Maria asked, seeing me turn.

"Not long." Traffic was light, and I knew all the backstreets. "How is he?"

"Terrible," she answered, exasperated. "He was injured when he arrived at Saint Francis. Dislocations in his knee, lower spine, shoulder, fractured skull, facial lacerations, two cracked ribs, broken hand, and that's just the start. The police said the car he was in was found underwater at the edge of—"

"I thought he fell off of a freeway overpass."

"Is that what he told you?"

"Yeah."

"Then that's what happened." She kept working. "Now he's managed to get even more mangled. Somehow he cut his hand, and it's stitched together with something that looks like dental floss—"

"It is dental floss," I offered. "The madwoman who did it has my daughter."

"You mean the woman who cut him, or the woman who rendered first aid?"

"Both. Same woman."

"I see. That was nice of her. I suppose."

Knottspeed groaned, and I realized he was regaining

consciousness right as I realized he'd lost it some minutes earlier.

"Where are we?" he mumbled.

"Do you know what day of the week it is, my darling?"

"One, or maybe four. Possibly B, or Y-6."

"The president?"

"John."

"Well, I'm glad you didn't hit your head again." She stroked his hair back. Knottspeed closed his eyes.

"I almost fell out of this tree." He took a breath. "That was a few nights back. I had an Indian with me. He's on a journey right now, looking for a piano. Feds'll never find him."

"Please, hold still Knottspeed. I can't have you wiggling so much."

I was surprised again. They were obviously in love, and she had called him Knottspeed. I'd thought his name was actually Anderson Smith. The name on the identity he'd manufactured for someone was, in truth, an identity he'd now stolen. Or borrowed. It was good that I didn't have to keep track of all of it.

"We robbed the guys who shot me," he said, as if reading my train of thought. "Might be why they were so pissed. I had to get this dipshit's daughter abducted and rescued at the same time, but I got us enough money now. For what we talked about. I tried to not get shot, Maria, I did, but . . . ahh."

"You've been shot only twice this time, you baby," she cooed.

"Twice?" we said together.

"One more bullet grazed the back of this skinny arm here," she said. "Doesn't count." She looked up at me and met my eyes in the mirror. "He's been shot before."

"Yeah, but it really hurts every fucking time," Knottspeed complained. "I just thought everyone should know."

"Then stop doing it," she said, trying to sound chiding about it. She was worried; I could hear it in her voice. If I could hear it, then Knottspeed most certainly could, but he seemed content enough to die right where he was. I somehow knew that he'd been hoping to get as far as he'd gotten at that moment, that the long periods when he'd been inside of himself had been dreams of where he was right at that instant. I'd never felt that way about a woman. I loved my children, but they were my flesh and blood. I'd never felt anything like that for anyone.

"We're . . . here?"

I looked back at Maria, uncertain. Even Knottspeed opened his eyes and widened them. We were in front of a white mansion with a white sports car in the driveway. The windows were ablaze with light reflected out of the white interior. A huge black man wearing bright-yellow Speedos stood in the doorway. He yelled something back into the house and sprinted to the cab.

"This is the right place," Maria said. There was something in the way she said the word "right."

The huge black man leaned in the back window. He was wearing purple eye shadow. He reached out one huge hand and laid it on Knottspeed's chest.

"Tay Tay," Knottspeed said weakly. "I brought you the money I owe you for that cab. I brought a cab too, so . . ."

"Knottspeed, you ignorant white fool," the black man scolded affectionately. "I told you like five times not to get shot again."

"I had a head injury. No memory of anything you said."

"Let's get you inside." The big man opened the door and lifted Knottspeed out of Maria's arms. I trailed them inside. I don't know why, really. My part in all of it was done, but for some reason I felt compelled to stay and see if he lived or died.

"He's touching my butt," Knottspeed whispered. "Pretty sure he's a homo."

"Shush," the big man said, hurrying.

Everything inside the enormous house was white. Bone on bleach on starch—white on white. It was appalling in almost every way, a lifeless place where seeds would forever remain seeds. A mousy bald man with glasses waited for us, dressed in a turquoise tracksuit that somehow made him look like a huge baby bird.

256

"Doctor," Maria said. "The patient."

"To begin with," Knottspeed began, "whoever your interior designer was needs to understand that—"

"Boy," Tay Tay scolded, "you zip it. An' I swear if you be drippin'—"

"In here," the doctor said.

We followed him into one of the many guest rooms. A shower curtain had been spread over the bed, and extra lamps were blazing. Tay Tay laid Knottspeed down, and the doctor looked at me.

"I'm Doctor Simon Resner. You?" Quick. Efficient.

"Jose Ramirez."

"Good. Please wait outside, Mr. Ramirez. Maria, scrub and glove. Clarence, get the big medical kit from the garage, and let's start with removing the clothes. I can already tell we're going to need a field transfusion, so let's compare blood types. And let's set the tray. I need all five of the—"

I closed the door as I left. I was panting. I walked slowly, dazed, not really seeing, through the spotless kitchen and into the dining room. There was a bar, so I poured myself a tumbler of something brown. I didn't recognize any of the labels, but it didn't really matter. I sipped without tasting. Maybe all the white around me had killed my taste buds. The homes of rich people had always scared me for some reason. They never seemed like the kinds of places where anyone should actually live—this place in particular. And I had just driven an extremely bloody fugitive up to the place, and the owner was performing emergency surgery on a shower curtain. I refilled my drink and went outside. There was a pool, surrounded by heavy white patio furniture. I sat down and stared at the shimmering water for somewhere between a minute and several hours, unable to find any train of thought at all. And I probably would have stayed that way forever, but my phone rang. I blinked and took it out of my suit coat, the suit that Knottspeed had bought as part of my disguise. The suit that had unshackled my napping, malnourished demons. I realized then that I was still wearing my sunglasses.

"Hola."

"Papa?" It was Raul. My son. My oldest boy. Raul, who would not wear his shoes until he was five years old.

"Sí, mi bebe."

"Papa, she's home. Laura is home. We're all home."

I sighed, suddenly tired, a kind of exhaustion that was totally foreign.

"Papa, Medrano—" Raul stopped. "Papa, what did you do? Where are you?"

"What do you mean, what did I do? I didn't do anything. Someone else did."

"Medrano is dead. He's dead, and so are most of his boys. The police are everywhere. The whole neighborhood is nothing but cop cars and helicopters."

"Are they . . . they aren't looking for black women, are they?"

"What? No! It's on the news. Medrano staged a robbery, like he robbed his own crib. Whatever was stashed there—and Laura says it was drugs and guns and money—it all belonged to someone else. They were pissed."

"I guess that happens," I said. I sipped. Dead. All the people who had been shooting at me were dead. If Knottspeed had been able to find out whom Medrano worked for, it would have taken a single phone call to light the fuse. Someone very smooth would have had to place that call, a sort of customer service king. The kind of person who was refined and elegant and used to secrets. Someone who could lie with as much authority as Knottspeed could. Someone like a concierge.

"Where are you, Popi? Is everything okay?"

I couldn't reply, because I didn't know. I couldn't remember anything of the actual streets that led to where I was sitting. The story hadn't ended, and if I were to tell it, I didn't know where to start, because I didn't know where it began.

"Boy," I said finally. "Boy, I had a long, long day. You could never guess where I'm sitting. Even what I'm wearing. Or what I'm drinking. Make something good to eat. Go water the garden. Moon water. I'll be home as soon as I get there."

The noise of the distant freeway was nothing more than a rain sound. I looked at the phone. A little after three in the morning. I had no idea what time we'd arrived, but I didn't feel like going in and asking anyone anything. I settled back in the lounge chair, and the tension in my back slowly moved into the cushions. I closed my eyes. The night breeze smelled like cooling roofing tar and lemon trees. The inside of my eyelids were streaked with afterimages, layered thick and jumbled and non-sensical. My heart slowed. My breathing grew regular.

Sometime later, the sliding door to my left opened and I started. Tay Tay and the doctor came out, both of them holding drinks and wearing different clothes. The doctor looked tired and had most of a suit on. The giant black man was wearing shorts, and there was a stunning white bandage on his arm, just at the elbow.

"How is he?" I asked, sitting up. They both sat down.

"A bullet struck his lower left side and passed through cleanly. I had to extract the one in his left leg. He's lost a lot of blood."

"Got it all back," Tay Tay said, glancing at his bandage. "Skinny little man is like a sponge. Thought I was gonna pass out."

"You still might," the doctor said. "Let's see what that drink does to you."

"I'm thinking the same thing." He drained his glass.

"So he will live." I didn't frame it as a question. I was not surprised. The doctor nodded.

"He will. He's been shot in the past, on more than one occasion. Clarence, what did you say he does for a living?"

"I don't fuckin' know. When he was at Saint Francis, the cops were asking that very same question."

They both looked at me. I shrugged.

"I just drive the cab."

"Jesus." The doctor drained his drink. He'd been full of confident authority when he was in his element, but now it was trickling away right before my eyes as he went from a man in charge, who knew exactly what he was doing and how to do it, to a man with a wildly eccentric gunshot victim/fugitive in his house, who was being attended by a strangely powerful and stunning Mexican woman, while the doctor sat drinking with an enormous, partially clad, and evidently gay black man and an impeccably dressed Mexican cab driver who was wearing sunglasses at night. I almost felt sorry for him.

"Refills," Tay Tay said. He didn't take our glasses, just went after the bottle.

"So how do you know Maria?" the doctor asked.

"I don't. Just Knottspeed."

"Knottspeed. He's . . . different than I thought he'd be."

"I don't know what you were expecting man, but nothing could prepare you for that dude."

"I guess not." The doctor shook his head, wistful. "Maria is special. Very special. I just can't, I mean . . . for one thing, he's so white. And he's a criminal of some kind. He has to be. And yet this saint of a woman is so clearly in love with him. The kind of love that makes you feel guilty to watch because it makes you feel shallow." He shook his head. "Makes you know it."

"Knottspeed is that way," I said. I had no idea why I was compelled to defend the man, but I was. "I can't understand him any more than I can fathom why cities are built or how anyone can play at sailing around the world."

"Hmm." The doctor looked up at the moon. After a while, "Were you there when he got shot? What was he doing?" He looked at me. It took a moment to answer, and when I did my words surprised me.

"He was saving me. My family. He loaned me his bravery, his insanity, his view of the peaks and valleys of wherever it is he lives—and he was generous, as you can see." I cleared my throat. "He was also helping an artist he knows, a young woman

260

who plays the violin in some gifted way. She cut his hand. And he was helping an actor find out something of his craft. He told me something about an Indian, and how they were both hiding, how they . . . escaped, I guess. More, probably. He was also setting up a monster, and he stole all of his money as part of a grand design. That was the part that cost him blood, not that he seems to care as much as most people about price tags when he's the one who's paying. He was standing between me and the bullets. Which is why this suit that he bought me looks better than his."

The doctor looked back up at the moon. "Now I understand." He sounded out of breath.

We sat like that for a moment. He looked up, and I watched the moon reflected in his eyes. I wondered what he was talking about, but I didn't ask. I just watched the light of the moon, caught there and bright, and that was enough.

"Found it," Tay Tay declared, emerging from inside. He held up a wine bottle. "The last of the white queen's white wine. Cost as much as a car, and worth about ten bucks."

"Let's drink," the doctor said, holding out his glass. I held mine out as well.

"Let's drink," I agreed. "It somehow seems fitting that we're about to finish off the last of a queen's hooch."

"It is," Tay Tay purred. "It is." He yanked the cork out and filled our glasses to the brim. I held mine up.

"To that motherfucker Knottspeed," I said.

"To Maria," the doctor added.

"To me," Tay Tay declared.

We drank, and then we finished off the bottle. Tay Tay went inside for a moment and then came back with a bottle of scotch and a huge platter of oysters. The doctor and I sipped and watched as he shucked them and passed them around. I was on my fifth oyster and feeling halfway ripped and better than I could remember feeling in years, when the sliding door opened and Maria emerged. I could tell instantly that Knottspeed was surviving, and that Tay Tay loved her and so did the doctor, each in his own way.

"He's finally resting," she said softly. "He talks."

"He does," Tay Tay agreed.

"And he just keeps on talking," I said. "I bet he talks in his sleep."

"So what now?" the doctor asked. Tay Tay filled his glass and handed it to Maria. She sipped without tasting.

"Knottspeed has amassed a small fortune. Some of it is with him, and some of it is hidden in various . . . places. He's wanted, now more than ever, so we have to find a way to get out of the country. I want to have a farm. Somewhere far from everything, but close to the ocean. Have children who play and sing and laugh like he does."

Tay Tay raised the bottle. "And they'll be like you, Maria, my dear friend. Put the two of you together, and . . ." He shook his head and drank. We all did.

"I can get you to the border," I offered. "From there, I don't know. Maybe a boat. A produce truck. I have a cousin in Nogales . . ."

"Maybe we can try to tap some longshoremen," Tay Tay mused. "Get you a hitch to France. I know some people."

"If anyone can find a way, it's Knottspeed," Maria said. She looked up at the moon just as the doctor had. He'd been watching her, and maybe he saw the reflection in her eyes as I had in his, glittering crescents of light from a distant object swimming through darkness all those incredible miles away, illuminating an eternal night with easy glory.

"I have an idea," the doctor said, rising. He held up one finger. "Just a moment."

The doctor went inside. We sat in silence. I drank and had another oyster. Maria looked into the distance, entranced by some vision in the same way Knottspeed had frequently been; I recognized the expression. Tay Tay looked almost asleep, as relaxed as I'd ever seen such a muscular person be. The night breeze had freshened with rosemary and eucalyptus dust. I closed my eyes and listened to the late and distant freeway, which was and always will be one of the loveliest of accidental musics.

When the doctor emerged, he was holding an envelope. He looked triumphant, alive, somehow different. He sat down across from Maria, then took the bottle from where it sat beside Tay Tay and took a healthy slug.

"That can't be what I think it is," Tay Tay said.

"It is," the doctor replied, "but it's value has . . . changed. It's something I was thinking about just the other day. It has poetry now. A new meaning."

"Figures," I said. I sat up a little. "What is it?"

"This," the doctor said glowingly, "is a present given to me that I didn't deserve. I didn't deserve it because it almost drove me mad, and no one deserves that. No one. It was sort of like a dowry for a nightmare, and now it isn't. Now it's clean. It's . . . remade. A different gift altogether."

"I'll be damned," Tay Tay whispered. "I think I'm gonna cry. Or laugh. I might throw up if I do either one."

The doctor held the envelope out to Maria. His hand was shaking. She looked at the white paper, dappled with shimmering fingers of pool lamp.

"Take it," he urged. "Take it and set us all free."

Maria took the envelope, opened it, and read. Tickets and a letter. She put them back in the envelope when she was done and rose and then gently kissed the doctor on the top of the head.

"Thank you," she whispered. He nodded, eyes bright with moon and water.

"No," he whispered back. "Thank you."

Maria exchanged a look with Tay Tay, who nodded and gave her a smile that seemed to come from his entire face. The big man leaned out and snatched the bottle out of the doctor's hand and clapped the smaller man on the back. Maria silently went back inside. The doctor and Tay Tay watched her go.

Then Tay Tay refilled our glasses. When my glass was finally empty, I realized the doctor was asleep, almost smiling as he rested, sleeping like a child.

"What was in the envelope?" I asked. Tay Tay looked at me and then glanced at the doctor. He spoke quietly.

"When Simon's wife left him, her new billionaire man gave him a present for letting him hit the gas on the divorce, for not making waves. In a lot of ways, it was the only thing the white queen ever gave him. And just like everything she ever touched, it didn't come from her at all. This white house with no children. Even Simon's job . . . he used to be a healer. And out of that entire curse, all he got was a private chartered jet ticket for two and a two-week stay at some rich people resort in Martinique."

"Huh."

Tay Tay looked at the doctor again. "Now look at him. Curse is broken."

"Another minor miracle."

"It sure is."

I don't know what the big man thought about after that. I thought about LA. I thought about my childhood, about the wild roses in my grandfather's backyard, about the house I grew up in. About meeting my wife, and where she was buried. I thought about a song I'd heard the night my first boy was born, a song on the radio, a song I never knew the words to, but I could still remember the melody. That's how I fell asleep too.

———————————

"Wakey wakey."

I opened my eyes. The sun had risen, and it was a little cold up in the hills where we were. The freeway at the bottom of the canyon was louder. I took my sunglasses off and rubbed my eyes. Across from me, the doctor yawned.

"What time is it?" he asked.

"'Bout seven, little after." Tay Tay was holding three white coffee mugs. I took one, and the doctor took one as well. Tay Tay wasn't smiling for some reason. He looked back at the house.

"I'll go check on the patient," the doctor said, rising. Tay Tay held up his hand.

"Don't bother. They're gone."

"What!" the doctor cried. "He was in no condition to move! Where'd they go?"

"Maria left a note. She called the jet service and booked it. Said Knottspeed had an idea, and he really wanted to get started. By now they're on their way to . . . Martinique. We can pick up the white car at the airport whenever. Long-term parking."

The doctor sat back down, eyes wide. He looked up at Tay Tay.

"Did they take any supplies?"

"Bandages. Some other stuff. Enough to get them there."

The doctor shook his head in amazement and then abruptly laughed.

"Fantastic," he said. He sipped his coffee and looked around. I got up and stretched.

"Nice to meet you guys," I said. "See you around."

The doctor cheered me with his coffee. Tay Tay nodded.

"Stuff to clean up in your cab?" he asked, obviously willing to help. I shook my head.

"Nah. I'm going to retire it. It's retired now, actually. As of this moment. Gotta go pack, which sucks. We're moving. Arizona, I think. Flagstaff. Better soil."

They nodded. The doctor snapped his fingers in sudden inspiration as I walked away.

"Tay Tay, let's go pick out some paint."

END

NEXT FROM

JEFF JOHNSON

AND

TURNER
PUBLISHING COMPANY

DEADBOMB
BINGO RAY

FALL 2017